A GLINT AM BONE[

by Ben Osborne

Copyright © Ben Osborne 2016

The right of Ben Osborne to be identified as author has been asserted by him in accordance with sections 77 and 78 of the Copyright, Designs and Patents Act 1988.

In this work of fiction all characters and incidents are either used fictitiously or are the product of the author's imagination and any resemblance to actual persons, living or dead, is purely coincidental.

CHAPTER 1

'What the hell is this?'

Danny Rawlings found it hard to take his widening blue eyes off the orange slab of Charles Darwins looking up at him. He hadn't seen this much cash since he'd been dragged round the Royal Mint on a school trip to Llantrisant.

But none of this added up.

Stony had led them to the Castle Keep pub and had even bought the drinks. That alone ought to have set alarm bells ringing.

Searching for answers, Danny looked to the furtive eyes poking from behind the upright of the open briefcase. 'There must be twenty bloody grand in here!'

'Nowhere near that,' Stony replied sheepishly and then disappeared behind the aluminium lid of the case. 'More like forty.'

Forty! Danny mouthed. 'And that makes it better how exactly?'

Danny could hear Stony shift his weight uneasily on a burgundy stool still smelling of leather since the refurb.

He looked again at the wads of notes, paper-banded into bank-counted thousands.

'They're in tens, which is good,' Stony reasoned. 'Have you ever tried to pass a fifty? They look at you like you're a shoplifter.'

'And you're telling me all this is mine?' Danny asked, voice smaller.

Stony appeared again, nodding.

Hearing the clink of empties being collected, Danny shut the case with a satisfying click and twitchily glanced over both shoulders. Landlord Len, a tall, hulking forty-something with short thinning hair and a small scar beneath his left eye, was doing the rounds now the lunchtime rush hour was over. He had yet to reach their table tucked in a dark corner, away from the fruity light streaming through the coloured glass that overlooked Cardiff Castle on the other side of the noisy one-way system snaking through the city centre.

'Please don't tell me it was a lucky bet that came in,' Danny said. 'You don't collect this kind of money from fifty-pence patents, even if you played up the winnings.'

'I do lucky 15s,' Stony said. 'Get double the odds for just having one winner down that new shop The Flutter House. Can't go wrong.'

Danny leant forward casting a shadow over the metal case. 'Stop messing, Stony. Where the hell did you get this from? And don't tell me you found it.'

'Like I say, I won it. Why is that so strange?'

'So you know how much is in there, but you won't tell me where it came from.'

Low on energy and patience, Danny slapped a wooden wall-panel beside him.

'Oi!' Len barked. 'Don't start acting all Bertie Big Bollocks in here, son. That wood was reclaimed from a galleon in the Bristol Channel well before the time when Cardiff was the world's largest port. Have some respect.'

'Thought I saw a fly settle,' Danny explained. 'Won't happen again.'

'Why the third degree? I reckoned you'd have been chuffed,' Stony said.

'Who made you do this?'

Stony sighed as if the game was up. 'An anonymous donor.'

'What?'

'Like a Secret Santa.'

Danny paused. 'But don't Secret Santas want something worth similar in return?'

'Not this one.'

'I just can't get my head round why anyone would give me money, let alone this much. Things are tight, but I'm no charity and I've been in racing long enough to know this smells bad.'

'Let's just say, it's a grateful colleague wanting to reward a job well done.'

'So this "donor" is using you as a middleman that I'd trust.'

'You'd trust him too,' Stony said. 'You've had dealings with him.'

'Then tell me who it is.'

'He wouldn't be anonymous then,' Stony said. 'Just take it, Danny, for my sake and yours.'

'You don't just take money off a stranger without questions.'

'It's hardly going to be a con, they're *giving* you money.'

'Why not give it to my face?'

'He said you'd be too modest to accept,' Stony said. 'And turns out he was right.'

'Too suspicious, more like.'

'Don't shoot the messenger,' Stony said. 'Same again?'

Danny really didn't need this right now on the eve of the Cheltenham Festival. His fist came down and the table shivered. Stony sat back down. Len looked over.

'That bloody fly again,' Danny called out. 'Think I got it this time.'

'What is it with the anger?' Stony asked.

'Just irritable that's all, low on energy.'

'You've lost more weight than I thought was possible. I mean, there wasn't much of you before,' Stony said. 'Must be eight stone wet through now. You're not—'

Danny shook his head. 'Nothing like that.'

'Then what is it?'

'You're not the only one that can have secrets,' Danny said.

He heard footsteps growing louder on the tiled floor. *Shit!*

Len had an eye for trouble, normally of the drunken variety, probably how he got the scar.

'You understand I can't have that panelling survive a shipwreck only to have it battered by a plank like you,' Len said and then put down the empties. With the sleeve of his flannel shirt, he wiped the glass of a framed picture showing Cardiff Castle above the fireplace nearby.

Last thing Danny wanted was a history lesson, least of all from a nosey barman with time on his hands. He sensed the danger of a conversation looming.

'What's the point of having that picture of the castle there when you can just look out of the window,' Stony asked.

Danny glared at his old friend. This wasn't the time for idle pub talk.

'It's the Castle Keep. Every pub needs a theme these days, makes us stand out from the rest.'

'Same with the races, put a Welsh Champions Day or a Ladies Day on the racecard down at Ely Park and you try getting a ticket,' Stony moaned. 'Gets as crowded as the Cheltenham Festival.'

'Speaking of which, you're both racing folk,' Len said and pointed at the poster next to the picture. 'Shown all this week, every race covered live.'

'Watch with a scotch?!' Stony said, reading the strapline penned at the bottom.

'Why on earth did the ad agency let you go?' Danny asked.

'Suppose you could do better.'

'Watch the horses with three courses,' Danny offered.

Len removed a spiral notepad from a shirt pocket and started jotting.

'I was joking,' Danny added but he was just thankful to see Len leave for the bar, no doubt to mock up another poster.

Danny noticed Stony needed both hands to keep his pint glass steady as he finished off the dregs of his Castle Keep's in-house Portcullis Blond Ale. His hair was now white as a veteran Desert Orchid. He looked like he was in deeper water than the oak panelling had ever voyaged.

'Ease down, Stony, it's not even dark outside,' Danny said.

Danny had presumed Stony was shifting his weight because of his not-so-new hip giving him jip again but now suspected it was the briefcase on the table rammed with cash that was stirring him. He reckoned changing the subject might help.

'Have you seen the decs?' Danny said. 'They're out forty-eight hours before the Championship races at the Festival. Left my smartphone in the car.'

'Blind Nye over there will have a racing paper,' Stony said.

'I thought you said he was blind,' Danny said and looked over at a gnarly old man in a brown suit at least a size too small. 'Didn't know they did a Braille version.'

'They don't,' Stony whispered. 'He used to come here every day with his wife, she'd read him the runners and riders and then he'd ask for the form of his favourites. Brilliant memory recall, until the accident.'

'Where's the wife today?'

'Bute Park, I heard,' Stony said.

'Lovely day for it.'

'Her ashes were scattered there. But that hasn't stopped him coming here most days, paper open on that round table, silently tapping his leg. Reckon he's imagining his wife was still reading to him.'

Blind Nye slowly turned his head and lowered his black shades to look directly back at them.

'It's a bit rough calling him Blind Nye,' Danny whispered. 'Aren't nicknames supposed to be a bit ironic?'

'It is ironic. Blind Nye isn't blind,' Stony replied. 'Lost his sight after a fall down the recycling depot and must've recently come back. I caught him playing darts here last month.'

'I was drunk!' Nye cried.

'And there's nothing wrong with his hearing either,' Stony said.

'A blind, drunk darter,' Danny said.

'He cleared the room quicker than he normally does,' Stony replied.

'Why pretend to be blind?' Danny asked. 'It's a hell of an act to keep up.'

'Let's just say, there are *benefits*.'

'Oh, I get you,' Danny said and took a sip of his coffee.

Nye's sudden silence spoke volumes.

'Nye, can we have a quick look at your racing paper?' Stony asked.

Nye downed his Guinness and rattled the bottom of the glass against his round table.

'Barman, give that gent a fresh pint of his choosing.'

Stony went over and slapped a tenner on the bar. 'And have one for your good self.'

'Bar Manager,' Len corrected. 'But thanks all the same.'

Stony wasn't one to flash the cash, usually because he never seemed to have any. Suddenly Danny wanted to check for slack in the paper bands around the cash.

Stony returned with the newspaper. As he flicked through to find the declarations page for tomorrow's runners, he stopped at the racing news section.

'Bad news, this,' he said.

Danny glanced over and saw the headline: Valleys Ace Carmichael Aiming for the Stars Again. Beside the full-page article there was a large photo filled with Toby Carmichael's fat head. He had tight greying curls around a bald crown and white-tipped mutton chops.

Clearly a stock photo, Danny thought, certain his hair was a bit greyer and neck a bit fatter now.

'Tell me about it,' Danny moaned. 'I think I know why all my best owners are leaving Silver Belle Stables. You'll notice he never does a full stable tour of his bright hopes to look out for, like all the other top trainers,' Danny said. 'Doesn't want a hack poking his nose round there and discovering what they're really up to.'

Danny pulled the paper closer and scanned the copy.

'Perhaps he's just good at what he does, Danny,' Stony said. 'Toby was alright to me when we rode in the Eighties, good luck to him. I never had you down as the jealous type.'

'I'm not,' Danny said, 'but this was a telephone interview, says in small print at the bottom there. He just does enough of these to keep the press happy and at arm's length. Surprised they could get his whole head in shot. Yet more publicity he doesn't even need.'

'But he trains Flat horses up at Arwen Vale,' Stony said, looking down at the paper, 'you're a National Hunt yard. Why let it bother you?'

'Some owners go where the money and the glory is.'

'Well, if they have left, they clearly weren't your best owners.'

'They still paid the bills on time and you can't blame them when Toby-bloody-Carmichael maintained a literally unbelievable fifty-five per cent strike rate on his rookie campaign in a code that has far bigger prize money than the jumps. The bastard picked up seven juvenile Group-race winners on the way.'

'Not that you're counting,' Nye piped up.

'There'll be even better to come when those two-year-olds have strengthened up to race as three-year-olds this summer,' Danny said, starting to regret not accepting that drink. 'It's Meg I'm worried about. When she thinks I'm not looking, I sometimes see her peering into the empty boxes. She'd never admit it, but I think she's scared we'll go under.'

'Toby might put the area on the map as a training centre,' Stony reasoned. 'One day it could become like a Lambourn, Newmarket or North Yorkshire. And anyway, this was the bad news I was on about.' Stony's finger jabbed the opposite page as he took the paper back. 'Look, there's been another jockey attacked at the racetrack. Apparently, the attacker claimed his fourth victim since the summer when Callum Doyle was jumped on after yesterday's Lingfield all-weather card. At least that doesn't affect you; the attacker seems to be targeting Flat jockeys.'

'And all four victims have been top-flight jockeys,' Nye piped up. 'So rest easy, boy.'

'Thanks,' Danny said, lip curled.

'No comfort to Callum, says here his arms and legs were viciously beaten, might not walk, let alone ride again. A young lad's career and perhaps life ruined, and for what? Some sick bastards in the world, aye.'

Danny heard his stomach growl and he glanced at the lunchtime menu. 'Probably a punter getting revenge for a losing bet.'

'No, it says all the victims had recently won a race.'

'Punter must've backed the second then.'

Danny held his stomach as it moaned loudly again.

'For Christ's sake, get some grub inside you,' Stony said. 'You haven't got a ride at Cheltenham this week.'

'I can't, I really can't.'

Danny returned to reading the article intently.

'Have a look at the runners,' Stony said. 'Give us some juicy inside info.'

'Wait a sec,' Danny muttered distantly.

When he finally looked up, Stony was grinning at him.

'What?' Danny asked, wiping his upper lip thinking he'd left a froth moustache from his cappuccino.

'You're bloody doing it aren't you,' Stony said, 'you're returning to Flat racing. It's obvious now: the weight loss, the obsession with neighbour Toby Carmichael, the fear about the jockey attacks. That's your secret!'

'Keep it down,' Danny said in a strangled whisper. 'I've taken out a dual permit as a trainer and passed the medical to renew my old Flat rider's licence. Seeing Toby clean up, I thought rather than sitting around moping, let's try to win the owners back, particularly since Ely Park now takes the hurdles down to race on the Flat over the summer. And Flat jockeys tend to ride for longer, look at Lester, rode Rodrigo De Triano to a Guineas win in his mid-fifties. I'm a youngster in comparison, though jogging in thermals every morning isn't getting any easier.'

'You even shaved off your long hair,' Stony said. 'There's dedication.'

Danny ran a hand over his prickly cropped hair. 'Every ounce counts.'

It took him back to the time he was an ambitious apprentice Flat jockey, straight from school to Lambourn, surviving on diet cola and coffee, and the help of a diuretic known in the lads' quarters as the pink pill.

'I don't miss being at the coalface of the sport, rather bet on them than be on them, now that's risky,' Stony sighed. 'Not many sports where an ambulance follows you around.'

'You must remember that buzz, Stony. It's what I'm made for, the thrill of winning; I even like the crushing despair of losing.'

'That'll be the gambler in you coming out,' Stony said. 'So what's Meg say about this all?'

'Not a lot.'

'Always said she's an understanding woman, taking on all that extra work,' Stony replied. 'She's a keeper, alright.'

'She doesn't know yet,' Danny said. 'That's why I said keep it down.'

'This deserves a drink,' Stony said and raised his glass. 'When's your first runner?'

'I haven't even got a Flat-bred in the yard yet but I'll be going to Ely Park's bloodstock sales in a few days to change that.'

'That deserves another drink,' Stony said and took another lengthy swig of his ale.

'Why are you hitting it hard?' Danny asked.

'I drink too much cos I think too much,' Stony slurred. 'Who was it said that?'

'You, just then.'

Danny suspected his old pal was trying to forget something, perhaps the answer was in the briefcase between them.

Danny thought it best to steer the conversation to calmer waters. He turned to the runners and riders for the opening day of Cheltenham tomorrow. In the odds table nearby, Powder Keg was a best price twenty-to-one for the Champion Hurdle, though was generally in at sixteen-to-one with most of the bookies.

'How do you rate your chances?' Stony asked, fishing for something in his jeans pocket.

'Well, the mare won the Welsh version, albeit in the stewards' room. But she's done everything right schooling on the gallops at home since. She's got to step up massively with the best of these. She's a stone worse off with the favourites Kiss Chaser and Lion's Share on official ratings.'

'Could've said that before I put twenty quid each-way on her ante-post,' Stony said, waving a crumpled betting slip.

Danny heard a scratching from behind. He looked back to see Nye taking notes on a bar mat. Nye looked back over, raising his black glasses again. 'Please, don't stop for me.'

Danny heard the bells in City Hall chime four times and felt ready to leave.

Wordlessly he picked up the case. Wherever the money had come from, Danny knew how it would look. He looked to the heavens.

'Careful, roll your eyes that hard, you'll see your brain,' Stony said.

'Doubt I've got one, taking this lot on.'

'So you'll take it,' Stony beamed. 'I could kiss you.'

'Don't, before I change my mind. And I'm doing this for you, not me,' Danny said. 'I'll find a safe place for this. I won't blow it at the sales just in case the donor has a change of heart and starts hassling you for it back.'

Stony finished off his ale, now glassy eyed.

Danny felt he was doing the right thing. He could see this money had proved a burden for his old pal. He tried to recall if he'd ridden or trained winners for any eccentric multimillionaires down the years, now wanting to spread their wealth. If this was a genuine gift, it would prove a useful cash injection to expand the yard.

'Where will you put it?' Stony asked.

'In the attic, I'll lodge it between crates of my dad's old 45s. Meg wouldn't go up there, reckons she's heard rats, and probably wouldn't know what to do with a vinyl record if she saw one. Anyway, best get back. Jordi will be thinking I've got lost. I know I'd be lost without him right now.'

'From Newcastle is he, the lad?'

'Jordi with a J,' Danny said. 'He's Spanish.'

'Send Meg my love and wish her luck for tomorrow, not that she'll need it. And Danny, thanks,' Stony said, glancing at the case. His shoulders and mood seemed to have lifted already, though that might've been the booze kicking in.

Danny picked up the weighty aluminium case full of cash. He had feared leaving the pub feeling guilty he'd succumbed to the demon drink but he was burdened instead with a pile of potentially dirty money.

As he parked up his red Mazda CX-3, Silver Belle Lodge was reassuringly quiet. It seemed Meg had already dropped the kids off with his mam for a few hours.

He entered the house with a click of the front door and lightly padded across the Welsh slate tiles to the staircase in the hallway. On the landing, he unhooked the attic door and lowered the telescopic ladder.

Clutching the case, his legs were in the landing and torso in the loft as he heard the creak of a door below. Shit!

Listening intently, he heard footsteps and then felt the ladder rising up at him.

'I'm armed and I will kill!' shrieked a women's voice.

Danny looked down at the square of light and then lost his footing, falling to the carpeted floorboards with a thud.

He leapt to his feet and raised his fists like a pugilist but saw Meg naked and shivering. 'It's me, Danny!'

The forearm crossing her panting chest barely hid her pert breasts and hard nipples. Her blonde curls were pulled back in a bunch. She hurriedly picked up the dry towel lying in a mess where it fell.

Danny lowered his fists and asked, 'Why didn't you bloody say it was you?'

'Cos I didn't know it was you!' she cried, wrapping the towel round her.

'You recognise these combats and trainers.'

'But I'd never seen you with a briefcase by your side,' she said. 'What's in it?'

'Nothing, it's empty.'

'Why are you hiding it up there then?'

'What's with the nudity? You haven't been at it with the milkman again,' Danny said, trying to relieve the tension.

'We don't have milk delivered.'

'I know,' Danny said and made a face. 'It was a joke.' He was tempted to look in the bedroom now.

'I was about to jump in the shower,' she explained, 'but reckon I'll run a hot bath now, I need a relaxing lie down after that.'

'Can I join you?'

She glowered at him. 'I didn't even know you'd gone out. I'd come back from dropping the kids off with your mam's for a few hours.'

'I told you I'd gone into town to meet Stony.'

'Well, I didn't hear you come in.'

'Old habits die hard,' Danny said. 'You knew I was a former housebreaker when you married me.'

'But you always slam that bloody front door, it normally wakes Cerys,' Meg said. 'Which makes me wonder what really is in that case?'

Danny looked up at the loft.

'Open it, Danny,' she said. 'If you don't, I will find it and I will open it.'

Danny unlocked and lifted the lid.

'Empty?!' Meg's eyes lit up. 'Are you kidding me?'

He could almost hear her brain composing the shopping list, topped by an Aga.

'Before you get any ideas, they're fake.'

'They don't look fake.'

'And they're not mine.'

'Where did you get them?' she asked, fingers skating over the notes.

'Stony.'

'He's always broke,' she said. 'That's how he got his name.'

'He had a big win.'

'You said they were fake,' she said, removing her hand from the case. 'Danny I don't like this one bit, get that money out of the house.'

'Can I just keep it safe for a few days?'

'No!'

'Well where can I put it?'

'Back with your friend Stony.'

'But—'

'I want that gone, do you hear?' Meg asked as she turned. 'By the time I've finished having a bath, alone!'

Danny waited for the sound of gushing water to mask his return to the loft. As planned, he hid the case between two crates of his dad's old LPs. Mam no longer had the record player but he wasn't ready to sell these on. He felt it would be like giving away one of the few remaining links he had left with his late father. The fact some of the album jackets were creased and torn at the corners, among them Dire Straits, Led Zeppelin, Pink Floyd, The Beatles, Bowie and The Jam, only added personal value. *Dad loved those records and so would he.*

In there somewhere, he recalled there was a signed Tom Jones record presumably mam took on an evening out in a workingmen's club when the legend perfected his act touring the clubs of South Wales pre-Vegas in the Sixties.

Out of sight, out of mind, he thought, as he tugged on the light cord.

CHAPTER 2

CHELTENHAM RACECOURSE. TUESDAY 16TH MARCH.

3.18pm. Danny felt he could do no more for this moment though months of planning couldn't ever have prepared him for the result.

He'd found a spot against the glass of the first floor balcony in the new Princess Royal Stand, about level with the furlong marker.

Off to his left, the weak spring sun lit up the rounded shoulders of Cleeve Hill in a blaze of greens and browns and the glowing honey Cotswold stone houses of Prestbury below. But the empty sky made it a day for thick coats and gloves.

That morning, they'd left Silver Belle Stables in blackness and after a trouble-free journey up there, it was still dark as they parked the van.

An official at the gates to the racecourse stabling checked his Identity Card and Validity Pass, along with Powder Keg's passport. The mare's black neck was swiped with a microchip reader. Danny was handed a plastic armband that read: *Race 3 No. 8*. He was then waved on. Even that early, the stables were a hive of activity, lads and lasses making sure their charges were settled in, fed and watered. Much of the powerful Irish contingent had travelled over on Sunday. Danny even had time to grab breakfast at the jockeys' canteen in the stable staff accommodation block by the stabling, though these days breakfast meant a thinly buttered slice of toast, with a banana as the treat. He didn't mind as he'd struggle to keep any more down.

Not long after, Powder Keg was given permission to have a quick blowout up the run-in and a pick of grass as a reward. Danny watched from the quiet of the stand as Meg and Powder Keg moved like champions as they breezed up the stiff incline, similar to the slopes of home, though he knew connections of the other ten runners would no doubt say the same about their representatives. Everything had gone to plan.

A cold gust snapped him away from his thoughts. He checked his watch again. 3.20pm.

He couldn't fight off a jaw-snapping yawn, though it was from tension not tiredness. He felt it more up here in the stands than if he were riding. It was something about the loss of control, and the fear for his wife and stable star he'd sent out to do battle.

If it wasn't bad enough, the trade paper's star tipster had flagged up Kegsy as a decent each-way punt. Danny wondered how many of the punters swarming the betting ring below had got on. He was confident they'd at least pick up on the place part of the wager but he felt added responsibility. Had he brought the mare to peak for the big day? Would the decision to rest her since winning the Welsh version pay off? She'd lack race-fitness but would be fresh, he reasoned.

He'd gone over again and again a routine he'd done a thousand times yet he was still convinced he'd missed something; a tiny detail which would mean the difference between winning and losing.

He felt the binoculars resting on his chest. He was too shaky to use them and would rely on the big screens standing in the Silver Ring and on the infield of the racetrack.

Meg was sat quietly on Powder Keg in her pristine white and red silks, that she'd ironed the night before.

Even from up in the stands, Danny could make out she looked to have Powder Keg calm and focused as they slowly circled by the two-mile and eighty-seven yards start pole on the bend, just a few strides from the home straight of the Old Course. There was over a lap between Meg and stardom. She'd barely slept this past week and was again up before first light, making sure Kegsy hadn't kicked out or been cast in her box overnight.

With it being just the second hurdle race of the meeting, the lush hallowed turf was like a green carpet and the official description of good to soft, soft in places made for perfect jumping ground.

There'd be no excuses today, he thought.

The crackle of anticipation from the packed crowd of the Tatts enclosure below grew to a chorus of excited cheers as the eleven runners walked in, some calm like Powder Keg, others geed-up by the crowd and fanfare like Kiss Chaser.

When the tape rose, the deafening roar felt like it could shake the foundations of the stand.

The field set off at a pedestrian pace. They'd agreed if they went a slow early gallop to sit up there. Danny looked for her red cap bobbing out the back.

Move her up Meg, Danny urged under his breath.

Just twenty or so strides into the race the first flight of timber was upon them. The leaders were keen enough, taking a healthy tug on the reins, as these accomplished Grade One hurdlers streamed over in perfect unison like a shoal of leaping salmon, almost as fast in the air as on the ground.

Meg began to coax Powder Keg on the approach, as if asking for a big one. It was more about finding an early rhythm at the first flight. There were no style marks awarded in this sport. The mare didn't pick up and her strapped forelegs paddled right through, flattening the board of timber.

'No!' Danny cried, despair lost in a wall of noise. There was a long run to the second hurdle to play catch-up, he thought.

As they galloped by the stands for the first time, Danny didn't need the binoculars to see Meg was struggling. It made no sense. Powder Keg's strength was her speed between the flights and efficient hurdling technique. Right then she was exhibiting neither. Meg administered a few gentle reminders with the whip and began to work the reins. But she was still out the back and becoming more detached with every stride.

Up ahead, last year's Supreme Hurdle hero Kiss Chaser and unbeaten warm favourite Lion's Share both pinged the second hurdle, gaining a couple of lengths on the rest.

But Danny's eyes were fixed firmly at the other end of the field where Meg had steadied Kegsy into the hurdle. They stuttered almost to a walk and the mare ballooned over the flight, treating the three foot of timber more like a fence. Sat back on the mare's flexed hind quarters, Meg straightened her short legs and pushed back, boots pressed firm to the pedals of the stirrup irons.

'What the hell,' Danny cried. The mare was acting like a petulant juvenile. It's as if the countless schooling sessions hadn't happened.

The field continued to climb as they banked left to embark on the only complete circuit, past the Silver Ring on their right. At least, the frontrunners were.

Danny's eyes flitted between Lion's Share now asserting into a clear lead and Kegsy in last. *Must be twenty-bloody-lengths.*

Right then, just about every emotion coursed through his body: concern, alarm, sadness, frustration, embarrassment.

They crested the rise, all except Meg, who was still desperately trying to stay in touch with the main pack, just to keep the mare competitive as they freewheeled down the back straight.

With only eleven runners and no confirmed pacesetter, the race-plan had always been to sit on the sharp end early. They didn't want to be caught flat-footed out the back when the pace quickened. Little did he reckon on them being flat-footed between the second and third flights of timber. In the exhaustive pre-race tactical planning, they'd gone through every eventuality bar this one.

Danny called upon the binoculars, as if unconvinced by what he was seeing with the naked eye.

A speedy jump here might ignite some interest from the mare, he thought, more in hope than belief.

But again, Kegsy's stride began to shorten into the take-off side of the hurdle. She then jinked right, almost ejecting her rider out the side door. Meg quickly reacted, shifting her weight more on the left iron, adding to the lead weight packing that side of the saddle, which contributed to the eleven-stone ten pounds every runner had to shoulder.

Her balance and poise as a dancer helped avert an unseating but it was merely delaying the inevitable. She was now a remote twenty-five lengths off the pace. Danny saw her arms begin to slow. She'd worked heavily on her fitness over the winter. This wasn't tiredness; it was the beginning of the end.

The speaker's blared, 'Lion's Share now by three, from Houseproud, another break to Kiss Chaser and Trebles For Show still in touch, but the same cannot be said for Powder Keg, whose jockey Megan Rawlings appears to be pulling up. They file over the fourth—'

Danny had tuned out. She'd pulled up and then dismounted alongside the packed coach park. That was more than he wanted to know.

He squeezed his way off the balcony, run down the stairwell two steps at a time and weaved through the distracted crowds of the picnic lawn below to the gate in the plastic railing.

From there he could just about make out the pair stood on the outer chase course. Her face was buried in her gloved hands. Clearly not keen on sharing to the world her private grief. They both knew this was her big moment, unfortunately 'moment' being the operative word. All he wanted was to reach her, comfort her, protect her.

'Fucking crooked twat, bent as the rest of 'em,' a short stocky man with a pink face slurred. Lager sloshing from his plastic pint glass. 'Get a refund for that pile of shite will I? Paper said you'd go close, didn't even get a run for my money, utter bollocks! You owe me twenty.'

'Go with your own opinion then, not a tipster,' Danny said and turned to security. 'Should he be drinking in this enclosure?'

The man was politely led away by a man in an orange hi-vis jacket.

'Stewards should ban you for life, do you hear?!' the drunk cried, beer spilling down his black puffa jacket. 'Life!'

Danny tried to blank him but that was proving hard. Abuse from irate punters was mercifully rare but it was always a risk, particularly when the bars were flowing and there was forty minutes between races to get the rounds in. The punter in him knew the frustration, but rule one of being a gambler was to take the rough with the smooth. He was left wondering if he'd just been confronted by the attacker.

He felt like straddling the plastic rail anyway but knew he'd make headlines for all the wrong reasons and get slapped with a fine he couldn't afford.

Once all the stragglers had safely completed, Danny ducked under the rail and sprinted across the track to discover the fallout. There were a handful of drinkers raising their beer to Danny, cheering him on with the distant beat of a live band in the Guinness tented village behind the Desert Orchid Stand in the Silver Ring. He barely heard them, too intent on reaching Meg.

He was concerned that she hadn't started to make her way back or even remounted. He feared Meg wasn't the only one in distress.

'Are you okay, love?' Danny asked and held her close. 'What happened?'

'Nothing happened, that was the problem,' she cried and pushed him away. 'She jumped bad and was never travelling, it's all my fault. It has to be. I must've lost my bottle. It felt like we were strangers.'

'Rubbish – it must be Powder Keg.'

'Don't you *dare* blame this little one!' Meg snapped.

He ran a hand down each of Powder Keg's legs feeling for any warmth. He checked the horse's flaring nostrils and mouth for blood but there was nothing to suggest she'd burst a blood vessel or bitten her tongue.

'It's just not our day, there'll be others.'

'Will there?' Meg asked sceptically. 'And I'll have the whole bloody summer replaying what I've done … or should've done.'

'If she's as sound as she seems we'll have plenty more chances before then.'

'What are you talking about Danny?' she asked.

'Now isn't the time,' Danny said. Either side, they led Powder Keg back.

'And I'm not a bad loser, just gutted for Kegsy,' she said, snotty.

'You didn't let her down. She's probably thinking – well, that was an easy day at the office, three hurdles, job done.'

She looked over at him and managed a smile that betrayed her wet eyes.

'Did you feel any lameness going down to the start or during the race?' Danny asked.

'I'm the one that feels lame.'

'We'll find you a dead cert to get you back among the winners soon enough,' Danny said, though he knew no words could change her mood right now.

'It's not the same. Kegsy is my idol.'

'I thought that was me,' Danny said.

She forced a teary smile.

'Come on, we'd better get back to the stands,' Danny said. 'The stewards are bound to ask questions, just say she didn't jump or feel right. We were one of the outsiders so there shouldn't be too many awkward ones.'

He could tell she needed a hug badly. This was the time but certainly not the place. With the race over, he knew the cameras would be zooming in soon. Tears make for great TV.

'It's disappointing, but do you know what percentage of horses actually manage to win a race in their whole career?'

'No stats, Danny, I'm not ready for stats right now.'

That was their last words trudging back and, with nothing else in the yard up to contesting at this level, months of planning for the festival was over in seconds.

Perversely, Danny reckoned it might've been good Powder Keg ran that badly. He wanted the yard's flagbearer to be its first Flat runner. But even he could sense now wasn't the time to broach the subject, particularly as she didn't even know the yard was branching out.

CHAPTER 3

Danny stared at the armed police officer in black guarding the main entrance to this large tented Sales arena topped by fluttering Welsh flags and stuck to the side of the main grandstand at Ely Park Racecourse.

He was left wondering if the UK's terror threat level had been raised.

The officer seemed to briefly eye Danny back with similar suspicion.

It was clearly a very public show designed to allay fears, though the sight of a trained killer gripping a fully loaded automatic firearm put Danny more on edge.

Danny looked away. He scanned the tiered amphitheatre already filling with consignors, owners, trainers, bloodstock agents, ex-jockeys-turned-reps, and spectators. Given it was the sale's first year, there was a healthy turnout. The dress seemed more country casual than smart. But many of the top owners liked it that way; they had little to prove, comfortable in their inordinate wealth. There were puffa jackets and jeans, with caps sporting logos for racing festivals and breeding operations from around the world, mingling with tailored suits and ties.

It seemed he was the only active jockey present. Danny picked up a discarded tabloid newspaper folded over the handrail in front of him. He read the headline: New Leads in Race to Find Attacker.

Suddenly Danny felt glad the armed police had turned up.

In the article, it claimed jockey Darren Cooper, a twenty-eight-year-old married father of two, had been questioned and then released without charge.

Danny was stood four rows back, looking down on the small sales ring of red asphalt with an island of hay in the middle, presumably to make the young, green horses feel more at home.

Up there, he could see without being seen.

The smell of fresh paint pricked his nostrils. It seemed the Ely maintenance staff had been up late putting the finishing touches to make the place ready to host some of the most influential and wealthiest faces in the business. They were clearly hoping some would be impressed enough to return with a high-profile runner on the new Flat track outside. Perhaps the BHA – the British Horseracing Authority – would then grant the racecourse a Pattern or Group race, also known as 'Black Type', as they were printed bold in the pedigree and form of sales catalogues and stud books.

The wooden boards moaned under their weight and looked like they'd been lifted from a local am-dram theatre, Danny was ashamed to admit. Ely Park wanted to become *the* place to be seen for both owners and breeders. The management were clearly high on ambition but low on budget.

'It's never good news when racing makes the front pages,' Danny heard. He turned and was glad to see a familiar face. Up until then, he'd felt like he was all alone at a party full of strangers.

'Mr Bernard,' Danny said.

'Danny... Danny Rawlings,' Malcolm replied belatedly, much to the apparent relief of both.

Malcolm Bernard was a short black man wearing a tailored cream linen suit with powder-blue shirt and pocket handkerchief and tie to match, same as the colours worn by his riders on the racetrack, though he wisely stopped short of a blue or green hat they wore to differentiate between first and second choice jockeys when two of his runners were declared for the same race, which happened quite often given the current number in his ownership. Malcolm was a self-made millionaire on the commodities markets in the Eighties boom and got out before the crash. Since then he'd seemingly played mostly on bloodstock rather than financial stock. Malcolm appeared to let his heart rule his head when it came to the horses. Danny could relate to that.

'Mind, don't much want to be reminded of the good news – Lion's Share romping home in the Champion Hurdle,' Danny said.

'I'm presuming your runner finished in behind then,' Malcolm said.

'Didn't even finish,' Danny replied.

Danny had ridden for Malcolm as a leading Flat apprentice back in his youth at Lambourn and even won a couple of small races for him. Danny hoped he had a long memory and could return the favour as he wanted to mine the high-profile owner for some dirt on Toby Carmichael.

'I had heard you're a National Hunt trainer now, so what brings you here to a Flat sale, young Danny? It's mostly drafts of yearlings and two-year-old horses-in-training in this catalogue. Unless you're looking for a store horse to keep back for the distant future, but where is the sense in that?'

'Nah, back in the Flat game too now,' Danny said and thought about offering his business card but reckoned a man of means would get that all the time and he didn't want to alienate him already. Instead, he added, 'I could ask the same about you, slumming it a bit coming here with the Doncaster Spring Bloodstock Sales and Tattersalls at Newmarket around the corner.'

He then silently cringed when realising his position as an ambassador of Ely Park, having helped designed the layout of the jump tracks.

'After a season or two of disappointments and false dawns, I need to replenish stock as it were, thought a new venue for a new start.'

'Well, you couldn't have chosen a better one,' Danny said.

Nice recovery, he thought.

'Prices still going up wherever you buy,' Malcolm remarked. 'You're paying for the breeding more than anything, fashionable bloodlines are going for crazy money, with so many mega-rich owners playing at the table in the hope to breed from them, rather than risk spoiling the family line with bad performances on the track.'

'It's a shame as many are retired at three, after just a handful of runs,' Danny agreed. 'The horses struggle to build a public following like the jumpers who keep coming back year after year.'

'You can't blame them as the money these Flat horses make on track is chickenfeed to what their offspring will make in these places. That and a seven per cent fall in the horse population since the financial crash, making the goods scarcer. Let's just say it's not a buyer's market.'

'But you're here, still got the bug,' Danny said.

'Looking at my dwindling bank balance, it's more like a wasting disease.'

Malcolm must be nearing pensionable age by now, Danny calculated, though he didn't smack of the type to need or desire the easy life.

Malcolm leant in closer, adding, 'And off the record, I'm thinking of making some changes to my rota of retained jockeys, wipe the slate completely. That Darren Cooper has shown more attitude than ability of late, a disruptive influence to the team. I'm already outsourcing a few of my fancied rides to replace Darren, see if results improve. I'm in this sport primarily for fun. It's certainly not for money given the current prize money level, as you well know. Last thing I need is a first choice jockey that's not onside.'

Danny picked up the newspaper again. 'Looks like you're a good judge of character. He was arrested yesterday.'

'Give me that,' Malcolm said and started reading. 'Funny, his agent failed to mention this. It claims here he was released without charge. He's still on the very last warning with me.'

'You're too forgiving.'

'Innocent until proven otherwise,' Malcolm said, shrugging.

Danny looked down on the red asphalt of the sales ring and the wooden auctioneer's plinth in front of fancy digital boards ready to flash up current bids simultaneously in pounds, guineas, US dollars and euros. Alongside was the wooden gallery where telephone and internet bids came in.

Off to his left was Toby Carmichael in double tweed and lost in conversation on his mobile.

A few tiers down and to the right, there was another new face on the scene; a slight man with strawberry blonde hair and wearing a silver waistcoat. He also had a phone pressed to his ear.

Malcolm followed Danny's gaze and asked, 'Do you know him?'

'Not yet,' Danny replied. 'Have you been introduced?'

'Never seemed the right moment, he's always on the phone. He looks too young to be a big owner, which makes me suspect he's a rep for one of them, or a bloodstock agent. Always good to suss out the enemy before embarking on a bidding war,' Malcolm reasoned. 'You'll learn that soon enough at these places. He might even be an anti-doping manager for the BHA, come to check the yearlings aren't pumped up on steroids as they're led through the ring.'

'I didn't even know they tested them.'

'Breeders need to make their product look its best to get the price, a tiny minority might resort to any lengths, including muscling them up with drugs.'

Danny looked over suspiciously at Toby, phone still glued to his ear. Was that his game?

'Toby Carmichael over there outbid me on two lots on the first day. The press dubbed him the Midas Man,' Malcolm said, finger pressing the folded newspaper now under his arm. 'Clearly hasn't lost his touch.'

'How much did he go to?' Danny asked.

'Oh, not a lot, ten thousand for one and twelve thousand for the other,' Malcolm said. 'Lovely looking brown colts, but I wasn't prepared to go any higher as their pedigrees lacked any quality.'

'I can't make comment,' Danny sighed. 'He's a neighbour of mine, albeit a valley away.'

'Well, if you're setting out, could do far worse than nicking a few trade secrets from him,' Malcolm advised.

Danny watched closely as Toby slipped the phone in his tweed pocket and then returned to thumbing the sales catalogue alongside Luke, his spotty teenage son, who kept trying to flatten his wild blond curls sprouting from beneath a baseball cap. Danny knew him as an occasional apprentice jockey who, after two seasons trying, had yet to win enough races to lose his rider's allowance, which explained why he appeared to be stuck in a sales ring on tea boy duty rather than riding round one of today's all-weather meetings at Chelmsford City or under the floodlights at Wolverhampton. It also explained the long face.

'And now's your chance,' Malcolm added.

'And now's yours,' Danny replied, seeing the waistcoated stranger also without mobile.

Danny approached from a blind spot and rested a hand on Toby's broad shoulder, leaving him no chance to escape. Toby looked around sharply and grunted, 'Oh, it's you.'

'Good to see you too,' Danny said.

'What do you want?'

'Wish you good luck, classy horses are hard to find.'

'For some maybe.'

'Got any tips for a novice at the sales?' Danny asked. 'Then I'll be gone.'

'Bid aggressively,' Toby replied. 'Even if you're near your limit, raise your paddle quick or raise the amount more than what's being asked. Scare the rivals in to thinking you are prepared to go much higher. They'll walk away sooner.'

Glancing down at Toby's catalogue, Danny caught sight of a mark made by hand against one of the lots at the top left of the opening double page.

Toby hadn't needed to tell Danny anything. The black ink circling Lot Two was enough. Toby closed the catalogue.

Danny needed to act as if he hadn't seen a thing. He recalled Toby's phone interview for the racing press and asked, 'When will you open your gates for the public?'

'Why the hell would I want to meet the public?' Toby asked dismissively.

'You need open days to attract new owners.'

'We don't need to attract owners and even if we did, they'd come to us.'

Glad to see the success hasn't gone to his head, Danny thought.

As Danny turned to leave, Toby grabbed his arm and said, 'Got what you came for did you?'

Danny tugged his arm free. 'Don't know what you mean.'

'I saw you looking just now,' Toby snarled. 'I dare you.'

'It's not a closed auction, I'll bid on what I like.'

Shaken, Danny quickly returned to the gap he'd left four rows back, facing the auctioneer's podium. From there, they couldn't possibly miss any of his bids.

The gangly auctioneer tapped the mic and welcomed the sizeable crowd to 'Day two of Ely Park's Inaugural Horses-in-Training and Yearlings Bloodstock Sales, we have eighty-nine lots catalogued for you in book two,' followed by the preamble of house rules before the bidding could begin.

Danny was busy searching the form database for Lot Two, a brown colt named Red Ink. Being a fourth foal by a low-grade winning miler out of an exposed maiden, with no notable full or half-brothers among the progeny, it didn't make for good reading. He was being sold by the trainer Ralph Carver to leave the yard. Danny felt flat. He was about to bid purely on the recommendation of another. That was his number one hate as a punter. He'd even preached against it to the angry drunk by the Cheltenham rails. But Danny was consoled by Toby's record of finding bargain buys for Arwen Vale. And if it proved a dud, Danny would at least then know Toby was up to something beyond shrewdly buying at the Sales.

The auctioneer began with, 'I'm the MC with the Hammer.'

Jesus, Danny cringed, fearing a rendition of Hammer Time. Where the hell did they get this joker from, a cruise ship? Let's hope he's not there all week. He groaned.

'It's about creating a buzz,' the man stood nearby explained.

'Is that what it's called,' Danny replied.

'Gets them in the mood to bid to their limits.'

'Wish he'd stop then, got one I'm interested in coming up,' Danny said.

The first lot came and went without Danny hearing a bid. He was too busy calculating how high he could go without breaking the bank, after taxes and fees. He knew sticking to a limit would be hard as his gambling instinct was always there bubbling beneath the surface. He'd much rather take a chance and suffer the loss than back out of a bid and then have to watch the horse go on to earn big money. He'd consider that a far greater loss – the one that got away. It's why he was hopeless at blackjack. He barely knew the word 'stick'.

Fourteen grand, Danny concluded, though he suspected that wouldn't even be considered a starting bid by many here.

'And let's move on to our second lot in our book of H-i-Ts. We have here a good-looking two-year-old brown colt called Red Ink, a Haymaker colt out of Charter Flight.' Danny wasn't surprised there was no mention of their achievements on the track or their progeny.

The horse walked calmly into the tent from stage right and was led slowly in circles round the ring. He certainly looked the part, Danny thought. He was a compact, muscular juvenile who appeared ready to run that day. He wanted a precocious early type if he was to make an instant impact and attract new owners to the yard.

His focus returned to Toby, who was slowly turning the bidder paddle in his hand. Danny knew he must have plenty of reserves after so many big races in his first season and a full stable of horses presumably bringing in training fees, though he had only seen a select few ever make the racetrack.

'Let's start the bidding at two thousand guineas, two thousand, two thousand, anybody like to start us off.'

Toby's round face looked relaxed. Danny began to wonder if it was actually lot two he'd circled.

'One thousand then to get things moving. One thousand please.' It was a question of who blinked first. 'No reserve on this, the colt has to go.'

A bid from the back broke the stalemate. Toby's paddle shot up. That's the reaction Danny was after. He quickly launched a counterbid.

'Three thousand to the gentleman facing, three thousand,' the auctioneer kept repeating to fill the silence and keep the energy up in the room.

'Four thousand at the back, new bidder … five thousand to me left.'

Danny saw Toby calmly raise the bid again to one of the bid spotters on the sales pavilion floor.

Danny mirrored the action.

'Six thousand to the gentleman ahead.'

Toby glanced back and gave a look when he saw who was bidding. He smirked dismissively as if to say, 'this is mine'.

'Seven thousand to my left … eight thousand straight ahead … nine thousand, yes madam … ten with you, sir, straight ahead,' the auctioneer said, looking at Danny.

Toby look of steely determination suddenly turned sour.

It's as if he'd realised Danny was hijacking his target horse, much like Toby had to Malcolm the day before.

Blissfully unaware, Red Ink kept circling, glossy brown coat shimmering under the rig of spotlights burning bright above.

'Eleven thousand now, on my right.'

Danny looked over at Malcolm, who was grinning as if relishing Toby being forced to pay more.

Danny raised his arm again. 'Twelve thousand, with you sir, twelve thousand.'

He looked again and there was now a gap where Toby and Luke had stood.

Danny quickly scoured the room. They hadn't moved, Danny reckoned, they'd left.

Danny had clearly got under their skin.

'Any more bids, twelve thousand … final warning.'

Danny held his breath. Down came the gavel loudly. 'Sold! Twelve thousand to you, sir, bidder …'

Danny raised the paddle one last time.

'Sixty-seven… to lot three we go—'

It was now time for Danny to slip away. As he stepped down from the amphitheatre, Malcolm gave him a knowing wink. Danny breathed in the fresh air as he stepped past the armed officer.

He confirmed his details and had a chat with the vendor in the makeshift sales office which was the information centre on race days. There was no point in sticking around as he had no more money to play with, proud he'd found the restraint not to eat into the mystery cash in the briefcase.

He approached the gates to the racecourse, just beyond a sign saying: NEXT MEETING: April 7.

He was lost in thought when Toby suddenly appeared from behind the ticket kiosk. Luke was nowhere to be seen, clearly been sent home or sloped off in a strop.

'No hard feelings,' Danny said.

'You think that was clever back there,' Toby said. 'Pretending to chat when you're really finding which one I'd marked down. You've cheated me out of a new recruit.'

'You could've carried on bidding,' Danny reasoned. 'You told me to bid aggressively and I only raised my arm once more than you.'

'Are you sure?' Toby asked as his open fist came up and lifted Danny clean off the ground. He might have a limp, but there was nothing wrong with his arms.

Danny was dragged behind the empty kiosk.

'And if I see you spying on my place, or bidding against me again—'

'Wha—' Danny spluttered. 'You'll attack me?'

Toby dropped Danny, who fell back against the wood of the kiosk. He then brushed Danny's shirt down and straightened the collar, as if to say 'let's both pretend this never happened'. That was no easy task as Danny's heart was still hammering like he'd just completed a three-mile steeplechase.

Toby said, 'Good luck with Red Ink. He's a looker, I'll give the colt that.'

Danny frowned. Toby said it like he meant it. That worried him more than if his words were riddled with sarcasm.

Why the sudden change of tone and character?

'You could've easily outbid me if you were that keen,' Danny said and then dry swallowed. 'My limit was set at fourteen K.'

'I'm surprised you couldn't have gone higher,' Toby said.

Danny pictured the briefcase hidden in the loft. He wondered if Toby was picturing the same.

The red mists only seemed to clear after Danny had asked, 'You'll attack me?'

Danny stepped to the side and grimaced as he held his neck. It was more painful than treading barefoot on a plug. 'I thought you normally went for the hands and legs!'

'It's just a flavour of things to come if I dare see you snooping near my place,' Toby said.

But surely Toby couldn't be the attacker, Danny thought. The four victims were young and fit and could've easily outrun him. And why hadn't he given Danny a good beating just now? He was certainly angry enough.

Danny was more scared by the thought he'd left Ely with just one unproven horse to embark on his Flat training career. He hoped the colt was as precocious as he looked or he'd be relying squarely on the shoulders of out-of-sorts hurdler Powder Keg to make an early impact as a Flat racer.

Suddenly the elation from winning at the sales ring had worn off. It now felt more like a hollow victory.

CHAPTER 4

'The day of reckoning,' Danny whispered into Red Ink's pricked ear as he finished tacking up. 'Don't let me down boy.'

The youngster's physique looked every bit as muscled and healthy in the spring sun as it had under the spotlights of the Ely sales ring. He clearly wasn't one that needed testing by the BHA anti-doping manager.

The brief chat with the vendor after the sale revealed that the youngster had already been broken in and extensively galloped at his former home in Wiltshire before the enforced sale due to a family bereavement. He certainly looked like an early type with those alert eyes and a gleaming brown coat.

Danny felt his stomach tighten. The stress of bidding had nothing on this. The time had come to take Red Ink out on his first serious piece of work. The moment he'd find out what exactly he'd bought.

There was a fresh breeze helping to blow away his bedhead after a sleepless night going over the moments he'd left Ely Park. He'd allowed Toby to intimidate him. In Danny's mind, he'd let Toby win again.

He led the youngster round to meet Meg, who was already loosening up Powder Keg over the three practice flights of timber at the foot of the gallop strip stretching right up to Silver Belle Woods by the ridge.

She had been surprisingly receptive to the new recruit, but then she was still under the impression the colt was there to go juvenile hurdling next season.

Meg had a face on. Danny suspected he'd kept her up too.

He then saw head lad Jordi trotting Zola the Shetland pony around the schooling ring with Danny's son Jack holding the reins.

It had been Danny's idea to introduce his son early to riding so it could become second nature; many of the best Irish jockeys grew up pony racing. He'd been giving the lad lessons in secret.

He presumed Zola was primarily here to keep best friend Powder Keg settled for this important workout. While it was a discovery mission for Red Ink, it was very much a recovery mission for Powder Keg.

'I've told you,' Meg said. 'He's too young.'

'Look, how old is Jack?'

'Six,' she replied.

'How old is Zola?'

'Five.'

'Well then, who's the senior one in that partnership,' Danny reasoned, as he climbed aboard Red Ink, who was already showing signs of greenness. He made sure to keep a tight rein. 'Anyway, Jack's been a lot calmer since he's started riding. The horses seem to relax him even more than his blanky.'

From there, Danny could see Jack riding with a lovely straight back and soft hands, just as he was taught.

'He has the Rawlings magic, no?' Jordi called over.

Danny laughed. 'Don't wish that on the lad.'

'He'll be taking my job soon,' Jordi said.

'And mine,' Danny replied.

'He's sucking up to you,' Meg said coldly, and turned Powder Keg to face the four furlongs of all-weather gallop strip on this first workout since Cheltenham. 'You're his boss and he's looking for rides.'

'He's our hardest worker,' Danny replied quietly.

'But I don't want him encouraging Jack on the pony. Wait till he's a bit older.'

'We'll talk about this later,' Danny huffed, turning Red Ink to face the path of loose dirt and wood chippings. 'I can't see Kegsy getting near this one, not over four furlongs on the Flat.'

'Race to the top wins.'

Shaking the reins, she suddenly stole a couple of lengths on Danny, who quickly reacted by urging Red Ink forward. The two-year-old soon hit top stride and was proving a handful as they drew alongside. He felt the colt hang a little to their right and hoped the greenness would soon disappear with experience.

Meg looked across and shouted, 'Mine's in second gear.'

Danny glanced over, replying, 'Mine's in first.'

The youngster responded willingly in Danny's hands. He knew it wasn't in any trainer's handbook to race against a far more physically mature rival in a gallop at such an early stage in Red

Ink's development but his competitive spirit drove him on. He wasn't going to lose this match.

He glanced over and saw Meg sat lower, rousting her charge along. Powder Keg's superior strength and stamina soon brushed Red Ink aside. Danny eased off when he saw the race was lost.

Meg was beaming as she pulled up. 'She's back!'

Danny was less effusive. He hated losing, however little was at stake. He was, however, glad Meg and her horse were both well on the recovery path. Red Ink wasn't blowing at all. It was an encouraging, if unspectacular, first piece of work. He still reckoned there was ability in there, but at this stage the colt just didn't know how to use it.

From up on the ridge, he spotted the gate open leading to the neighbouring Mills' estate which was up for sale. Danny had an idea. 'You said to the top, the highest peak in these parts is up on Pen-y-Bryn.'

'But that must be another mile from here,' she said.

Danny rousted the reins.

'You cheating git,' she called after him. Danny smiled when he saw she'd taken the bait. His competitive spirit remained undimmed in his bid to exact revenge.

'You jumped the start back there,' Danny shouted back. 'After that, anything else is fair game.'

Danny took it steady downslope. He already had a maiden at Bath earmarked to introduce the youngster. The ability to race at altitude over undulations was a plus at that spa track. This spin would do both their confidence the world of good.

He never felt more alive than with the fresh air brushing over his face and cropped scalp as he moved in perfect unison with the powerful half-ton animal beneath and the valleys a blur of green on all sides. It made him keep coming back. It felt like the most natural thing in the world; the only time he could truly escape everything.

It certainly made up for all the black, freezing mornings, the miles of jogging laps of the estate in three sweaty layers, doing five lots in howling winds and sleet stinging his body; the hours of wasted life inching towards roadworks, only to see the yard's sole runner on the card tailing off in a race worth just two grand to the winner and then return to the reward of a dinner fit for a rabbit with the sky as black as he'd left it in the morning.

And yet, he wouldn't swap any of it for a desk job in some grey stuffy office working for someone he despised. That's why he had to make this move to the Flat work. He dreamt of emulating just a fraction of the success enjoyed by Carmichael.

'You paid twelve thousand for that,' Meg shouted as she appeared on his left and gave a cheeky smile. 'Kegsy's got more speed than him and she's a hurdler.'

They slowed by the gate in the hedge hiding the Rhymney road. Danny opened the gate and led Red Ink to the gate on the other side of the road.

'Are you sure about this?' Meg asked, following close behind. 'Boy racers bomb along here.'

'We're walking across the road not along it,' Danny explained. 'The Mills family are selling up, their livestock has already gone through the sales ring. It's vacant land we can use.'

'But she might slip and strain on a divot or a cow pat.'

'That's virgin turf, no horse has galloped over these fields for centuries,' Danny lied. He'd gone up here several times, the quickest route to Pen-y-Bryn. 'It's like discovering another Newmarket heath and the views will make you weep.'

Danny dropped the latch of the second gate behind him and then remounted.

Soon they'd crossed Mills' estate and were free to gallop on open heathland.

As the climb grew steeper, Danny asked Red Ink for more but the youngster was laboured in his response, merely plugging on at the one pace.

Suddenly Meg tried to take a shortcut by clearing the corner of a widening stream that snaked from a natural spring higher up but the mare's back heels made a splash.

Meg sat lower in the Martini glass position and recovered well. Sat on the non-jumper, Danny was forced to take the longer route round and fell further behind.

Red Ink's hooves pounded the spongy turf as they closed in on the peak. Although blowing hard and losing ground, the youngster appeared to be relishing this as much as his rider, surprisingly undaunted by the rugged surroundings. Everything must have seemed new at his age. But there was no way they were getting any nearer to Powder Keg, who'd surged well clear, stamina only now kicking in as they loomed in on Pen-y-Bryn, which meant 'top of the hill' in Danny's very broken Welsh.

Meg punched the air, seemingly as invigorated by the change of routine as the mare between her legs. As she slowed to a walk at the peak, she glanced back. Danny read her lips, 'Yes!'

Red Ink had once again come up short, blowing hard. Admitting defeat, he slowed to a walk.

She stood up in the saddle and her pert bottom did a victory wiggle. Secretly Danny found the sight sexy as hell in those tight jodhpurs. Yet, even after years of telling her, she still seemed completely oblivious to her own natural beauty. She'd always laugh it off. It made her even more attractive in Danny's eyes. He certainly knew how lucky he was. That's probably why he was so anxious to have her blessing for taking out a dual licence.

Low on energy, Danny gasped begrudgingly, 'I'll give you that one.'

Face lit up, she fist-pumped the air again. Powder Keg didn't react. Danny had noticed the unbreakable bond develop between those two. It's as if they could both read and second guess each other, like an old married couple.

'Two nil, get in!' she cried. 'Bet you'll want to double or quits to the Brecon Beacons.'

The pair then sat on horseback silently drinking in the savage beauty of the neighbouring valley. It took Danny's breath away almost as much as the crystal clear air up here. Careful to avoid the patches of gorse bushes and rocky outcrops they slowly descended to take a closer look, keeping well away from the steeper slopes.

She asked, 'How come you know this path so well?'

Danny shrugged. 'It was you that won the race.'

'I got up close home, you led me here.'

'I didn't have much control,' Danny said. 'This one was running away with me, must've spooked and bolted at something.'

Meg stroked her chin strap. 'Remember the boy that cried wolf.'

Danny wasted no time in removing compact zoom binoculars from his jacket and looked down on Toby Carmichael's yard nestled at the floor of Arwen Vale which aptly meant 'beautiful' vale in Welsh.

Among the purple heather and brown brambles, Danny took in the radiant green of the sweeping valley slopes below.

'It's not ideal with all these rocks and brambles, what if the horses step on something. Thoroughbreds aren't the same as hardy mountain ponies,' Danny heard Meg say somewhere behind his right shoulder. 'What are you looking for?'

'That's the problem, I don't know.'

'I don't feel good about this.'

'We're not on his land,' Danny said. 'That wire fence down there tells us that.'

'We're not on our land either. It's still trespassing.'

'Only if we're caught,' Danny said.

'You're not still stalking Toby Carmichael? He's enjoyed success, so what?'

'I've been a trainer years longer than him,' Danny said.

'Exactly, he should be learning from you,' Meg replied. 'So do you really want him to see you up here spying on him?'

'You're supposed to learn from your mistakes,' Danny said. 'If that's right, he made no mistakes on his rookie season.'

'And that means he won't improve this season.'

'Stop being so positive.'

'You told me that, "big yourself up, don't beat yourself up",' she replied. 'If you don't you'll go mad at this game, that's what you said.'

'But he's having success with bargain bucket buys that should rightly be lining up for Southwell sellers on a rainy Monday, not Group races at the Grade One tracks.'

'It's just a regular yard that's enjoying a winning streak, Danny. We've been there when Salamanca was in his prime. Where's this jealous streak come from? I don't like it.'

'I'm not jealous, just baffled.'

'Well, stay baffled, I don't want you going round there making enemies, like with the Mills' on the other side of the valley.'

'I need to,' Danny said.

'Why?'

'They've stolen five of our best owners in recent months, others would've probably gone if they hadn't been behind on their training fees and they know I'd take them to court. He's stolen the owners that pay bills. A business can't live on bad debts.'

'Even if you're right, we'll get new owners.'

'Doubt it, the wealthiest are in London and the Home Counties. They want to watch their horses working on the gallops and racing in the South-East tracks, like Epsom, Sandown and Lingfield.'

'There's plenty of money in Cardiff if you look hard enough,' she reasoned. 'Fastest growing capital in Europe I heard.'

'But they're investing in football or rugby.'

'The racing scene in Wales is hotting up with a handful of big yards,' she said.

'National Hunt yards, nothing like the same on the Flat.'

'We've got Powder Keg.'

'Just one star, that's it.'

'Most yards would die for *just one star*.'

'But Toby's got a galaxy in that stable down there.'

'Danny, we've got Jack and Cerys while he's rattling around in there with a son that hates him. Toby can never beat us.'

'It drives me on to do better.'

'It also means you'll never be fulfilled, ever fully happy.'

Danny tracked two jockeys riding out on a gallop strip circling the island of woodland in the middle of Arwen Vale and then handed over the binoculars. 'See the rider with the black hair, that's Darren Cooper. He normally rides in the colours of Malcolm Bernard.'

'Perhaps he's doing a bit of freelancing, it's not easy to scrape a living as a journeyman jockey, travelling costs are insane,' Meg said.

'He'd never moonlight for us,' Danny said.

'Cos he's not wearing a hat?' Meg queried.

'Cos I've heard he's a disruptive influence,' Danny said. 'Perhaps Toby sees something of himself in the lad.'

Meg returned the binoculars. 'Looks like he can ride, he's gone clear in that piece of work.'

'Not saying much, I reckon little Jack could beat the other rider, Luke, that's Toby's son.' Clearly Luke was as listless in the saddle as he was as Toby's tea boy at the sales ring. 'Toby has too much business brains to put him on one of his runners though. Still, I'd rather work with him than Darren.'

When the galloping horses disappeared behind the woodland, Danny zoomed in on the tall wire fence marking the boundary of Toby Carmichael's estate, a foreboding wall of mesh topped by rolls of razor barbs.

'It's more like Area 51 than a racing yard,' Meg said.

'Probably holds as many secrets, too,' Danny said. 'I'm getting flashbacks of the time I served at Ringwall prison.'

'Perhaps it's there to keep the inmates from escaping, rather than intruders breaking in.'

'If it's the millions of pounds in horseflesh, why is there twenty thousand volts pulsing through a wire that close to the gallops? I heard a buzzing when I got closer once and the handful of grass I threw at the fence was frazzled before it hit the ground.'

'Bloody hell, that's a bit out of order,' Meg said indignantly. 'What if cattle came to graze round these parts?'

'Doubt he'd care,' Danny said. 'If a cow leaned on that, the Carmichaels would be dining on chargrilled steak for a month.'

He panned the binoculars across the vale and caught sight again of the criss-crossing gallop strips, looking like veins that fed the heart of the training complex somewhere beyond a large wooded area.

Over on the opposite slope, Danny stopped panning when he spotted the grey spoil and scree around the mouth of a cave or mineshaft. He knew centuries of mining had left these hills riddled with tunnels, like woodworm.

The opening to the cave was boarded up but he could see Toby's old hack had been tied to a boulder nearby.

'Bastard's in there again,' Danny whispered.

'In where?'

'I don't know for sure, but he keeps something inside the hill,' Danny said and then panned right. 'Crate of steroids I bet.'

'Yes, yes, Danny,' Meg sighed. 'I've heard it a thousand times, he's up to something, let's leave it at that … just something. Let them be, Danny, I never married a sore loser. Anyway, it's none of our bloody business, literally – he deals in Flat racers, we're jumpers and bumpers only.'

There was a pause. She watched as Danny turned Red Ink. He needed to face her for this. Having kept this secret for over a month, it's the least he could do.

'What?' she asked nervously, as if sensing a big reveal.

Meg then looked down at the juvenile and back up to Danny, who was pulling out his dual licence.

'Well, you know we've got plenty of vacant boxes in the new stabling block,' Danny said. 'I've got a plan to fill them.'

She turned Powder Keg slightly, as if it was her about to flee the scene. 'What are you saying?'

'I think we'll be more in competition with Toby than you might think.'

'We're adding Flat horses,' Meg said.

Danny nodded.

'You haven't even got a—'

'I got my permit from the BHA last week, all we need now is fresh bloodstock,' Danny said. He glanced down at Red Ink between his legs. 'This is the first of many I hope.'

'But it's a different skill,' Meg said. 'The horses work to a different regime.'

'The Flat horses will be racing-fit galloping the slopes up here and the fresh air works a treat. It hasn't done Carmichael's lot much harm. The ponies these thoroughbreds stem from once roamed these lands.'

'But Powder Keg outpaced Red Ink, who is our only buy for the Flat,' Meg said. 'And we've got two kids, Danny. It would be nice to see them grow up. We work fifteen hours a day, seven days a week over the winter with only three days off over Christmas and even they're busy, preparing for the Boxing Day schedule of meetings.'

'We'll get a child minder, Jack will be okay, you've seen how he gets on with Jordi,' Danny explained. 'We can just about afford not to, but prize money on the Flat is twice that of the jumps and the training fees we can charge are higher. This is a game of risks. If we play safe, Silver Belle Stables will slowly sink.'

'I know the risks,' Meg said. 'I worry every time you leave for the track with a ride.'

'What do you say? Let's do this.'

Meg paused.

Say something, Danny thought, anything.

He felt it was time to place his trump card on the table. 'You know you were dreading a summer post-morteming the Cheltenham flop. Well, dread no more.'

'You're telling me we're switching Kegsy to the Flat.'

'I reckon it wasn't lameness or the conditions that made her run so bad, and it certainly wasn't the jockey,' Danny said. 'You said yourself she outpaced this Flat-bred late on in that gallop and her pace between the flights of timber was always her most potent weapon. She's the most intelligent in the yard and returned from Cheltenham sound as a pound. It makes me think she'd just got bored with the game. You said yourself, she never jumped a twig and was always off the bridle. I'm convinced a switch of codes would reignite her interest, a change is good as a rest. Look at how she climbed that hill. If a change of routine did that, just imagine what a different track on the Flat would do.'

'I guess the Flat season is longer than the jumps,' she conceded after some thought, as if coming round to the idea.

'And there's all-weather,' Danny said. 'We'd be an all-year-round operation, none of this on and off season.'

'And Flat racers pick up fewer niggly injuries,' Meg added.

Danny felt he was winning her over. 'So you're onside.'

'But—'

'No buts,' Danny said. 'A Group Two on the Flat returns way more in prize money than a Grade Two over hurdles. She's your horse and I'll understand if you want to rest her, but—'

'I thought you said no buts,' she replied, grinning.

Danny smiled. 'We'll make this work, love, I promise.'

'Danny, you know I'll back you to the end,' Meg said.

'So you'll back me in this.'

'Would it make any difference? It looks like we're going ahead anyway.'

'We're a team, you have to be on board with this.'

She nodded.

'Best news all day that is.'

'But it's not even eight in the morning,' Meg said.

'This one will be ready for a Bath maiden on Guineas weekend in early May, and all being well Kegsy will go for a race later on that same card, there's a conditions event where she'll be thrown in at the weights with her sex allowance and no penalties to carry for all her hurdle wins.'

'Now I see the real reason for this new obsession about catching Toby out,' Meg said. 'It wasn't that you were worried about him stealing our owners, jump owners don't tend to switch to the Flat just because we've had a cold patch. You want our biggest competitor down there off the scene as we try to build the Flat side of the business.'

'I learnt as a punter, like most things in life, if it's too good to be true it probably is,' Danny said. 'Toby's strike rate is fifty-five per cent. *That* is too good to be true. Either Toby is incredibly lucky or incredibly skilful. Given most of the purchases are under ten grand, I'm going for neither. There's something else behind this. Somehow he's cheating the game, Meg. I'm not doing this for personal gain, I'm thinking of all the owners and punters of the rival horses getting beat by this yard. On the world stage, British racing has a reputation as being as clean as it gets, and it would only take something like this to ruin everything. Unfortunately, the answer is behind that bloody electric fence.'

Danny sat with a military bearing, as if he'd just delivered a Churchill speech.

'But it is a bit about us,' Meg said, spoiling his moment.

'Only a bit,' Danny said, shoulders dropping slightly.

'Do you think we should go now?' Meg said more as a request than a question. 'This feels awkward, it's like staring into a neighbour's window. And I need a coffee.'

'They can't see us up here,' Danny said.

Suddenly, a loud clap of gunfire shot from below, bouncing off the walls of the valley. Instinct made Danny duck. He then zoomed in to see Toby stood by the mesh of the wire fencing on his old hack, rifle cocked like a sheriff on patrol.

His hack had stood rooted to the spot as a dungeon of crows scattered from the woodland. The gelding had clearly heard gunfire before.

The same couldn't be said for Red Ink, who'd reared up on his haunches, whinnying. Danny gripped the reins. He wasn't scared of unseating but he didn't want the youngster running wild among all these rocks and brambles.

'Let's get out of—' Danny said but his voice was drowned by another loud bang.

Red Ink reared again and then bolted for real this time.

Danny hugged the colt's neck as he tried to catch the flapping reins he'd let slip. He quickly grabbed them and sat back but the horse was running on instinct alone.

Danny couldn't control the speed but could control the direction. His strong arms managed to point the galloping runaway in the direction of home, though less comfortably than before as the saddle had begun to slip. When he lost one stirrup, he kicked his boot out of the other. It was easier to balance his weight with both feet out of the irons. Danny was now effectively riding bareback.

Didn't want a third child anyway, he grimaced, feeling every bump and false step as they careered back down the slope.

He didn't know what scared him most – being shot at by a deranged neighbour or being perched on a juvenile going berserk. It felt a lot worse than the loss of control he'd experienced in the stands at Cheltenham.

At least Meg wouldn't question if he was crying wolf this time.

CHAPTER 5

BATH RACECOURSE. SATURDAY 2ND MAY.

1.59pm. Danny was being led in on Red Ink, who was set for stall three of nine, as the post-time came and went for the opening maiden.

Ahead lay the one mile and five yards of lush turf covering this left-handed oval track, best known for being the highest Flat racecourse in Britain. Some reckoned the air was slightly thinner up here. It was a track for course specialists, often favouring those used to training at altitude over undulations. Based up in the Valleys, Danny hoped this would become a home from home for his runners. They'd even brought the weather this time. The spitting sky was grey as the Welsh stone farmhouses peppering the remote hills of home.

While the turf action kicked off at Doncaster's Lincoln meeting in March, most in the industry viewed the Guineas meeting staged at Newmarket this weekend as when the campaign gets going properly.

Despite having been regularly tested in the replica stalls back at the yard, Red Ink appeared to be having second thoughts on his big day. Perhaps he was picking up a different vibe. Race days were a good deal more frenetic than the pace of the daily routine back home. Red Ink clearly knew something was up.

The stall handler bent and showed Red Ink a pick of grass. Danny could've been excused for being tempted by the offer. Dropping to over a stone below his natural weight was only half the battle, keeping it off had proved just as hard. Exhaustion and hunger haunted his every waking hour.

When Jack once asked, 'Daddy, why you so grumpy and sad?' he felt like flopping back on the sofa and crying. He somehow kept it together, knowing how it might look to his son.

Danny adjusted his goggles and filled his lungs with cool, damp air. This was the moment he'd been working for in recent months, though expectations weren't high, least of all in the betting ring where his mount had drifted out to twenty-five-to-one on the electronic bookie boards glowing orange.

They'd clearly sent a mole to see his homework, Danny thought wryly.

Right then, he felt like being sick. He didn't think fear would be a thing on this belated comeback to the Flat scene but the doubts had crept in. Would he still cut it after all these years away?

It's not as if he didn't have experience on the Flat, he kept telling himself, and it was just like the jumps but without the problem of jumping. Except, deep down, he knew it wasn't the same at all. Everything unfolded that much quicker over the shorter trips. It was more about searching out the firmest ground and avoiding getting boxed in behind runners as the pace quickens.

Danny glanced on both sides. To the left, he saw Darren Cooper, with his high cheekbones framed by black foppish hair, sat quietly staring through the grilles of stall two on Shoehorn, who remained steady at three-to-one in the betting market. He was in the colours of leading owner Malcolm Bernard – white with powder blue trim and matching cap. He blanked Danny, probably still going over the police interview.

On his right was Ryan Lawson, who was also facing ahead in red and green diamond silks with matching hooped sleeves and white cap. A rising star of the weighing room, he was sitting on the Toby Carmichael-trained and owned Fat Suit, a handsome brown colt possessing plenty of size and scope.

He was markedly similar in appearance to Red Ink. But given Fat Suit was the well-supported even-money favourite, Danny suspected that's where the resemblance ended. That better-fancied rival had clearly shown a great deal more promise galloping round the woodland in the neighbouring valley and the fact Toby had been seen on track was a pointer in itself to Fat Suit's chances. Carmichael wouldn't travel here for the fun of it on a day like this, most punters would presume.

The stalls rattled and rocked slightly as the last of the runners were loaded and the starter climbed his rostrum.

Red Ink had begun to get restless, drum brushing the side bars of the stall.

As the bars sprung back, there was a chorus of jockeys' growls as they coaxed their inexperienced horses forward in the hope of grabbing a decent early pitch.

After a few strides, Red Ink had already fallen behind those either side.

Danny had at least bagged a rail berth to save ground on the bend, albeit in rear, as they began the three-furlong climb before the left turn.

Red Ink was soon travelling better than most, clearly benefitting from the hill-work at home. Danny had gained a few places into sixth as the field banked left before negotiating a more gentle turn into about four furlongs of home straight. Up front, he could see the bobbing blue and white caps of Shoehorn tracked by Fat Suit as they embarked on the downhill stretch to the red lollipop stick of the finish line.

Danny began to ask for more as he sat lower shaking the reins, but Red Ink simply wasn't picking up. Greenness made the colt edge off a true line, right then left. He put the whip down.

Passing the two-furlong pole, he got broadsided by a meandering straggler on his outer. It was clear he needed to become more spatially aware and react to runners around him during the race as he'd forgotten how much tighter they grouped on the Flat, with many runners still holding a live chance late on. Unfortunately that wasn't the case for Red Ink, whose race was already run entering the final furlong. He eased down.

Danny was merely a bystander as he watched Fat Suit switch out wider and lengthen clear of Shoehorn for an emphatic win. Winning jockey Ryan Lawson hadn't even needed to call upon his whip.

Over the speakers, he made out the commentator chirp, '— and it's yet another impressive recruit for Carmichael's all-conquering Arwen Vale yard.'

Bastard!

What the hell had Toby seen in Red Ink at the Ely sales ring?

Danny felt frustrated. Not at the horse but that he'd allowed himself to rely on another's opinion and not trust his own. He'd preached exactly the opposite to the whining punter by the rails at Cheltenham and was now paying the price.

The colt hadn't even shown enough to suggest that with natural progression, he could win a race, whatever the grade. Racing was often a matter of managing hope with expectation. Right then, Danny held little of either for Red Ink.

Back in the parade ring, Danny handed Red Ink over to Meg.

'Oh, well,' Meg sighed. 'It was an education.'

'For both of us,' Danny replied.

Meg led the colt away to be hosed down in the racecourse stabling.

Danny then returned to the changing room to prepare for the feature event, a two-mile one-furlong and thirty-four yards conditions event which had long been earmarked as the ideal introduction to Powder Keg's second career as a Flat racer.

Danny approached the Roman pillared entrance beneath the lettering Bath Racecourse and a green gilded clock set in the grey-yellow Bath limestone of the main stand. He crossed paths with Ryan Lawson, who clutched a small silver medal, having come from posing for photos by the winner's podium in the parade ring.

Danny offered a gloved hand in congratulations. He was a new face to the Flat weighing rooms and wanted to make friends not enemies.

Ryan was short even for a Flat jockey, with cropped hair and green eyes. 'It was a Bath maiden,' he said sarcastically in his scouse accent as their hands barely touched.

It's only then Danny realised the race held more significance to him on his big comeback than others riding in the race, least of all the likes of Lawson. It left Danny wondering why the hell the lad was messing about at this low-key meeting when Newmarket was on. Probably retained by Carmichael and contractually left with no option but to steer home a minor winner here. That would explain the slight attitude in Ryan's reply.

Probably thought I was the one being sarcastic with a handshake.

'Wasn't being off or anything just then,' Danny added.

'It's not you,' Ryan replied. 'It was just an armchair ride, feel guilty picking up my riding fee let alone winner's percentage, but don't tell anyone that. As they say, fortune favours the fortunate,' Ryan said cheekily. A twinkle had quickly returned to his green eyes.

In the weighing room, Danny found a quiet corner. It wasn't difficult as most of the jockeys were huddled in varying degrees of undress staring up at a TV screen on the wall showing Newmarket, probably wishing they were there too.

Danny wasn't one of them. He'd dropped his wasted body on to the bench, back against the wall, trying to get his head straight for Powder Keg in the next. He glanced across at a young jockey he knew only as Chris in the corner opposite, staring at the tiled floor, alone with his thoughts. He was the smallest and palest in the weighing room and that alone was quite an achievement. With an overbite, reddish hair, freckles, gapped teeth and glasses, it wasn't hard to feel sorry for the lad, a bully's wet dream. He wouldn't have lasted a term at Danny's old school in Rhymney.

When Chris looked up, Danny looked away.

'Weighed in, weighed in,' came over the crackly speaker above his head. 'Horses away, horses away.'

As Danny changed into Meg's red and white colours, he hoped the steam from the gushing showers over the walled divide might help him sweat off the extra few ounces to make the correct weight for Powder Keg, who was allowed to claim allowances for being a winless mare.

On the TV, the presenters had moved on to a preview of the 2000 Guineas. Right then, Danny had no interest in Group Ones on the Flat. At the current rate, he was unlikely to be saddling anything nearly good enough to even contest let alone win at the highest level this summer.

Danny kept an almost meditative state as he imagined in his mind's eye every conceivable race-plan, reacting to each scenario in a different way, but making sure the result was always the same: first, number seven Powder Keg.

'Move!' Danny heard. Only then he realised Darren Cooper had returned to the changing room and was ordering Chris, who was slouched even lower, like a spider making himself small. But it didn't matter what the lad did, Darren had already noticed him. 'This is my spot.'

'There are loads of others free,' Chris replied, little more than a whisper.

'But none are this one!' Darren snarled.

Chris couldn't keep his eyes off the floor tiles, as if wanting them to swallow him up whole.

Darren removed his riding cap and grinned as he messed up his hat hair as black and shiny as Powder Keg's mane. From where Danny stood the other side, it looked like Darren was actually enjoying this. The same couldn't be said for Chris.

'Hello?!' Darren called out deliberately as if talking to a young child, knuckles rapping Chris' scalp. 'Is there something wrong with your hearing or your legs?' Chris sniffled. 'Well, which is it?'

It's as if Darren was asking for an audience. One by one the other jockeys in the room turned to watch.

Chris quickly wiped his eyes with the back of his hand.

'Oh man up, acting like the poof you are, Chris Ramsbottom,' Darren said, making himself laugh. 'Chris Rams… bottom, gets me every time. You're the gift that keeps giving. You must come from a long line of Ramsbottoms.'

'I chose it. It's my mother's maiden name,' Chris said, as if another nerve had been struck.

Danny had wondered if this was more about Darren losing the previous race, but if he reacted this badly from losing a minor maiden, he was in the wrong business.

Darren said, 'What? Don't want to leave? The door's over there. I know you prefer the tradesman's entrance.' Darren's laugh again helped filled the silence. 'Do you get it? Because you like to take it up the wrong 'n.'

Danny now knew Malcolm was underselling it when he'd described Darren as a disruptive influence.

Chris grabbed his towel and stood.

'Oh, quick, call for Mummy Ramsbottom, he's running away.'

'Wouldn't give you the satisfaction.'

'No, look, lads, he's going for a shower, backs to the wall,' Darren said. 'All this time I wondered why you were finishing last in races. It wasn't your weak wrists; it was to get an eyeful of the view from back there.'

Danny felt an atmosphere as the room fell completely silent, like watching a stand-up comedian dying on his arse. Yet there were no hecklers in there, probably too scared. He last saw Darren's type at school. They played on fear, forging friendships solely on the promise that they wouldn't be the next target. It was a small-scale protection racket.

Danny knew something had to be done. Someone had to say something.

But Darren had strength, reach and youth on his side. Danny only had his air-cushioned whip, designed specifically not to inflict damage.

Standing tall with shoulders back, Danny shouted, 'Enough!'

Darren didn't immediately react. It's as if he couldn't quite believe anyone would dare interrupt him in full flow. When he did look over, Danny added, 'For fuck's sake, Darren, the Seventies want you back.'

'Danny Rawlings,' Darren replied, 'I'm surprised they've not asked you first, you're the only one in here alive back then.' There was some nervy laughter from somewhere. 'Failed punter, failed jump jockey, and now trying to steal some of our prize money, boys. Could've guessed you'd side with the queer, stick together your type.'

'*Our* prize money?' Danny questioned. 'There's no us and them, we're all jockeys.'

'That's a matter of opinion,' Darren replied, smirking. 'Anyway, calm down, grandpa, who said you could join our argument?'

'An argument has two sides, this is abuse.'

'I never touched him.'

'You've never heard of verbal abuse then?'

'I'll show you abuse,' Darren said. Danny backed up against the wall as Darren came storming over and grabbed Danny by the silks.

Chris shrieked. 'Stop it!'

Darren glanced back over his shoulder, seemingly surprised his first victim had suddenly found a voice.

While Darren wasn't looking, Danny glared at Chris and rapidly shook his head, mouthing, 'No.' He didn't want the young lad getting anymore grief.

But Darren let him go, as if it all had been one big mistake. He just walked out of there to a stunned silence.

There was a few seconds where no one knew what to do or say. All the years Danny had frequented the changing rooms at racetracks, he'd never seen anything like it.

The crowd soon dispersed as the show was clearly over. Danny found himself alone with Chris, who took off his specs and carefully placed them in their case. He pulled a dust cloth from inside and dabbed his cheeks with it, snapping the case shut. He then set about putting in his contact lenses.

'Do you mind not looking, it's just I shake when being watched.'

Danny suspected he knew why the lad hadn't made it, and never would, in the pressured world of a modern-day jockey.

'I reckon my glasses were the only reason Darren didn't thump me,' Chris said.

'Only to avoid shredding his knuckles, not your face,' Danny replied and then leant in close. 'People will think Darren's a bully, but it's also important to remember he's a cock.'

Chris let out a snotty laugh.

'That's the spirit,' Danny said. 'You okay now?'

'Shouldn't it be me asking that?'

'He's all talk. Seen his type before,' Danny replied. 'All mouth, probably a frustrated virgin.'

'He's married, with three kids,' Chris replied coldly.

'He should know better then.'

'I've had worse confrontations,' Chris said.

'Really? When?'

'When I tried to tell my father that … I couldn't form those simple words, "I'm gay."' Chris looked up. 'I'd rehearsed it so many times, the words didn't seem right anymore. They didn't even seem like words, I just had to form these noises to let my father know. He'd beat me for losing a race, he'd kill me for this. He used to say, be a man, grow a pair.'

'So what did you do?'

Chris straightened his arm and a rainbow wristband fell from his silk sleeve.

'Clever.'

'Would've been, but Dad didn't know what the colours symbolised, reckoned I'd joined some hippy troupe.' Chris made himself laugh. 'Seems funny now, but I was at my lowest right then.'

'At least there was no more pretending.'

'He tried to beat the gay out of me, like it was some disease.' Chris looked up at him with sad eyes. 'I think I prefer pretending.'

'Don't let Darren rake up bad memories,' Danny said. 'Look, you're welcome to do some work riding down at my yard, can't guarantee you'll sit on any pigeon catchers.'

'Thanks, but no thanks,' Chris said. 'The day I become a charity is the day I walk away.'

'You'd really do that?'

Chris wiped his pink eyes and nostrils, muttering, 'Bloody hay fever.' He cleared his throat. 'I've been thinking about it for a while. It takes guts, though. Maybe Darren's right, I am weak in the head.'

'Darren's type is never right.'

'But it turns out riding really isn't for me, hasn't been for some time.'

'What else would you do?' Danny asked.

'That jockeys' retraining thing put on by the BHA.'

'JETS?' Danny asked. He'd looked into the Jockeys Employment Training Scheme himself when last suffering a slump in form a few years back.

'I've already completed a course, and I want to stay in racing, just not with …' Chris stopped. It's as if he couldn't even say Darren Cooper's name. 'It's just, in here people only notice me when I get picked on.'

'Get out if you're not happy,' Danny said. 'This game's not for everyone.'

The speakers sounded, 'We have a jockey change for the two thirty-five, our second race. Darren Cooper will now be riding number three on the racecard Spirit Kettle.'

Clearly Ryan Lawson had seen sense, Danny thought, probably clocked off early to head for Newmarket's One Thousand Guineas meeting on Sunday.

Danny welcomed the news. He reckoned it was a boost to the chances of Powder Keg. He'd much rather have Darren Cooper on board his biggest threat than the in-form rising star Ryan Lawson.

'Shouldn't have any more aggro from Darren today,' he said, 'seems he's just landed a plum ride on the second favourite in the next.'

'Only if he runs well,' Chris reasoned.

'Not too well,' Danny replied. 'I'm on the fav.'

Still shaken, Danny tried to regain his composure for what he felt could turn out to be career-transforming moments for both the horse and her trainer.

Discreetly, he checked himself out in a mirror as he straightened his silks on the way to meet Meg, who by now would be parading her mare for the paying public.

Let's do this!

CHAPTER 6

'He tried to bloody kill us,' Meg said, staring intently at Toby Carmichael close by.

'He tried to scare us,' Danny replied. 'They were air shots. Toby might be evil but he's not stupid.'

Toby was handing out instructions to last-minute jockey replacement Darren Cooper, who'd quickly changed into the yard's red-and-green diamond silks which had already graced the winner's circle after the first race.

Danny was adjusting Powder Keg's girth to a comfortable, yet tight, fit. Last thing they needed was for the saddle to slip. Danny knew a bad experience could leave its mark for future outings.

'Well, his wife Molly died not that long ago,' Meg said.

'Local paper reported it as suicide,' Danny explained. 'She was clinically depressed. They even found a note on her.'

'All the same, makes you wonder,' Meg muttered.

'I thought you said we weren't to mention the C word.'

Meg's face froze as if she'd seen Molly's ghost over Danny's shoulder. He turned to see Toby, shadowed by a suited Luke, whose blond curls had been tamed by water.

'Alright there, Toby?' Danny asked casually, trying to figure out if Carmichael had overheard any of that.

'Found a note on whom?' Toby asked sternly.

Danny felt his face burn and brain cramp. 'Do you make a habit of listening in to private conversations?'

'I do when they're about us,' Toby said.

'Mam wasn't right in the head towards the end,' Luke said.

'We understand,' Meg said.

Toby leant in close. Danny could feel and smell the warm breath. 'I only hope your Powder Keg performs better than your first runner,' Toby whispered. Danny felt like shoving him away. 'Seemed I dodged a bullet with that... one.'

'Red Ink is sure to improve for the experience,' Danny replied.

'He'll need to,' Toby said and left to the sound of the brass bell signalling jockeys to mount.

Danny watched Toby meet up with Darren again.

Malcolm was also over there in his trademark cream suit with blue hanky and tie. He'd got the third favourite Mood Music running for him.

Danny saw Toby and Malcolm briefly exchange words and then both laugh. Malcolm was probably glad to see Darren off his hands, Danny reckoned, while Toby was relieved to find a replacement in time after Ryan's no show.

Danny took Powder Keg down quietly to the start. The stalls for this two-mile one-furlong and thirty-four yards contest – the furthest they raced at Bath – were positioned at the start of the straight sprint track. At the finish line, runners would then go out again and complete a whole lap with the lollipop marking the finish second time around.

He hoped Powder Keg would emulate great hurdlers of the past to make an impact on the Flat, like Kribensis and Morley Street. He'd soon know if those hopes were pure fantasy.

'Jockeys, ready!' shouted the starter, palm resting on the mushroom button on his rostrum.

On the ping of the gates, Powder Keg broke smartly and was quickly into stride. She seemed eager to be out of that alien metal contraption. Danny was pleased she'd settled into an early rhythm out in the lead. From there, he could dictate matters rather than be dictated by others.

With no hurdles in sight, perhaps she thought it was a regular gallop at home. If he still held the lead on the final turn into the home run, Danny reckoned she'd be very hard to pass.

As they galloped by the old grandstands and the newer grey corporate boxes tacked on, Danny could pick out individual cheers among the small, largely local, crowd urging them out on the only complete circuit.

A far cry from the Cheltenham roar, Danny thought, but hearing his name among the shouts almost meant more than a deafening wall of noise, something like a musician playing an intimate gig rather than a stadium.

Wherever the race, Danny always felt the same: the adrenalin, the anxiety, the fear, the buzz.

They banked left at the lowest point of the track and then set about the largely uphill backstretch.

Powder Keg was changing stride patterns to keep balance and momentum; Danny just had to sit still and not upset that natural rhythm. It's as if he'd flicked an autopilot switch and could actually enjoy the ride.

With no big screen to call upon and the distant commentator now just a garbled noise, Danny glanced back for a few strides. He had two lengths on nearest pursuer the Malcolm Bernard-owned Mood Music and a similar gap back to Darren Cooper's Spirit Kettle sharing third on the outer with Crestfallen.

Danny already had his finger hovering over the button. *When to go?*

He then spotted the offshoot for the one-mile start where Red Ink had begun his career. They'd only completed just over half the race. Eagerness to win like the champion he knew she was risked losing the race. Going for home this early, she'd be a floundering mess by the closing stages. She was a proven stayer not Pegasus.

All the while, he was trying to second-guess any challenge from behind. As they crested the rise on the farthest point from the stands, Danny knew there was about five furlongs left. The mare was still travelling sweetly. He was so sorely tempted to ask her to seal it, getting first run on the rest.

They negotiated another sharpish left. Powder Keg's nimble legs and compact, neat action adjusted well to the cornering and change of direction and gradient. She darted round there like a railing greyhound from trap one.

He started to see the distant grandstand come into view. He gathered up the reins.

It's then he heard the snorts of air and thud of hooves by Powder Keg's flank. A rival was trying to catch them off guard, sleeping on the job.

He turned his head to see Darren riding for his life, throwing his arms, legs and whip at Spirit Kettle, whose glossy bay neck edged into the lead.

Danny didn't panic, confidently holding the rails pitch as he sat lower.

Time to finish the job, he thought, come on girl show us what you got.

Clutching the bunched reins, he pushed her plaited mane as she lengthened her stride beautifully, bravely extending her forelegs on the descent while her powerful hind legs propelled her on.

It was if she answered, 'you want it, you got it.'

Danny no longer heard Darren or Spirit Kettle.

Some karma for his behaviour in the changing room, Danny thought.

Passing the furlong marker, Danny looked back again. Since making the final turn, Powder Keg had put five lengths between her and the rest. *She was back big time!*

He felt like punching the air but managed to keep both hands firmly on the reins. He was steering home precious cargo. He wouldn't take his hand off the wheel driving with Jack and Cerys in the back of his Mazda CX-3 fearing a blowout. He felt a responsibility for Powder Keg, who could quite easily spook and jink at one of the course photographers in bright green bibs pointing a long lens over the rails. He knew Meg would be on springs looking from somewhere up in the owners and trainers area of the stands.

'It's Powder Keg by six lengths, value for more,' came over the speakers.

That was a cue for Danny to apply the handbrake by tugging on the reins. The mare's head immediately came up. She wanted more, still galloping her heart out, even after seventeen furlongs. The finish post was a streak of red as they flew over the line. She'd clearly been lit up by the change of scenery and code here. Danny felt she could've carted him at the same speed down to the historic spa town far below.

'Have we seen a Cup horse in the making here? Mightily impressive that's for sure,' added the course commentator. Danny didn't want to stoke the hype machine any more. There was enough pressure in this game without manufacturing it. He certainly wouldn't reveal that her next stop would be the Yorkshire Cup in a few weeks.

His days as a hardened punter told him they'd only beaten a failed middle-distance handicapper and an exposed maiden winner, but she couldn't have done it easier and she'd learn more from the experience than the others.

He'd rehearse that line for the waiting hacks lurking near the winners' circle, hoping it would be enough to fill their copy and for him to make a quick getaway.

Unfortunately, he was also called in for a grilling from the Stewards, too. Danny explained away the apparent dramatic improvement from the Cheltenham flop by saying, 'A switch to the Flat had got her interest back and the ground conditions and track suited her perfectly in a race she was entitled to win on the pick of her hurdling form.'

They ordered a routine drugs test but no further action would be taken.

It still meant Danny had to scrap the quick exit. He'd left Meg to load Red Ink and Powder Keg into the van while he grabbed his things from the changing room.

They'd arranged to meet up in the car park by the golf course outside the gates to save time with the aim to beat the rush-hour traffic around Cardiff near the journey's end.

By the time he'd returned to the back of the grandstand Darren was already out of Carmichael's silks. He was leaning against one of the Roman pillars in a white sleeveless vest and matching breeches. His tattooed right arm held a phone to his ear.

After suffering his second defeat in two races, he half expected Darren's free arm to stick out as a barrier, just for the sake of it. But Darren didn't even look across, as if Danny no longer existed.

He'd clearly simmered down from earlier, Danny thought, probably calling mummy.

Entering the changing room, Danny smiled at Chris as he went to his saddle tree. In his kitbag, he stuffed his socks, deodorant, goggles, silks, talc, towel and breeches. He zipped it up and then his blue Silver Belle Stables fleece. He'd shower when he got back.

He slung the bag over his shoulder and left with, 'I meant it, Chris. Call me if you want some work.'

Chris smiled back.

As Danny made for the exit gates of the racecourse, he swore he heard a groan. He stopped. He feared it might be a sore loser drunkenly meandering from the hospitality tent taking the effort to tell him they backed the runner-up Spirit Kettle. But

Danny appeared to be alone there. He was about to carry on when he heard the same guttural groan, louder and longer this time.

He thought it must be gusts whistling between the Tote offices, toilets, burger van and betting ring manager's office, more like a windowed shed. Danny went over and made a visor with his hand as he peered through the window. The office appeared empty; clearly the betting ring manager was on his rounds dealing with problems or disputes between the bookies and punters on the other side of the stands.

'Help!' came from the other side.

Danny rushed to the rear, dropping his kitbag as he went. There, he could see a slumped jockey in full costume wearing the Carmichael colours of green, red and white silks. He was propped up by a sheltered stone wall. His breeches were also red. The last time he'd seen red breeches was in the Shergar Cup. This wasn't Ascot.

'Ryan!'

It was Ryan Lawson, runaway winner of the opening maiden. The ups and downs of racing had never seemed so stark.

The fallen jockey's bloody hands came up to mask his screwed-up face. He clearly couldn't bear to look at his legs.

Danny looked down for him. *Holy shit!*

Ryan was making a weird demonic groan, like a witch doctor speaking in tongues.

Danny extended a comforting arm around the young lad's shoulders. He appeared unharmed above the waist. 'What the hell happened, Ryan? Ryan? Stay with me, Ryan. Don't shut your eyes, Ryan, count from ten to one, do it, now.'

'Are you the doctor?' Ryan asked.

He was clearly in shock.

Ryan's finger dripped red as it pointed at the DR initials on Danny's fleece.

'No, it's Danny Rawlings,' Danny said. Ryan had recognised him just minutes after the maiden win.

Danny reckoned it wasn't just the knees that had taken a blow. He checked Ryan's scalp for a lump or blood. Nothing.

'I'll get the medics, there's a St John's ambulance just over there.'

'Ruffie,' Ryan slurred. 'I'm on Ruffie.'

Danny looked up at the flat roof of the shed. 'Have you been drinking?'

Ryan shook his head angrily. 'Ruffie.'

Danny looked again at the breeches and saw a bone protruding through one of the several rips. His legs were bent in a place where they shouldn't. There was no way he'd do that damage from a single level fall.

Ryan was victim five.

'I'll get help, don't you dare pass out on me, Ryan.'

Only then Ryan also dared to look down at his mangled legs. The whimpering turned to wailing and his grip on Danny's hand began to hurt. Danny needed him to keep calm, or he'd go into shock. 'They're not as bad as they look.'

'It's not how they look,' Ryan cried. 'I can't move them. I can't bloody—' He stopped and pinched his eyes.

Danny paused. He was torn. He didn't want to leave the kid alone at his lowest hour. But he had to get help.

The ambulance was parked up by a red brick wall below the picnic area and betting ring. It was as empty as the betting ring manager's office. The medics were clearly doing a tour of the stands strapped with first aid backpacks.

Danny shouted over to Darren, who was still on the phone. 'Ring for an ambulance.'

Darren shook his head.

'End that fucking call or you'll need an ambulance,' Danny shouted.

Darren removed the phone from his ear and appeared to dial. He shouted back, 'What's up?'

'Jockey down,' Danny shouted, 'bad leg injury, passing out.'

Darren grimaced. 'Who?'

'Just call them!'

There was another groan, as if Ryan had heard the message too. Danny just hoped Ryan wouldn't face a life of pushing wheels, not horse's withers, as he rushed back behind the shed. 'Help is on its way.'

Danny held Ryan's blooded and shaky hands as they waited.

He blew out when he saw the flash of blue lights and a medic appear.

'What's your name, son?'

'Ryan.'

The lead medic snapped on an oxygen mask. 'Breathe deep and slow, Ryan.'

The medic looked to Danny. 'Did he mention anything he'd taken? Any alcohol?'

'No,' Danny said, shaking his head. 'He said something about Ruffie. I'm on Ruffie.'

'Are you sure?'

'Yeah,' Danny said. Ryan was also nodding. 'What is it?'

'Street name for Rohypnol.'

Danny had heard the name in a TV report about date rapes.

'Can't promise you that, Ryan. But we can sort you out with a dose of morphine, ease the pain while we stretcher you to the ambulance, get you checked out properly at Bath General.'

Ryan nodded, mask steaming up as he noisily filled his lungs.

'Who made the call?' the medic asked.

'Darren Cooper,' Danny replied.

'Good job he did,' the medic said.

Danny looked over at the pillars. 'Looks like he's already left, though.'

'On three.' The medics lifted the stretcher and were gone.

Danny stayed back to make a police witness statement before finally leaving with Meg and the two horses in the back of the van. She'd rested the silver winner's plate on the dashboard and couldn't take her eyes off it, beaming all the way home.

Danny was only thankful she'd been spared the sickening scene leaving the racetrack.

CHAPTER 7

Early next morning, Danny's fists banged the red paint of Arwen Vale's front door.

He could smell the acrid smoke from here. He backed up enough to see the black billowing column reaching up to the empty sky, tall enough to be seen a valley away. It's what drew him there; the fear Carmichael's horses could be in distress.

He'd only tried the door as he didn't want to be accused of sneaking around the yard without consent. Toby's threat by the Ely Park kiosk still lived large in his memory.

Fuck it, Danny thought. The horses were more important than their opinion.

He sprinted for the stables round the back. But when he checked, the grass island framed by boxes on all sides was deathly quiet. A few of the more inquisitive horses poked their heads over the V in their stable doors, checking out the new visitor. It seemed Danny was the only one distressed in there.

He looked up at the mossy tiles and air vents of the stable roof and soon realised the smoke was coming from behind the stable block.

Danny sprinted round and was met by a small unmanned bonfire

As he neared, he could see through the shimmering heat and fumes, there looked like a piece of material not yet consumed by the licking flames.

Using a crooked twig he found under a nearby tree, Danny skewered the material. It looked like a white hanky.

Must be Toby's, Danny reckoned, Luke would use his sleeve.

As he felt its warmth, he noticed it was covered in dark brown spots.

Toby must've had a nosebleed, he thought.

He was about to chuck it back on the fire when he recognised the sky-blue trim on white in parts where the soft material hadn't been singed brown.

This was no hanky, but part of something bigger, Danny realised, the silks of Malcolm Bernard.

His fingers skated over the material. It certainly felt like the mix of drag-resistant Lycra and polyester used in modern-day silks. It weighed nothing in his palm. No wonder, as a whole set of silks weighed about one hundred and fifty grams in this weight-conscious sport and this was a mere fragment. If it wasn't for its warmth, he couldn't readily tell he held it at all. He'd last seen them being worn by Darren Cooper finishing runner-up in the opener at Bath, just minutes before the vicious attack on the winning jockey Ryan Lawson. Owners had to design their unique silks to distinguish their runners in a race from a choice of eighteen colours, twelve sleeves and twenty-five shapes.

Although it was limited compared to the infinite palate offered to owners by the US Jockey Club, there were more than enough combinations of colours and designs to suggest it was almost certainly Malcolm Bernard's silks.

Had Darren got his sick revenge for getting beat? Having got a spare ride at the expense of Ryan Lawson on Spirit Kettle in the next race, Darren certainly had the motive. And the earful of abuse he'd dished out to Chris between races suggested he was up for a fight.

But why would Darren go on an angry homophobic rant? He'd only then become the prime suspect. Everyone there wouldn't forget the show, Danny thought, unless that was the point. Putting on such a public display of hate would place him firmly in the weighing room, rather than butchering Ryan behind the betting ring manager's office. He'd have a dozen reliable alibis in the changing room. Danny held the silk knowing his fingerprints were now all over the evidence.

There was thirty-five minutes between the maiden and the conditions race, more than enough time to physically attack Ryan and then verbally attack Chris, particularly as Darren had finished runner-up in the opener and wouldn't need to collect a jockey's winner's medal at the podium in the parade ring or give TV and press interviews.

'You!' Danny heard from behind.

As Danny turned, he deftly slipped the burnt silk down the back of his jeans with a pickpocket's touch.

It was Darren sat on a strapping brown colt.

Danny said, 'I was just thinking about you.'

'Get away from the fire!' Darren ordered angrily.

'It's why I came,' Danny explained. 'What the hell were you thinking starting it here?'

'I scorched the surrounding area. Don't want grass fires like they have above Port Talbot.'

'So it's your fire, then?' Danny questioned. He wanted Darren to volunteer a confession, albeit unwittingly, to the brutal attack on Ryan Lawson.

'It's my responsibility, yeah,' Darren said.

Danny watched orange embers float about like fireflies near the timber-framed stables.

'A gust in the wrong direction and that will go up in smoke,' Danny replied, 'then you'll have a fucking bonfire.'

Darren refused to dismount, as if he wanted to keep talking down to Danny. There was a moment of awkward silence broken only by the crackle and hiss of the roaring yellow-orange flames. Danny reckoned both were wondering what the other was doing there.

'I thought you were retained by Malcolm Bernard. Moonlighting are you?' Danny asked.

'I was asked to work some of the new recruits here and when Mr Carmichael calls, you don't hang up,' Darren said. 'Nothing in the contract says I can't tend another trainer's fire.'

Destroying evidence more like, Danny thought, feeling the silk warming his arse. 'Well, it's clearly paying off; you got the spare on Spirit Kettle.'

Feeling the back of his neck burn from the fire, Danny came over and slapped Darren's mount on the rump.

'Don't pat him there.'

'I guess you hit him there.'

'I don't hit horses, I'd hit humans though,' Darren said pointedly.

'You make it hard for me to like you,' Danny said. 'Has Toby given you permission for the fire?'

'He has,' Danny heard another voice, deeper. Several seconds later, Toby hobbled into view from behind the grey stone perimeter wall of the stable block. He glanced up at Darren on horseback and Danny, both not far from the fire. 'What is this, summer camp?'

'I was just explain—' Danny started saying

'Did *you* have permission to be here?' Toby interjected.

'I was worried about the horses.'

'Well, rest assured, they're thriving,' Toby said. 'I would be more concerned about your own.'

'Results will turn,' Danny said. 'Can I look in at them on my way out? It'll help calm Meg. I put her off calling out the fire brigade.'

Toby paused. 'Very well, but I'll be your guide.'

'I'll be fine by myself.'

'But I won't be fine with that.'

Danny didn't argue. He knew Toby hadn't even offered a stable tour for the press, let alone a rival trainer. Stable tours had become a common feature in trade papers, allowing punters to find out the latest on their favourites, the stable stars, the promising recruits and the 'dark' horses to look out for.

Danny felt Toby wasn't the type to be bothered about either connecting with racing fans or appearing more transparent and welcoming to attract new owners.

Slowly, Danny and Toby made their way round to the grassy stable courtyard.

Toby's limp became less apparent as his pace quickened by the half-open stable doors.

Inside the gloomy first box, Danny could make out the glossy brown coat of a fine stamp of a two-year-old filly, seemingly healthy as she was happy. She was stood quietly in a thick bedding of clean hay, with full water and feed trays. Danny pulled his head from in there and read the brass nameplate. It read: Drunken Mistress, Sire: Good To Go, Dam: The Plan Has Landed. Danny hadn't heard of the sire or dam. He looked over at Toby, who had already carried on to the fifth stable door in.

Toby said, 'Let's keep moving, or we'll never be done. Unlike you, my time is money.'

'Tell me more about this one,' Danny said.

Toby arched his bushy eyebrows and sighed. 'She won her maiden well and is going for a Listed race at York's Dante meeting. You'll see her win in the flesh. I hear your only star Powder Keg's going for the Yorkshire Cup later on the card. Longer term, this one will hopefully make a lovely broodmare.'

'Not much of a pedigree to go on,' Danny said. 'She'll have to do the business on the track for her progeny to make money at the sales.'

'Her family line will improve once the breeding industry sees her true ability,' Toby said confidently.

The horse trustingly came forward into the daylight and Danny patted her neck.

'Don't pat her there.'

Darren had said something similar when he patted the rump of his charge.

'Have you created robot horses and you're worried I'll flick the off button?'

'If I could build robots that beautiful and elegant do you think I'd be stuck watching them at dawn in the dark and cold?'

'What is it, then?'

'I don't risk the crossing of diseases or viruses from another string of horses.'

'My horses are healthy!'

'That's even more worrying for you,' Toby smirked. 'Some of these are as valuable as paintings by the masters, you wouldn't touch them.'

When Danny stopped at the neighbouring stable, he heard another loud sigh from Toby. Inside was another brown youngster, a colt this time, as pleasing to the eye as the filly, again with no distinct markings or whorls.

As he slowly made his way round the courtyard, it became clear all the horses appeared to be in good order, as you'd expect for a high-profile yard in great form. But to Danny something still didn't feel right about the place. Aside from the fact they were all modestly bred yet good looking, all twenty-eight horses were a variation of brown, from dark bay to brown.

There wasn't a chestnut, roan, grey or black horse to be seen.

'Are we done?' Toby asked, tapping the steel tip of the cane on the tarmac.

'Nearly,' Danny said and looked in the last of the stable doors.

Suddenly, he smelt a woody smoke. He was about to sprint back to check on the bonfire when he saw Toby's wet lips were sucking on a Cuban cigar. The ghost of a smile spread across his fat face as he blew smoke into the crisp morning air.

Danny looked on with a mix of shock and disgust. 'Like I said, I was afraid the smoke would harm the horses.'

Toby carried on puffing clouds with apparent glee.

Danny didn't want to be there anymore. Perhaps that was Toby's aim.

'I treat our horses better than I treat Luke,' Toby explained. 'This place is more like a luxury hotel, nothing but the finest feed and room service. A sauna, solarium and a swimming pool are being planned for next summer. And one look at our jockey's use of the whip show they are also treated with the respect their ability deserves out on track.'

Danny turned to leave. 'I've seen more than enough.'

Halfway down the tarmacked drive, Danny heard a young voice shout, 'Where you going?'

Luke Carmichael was scraping his wellies by the kitchen door at the side of the lodge.

'Home,' Danny shouted back.

Luke came jogging over. It was clear he was suffering a bad skin and hair day. His sweatpants and diamond padded coat were as mud-spattered as his boots. 'You'll be back for the yard's do.'

'We haven't been invited.'

'You have now,' Luke said and smiled, scratching his spotty chin. His fingers snagged on his greasy blonde curls. 'It only happens once a year like. For owners and trainers and staff to have a bit of a laugh, there'll be music, booze, I'll even mix up one of my legendary punchbowls.'

Danny felt a bit sorry for the lad. He didn't appear to have any friends and his father clearly hadn't the faith to try him on one of the yard's runners. Carmichael could never be accused of keeping it in the family.

'When?'

'Fortnight on Thursday,' Luke said.

'Will Toby be okay with this?'

'Just show up at the door, he can't turn you away.'

'Go on, then.' There'd be no problem finding a babysitter on a weeknight, he thought, and Meg could do with her first evening out since having baby Cerys.

'Oh, it's an Eighties theme, dress and music.'

Now he says, Danny thought. Luke headed back to the trainer's house.

Danny carried on out of there when he realised he was alone at Arwen Vale. Inside the electrified boundary of an estate he'd often looked down upon from afar. He reckoned he'd have few better opportunities to satisfy his morbid curiosity about this place. It was like casing the joint all over again.

Further along the driveway, Danny shortened his stride, occasionally glancing back. Luke was still scraping his boots. He wasn't far from the line of trees blocking out the Rhymney Road when he turned to see Luke had gone, hopefully for an overdue shower. There was no way Toby would allow his son to stink the place out, Danny reasoned. He swiftly changed course and, keeping low, ran across the grass lawn and dirt gallop strips before finding some shelter from the wooded island.

Danny skirted round the trees and sprinted again for the boarded-up mouth of the mineshaft at the foot of the hillside he'd previously seen from up on Pen-y-Bryn. He expected the next lot to come galloping from behind the trees any second. Out in the open, he felt like he was running naked, completely exposed.

Stood outside were wooden beams, covering much of the mouth, and propped by a bolder and scree to the right was a red and white sign freckled with orange rust that read: KEEP OUT: PITMEN WORKING DOWN MINESHAFT.

Danny peered into the blackness between gaps in the wood. 'Hello?' he called out but it was his own voice that echoed back. Danny reckoned his dad was alive the last time pitmen ever ventured in there.

Danny could see the iron nails holding up the top wooden bar had been loosened. He now knew how Toby managed to clamber over. Danny didn't need to lower the top board. He could hoist himself up and slither his way through the gap. With the minty green light from the screen of his smartphone, Danny stepped into the darkness.

CHAPTER 8

As Danny moved deeper into the hillside, the natural light faded fast, the dripping water grew louder and the air felt colder.

It had soon become painful to walk in there. He guessed it was spoil or stones knocking against his ankles.

He stopped and shone some light from his phone down there. He was in fact standing in a scattering of bones, cracked and broken.

What was this place?

Off to his right, he heard something. He quickly pointed the phone over there and saw two small beady red eyes looking back into the stark light.

It was a rat sat perched on a natural ledge in the cave wall. The biggest rat Danny had ever seen, more like an otter.

He stepped back, scattering the bones some more.

Clearly not short of a meal in here, Danny thought.

With a click of claws and clack of bones cascading down jagged rock, the rat scampered for cover.

He kept the light on the wall. Even from there, he could make out a red marking on the rock. Taking a closer look, his fingers skated over the ochre carving.

A speared reindeer.

Merry Christmas kids, Danny thought.

He also noticed there was no trace of any rails on the ground where they'd cart coal and spoil out of there.

He turned the torch deeper inside. The light ended in a dull grey reflection about five yards ahead where the tunnel ended.

This was no mineshaft.

He then shivered. Now more than at any point, he felt like he shouldn't be here.

What the hell made Toby want to keep coming back?

Having come here for answers, he didn't want to leave with more questions. He returned to the barrier covering the cave's mouth in search of a phone signal. Partly shielded by the wooden boards, he searched online for: south wales valley caves. He clicked on a university article from some historical society.

Holes like these were cut in the hillside when glaciers carved out these valleys in the last Ice Age some fifteen thousand years ago, Danny read. He'd regretted not turning up for Geography now.

Further down the article, he saw a photo of a hillfort in the region, with dry-stone rampart at the entrance. Danny looked out on the piles of broken stone and shale around the mouth of this cave.

He heard the distance rumble of hooves. When he clocked two horses circling the woodland on the gallop strip, Danny ducked for cover behind the wooden barrier.

Scrolling down the silvery phone screen, he saw strikingly similar rock art to the reindeer on this cave wall. It was like he'd taken the photo himself.

He kept reading. Apparently, in the River Elwy Valley, they'd found seventeen teeth from five prehistoric individuals in a cave. He glanced back at the bones here.

They've got nothing on this place, he thought.

Other sites in the region had returned ivory bracelets, hand axes and carved animal bones, kept by the hunter-gatherers taking shelter here thousands of years before the Romans invaded.

This cave should be a museum, Danny reckoned. Perhaps Toby was the keeper entrusted with looking after it.

Danny returned to the bones, half expecting to find a mammoth's tusk. He stuck the phone between his teeth to free his hands as he carefully examined them. Many were unrecognisable fragments, none of them had carvings.

Fearing he'd pushed his luck already, Danny glanced at the circle of light made by the cave's entrance. Toby was probably out there somewhere on the gallops watching the morning lots.

He was about to stand and leave when he uncovered a larger bone. It was part of a skull with a large cranium, eye socket and nasal bone. It had been split down the middle. Despite holding only half the skull, Danny could already see it was a horse.

If Toby had discovered a long lost concoction or some voodoo charm to improve results, it didn't do this poor sod much good.

He knelt again and with torch in mouth, he slowly combed the bones until he found the missing half. He slowly pushed the two halves together, dovetailing perfectly. It's only then he could see there was a hole between the eye sockets.

'A bolt between the eyes,' Danny whispered mournfully.

Until then, Danny didn't think his opinion of Toby Carmichael could get lower. Was he putting down horses that didn't make the grade?

He wondered just how many horses died in the making of Arwen Vale. It would partly explain the miraculous strike-rate in Group races.

But why not sell them on? There were plenty of trainers specialising in turning round the careers of castoffs from the top yards.

This alone was enough to get Carmichael's licence revoked, he reckoned. With some luck, Carmichael could face criminal charges for animal cruelty, enough to take him out of the sport long enough for Danny to get some owners back.

His smartphone flashed white as he took a photo as evidence. He now had a better idea why Toby returned here.

Putting the skull down, Danny felt he'd seen more than enough.

Back at the barrier, he hung fire for another galloping lot to disappear behind the island of trees and then made a break for the driveway.

Clambering over the front gates with a clatter, he heard the whir of CCTV cameras high up on poles as they tracked his every move.

Danny sprinted back up the Rhymney road suspecting he was now a marked man.

That evening, Danny poured the last of the wine and sat crossed-legged on the rug by the inglenook, warming his face in front of a roaring fire.

Laid out on the hearth rug he had the architect's plans to regenerate the Ely train station on the footprint of the old platform that used to serve the first incarnation of the Ely Park Racecourse.

With takings at the turnstiles up, a new sales pavilion and a busy summer of Flat meetings added to the roster, there was no better time to improve the transport links.

Apparently, back in the 1930s when the old Ely Racecourse was thriving they'd put on a train service direct from as far afield as Birmingham on race days, allowing connections to travel their horses straight to the track. They'd even built a coaching house behind the station to feed and water the new arrivals before the half-mile walk to the racetrack.

He'd been down there many times though little of the original buildings remained as it was a victim of the 'railways genocide' back in the Sixties. He recalled his dad saying they'd done something similar to the mines a few decades later.

In this age obsessed with progress, Danny felt sometimes it was best to look back in time for answers.

Waiting to see whether town planning would green-light the project was worse than waiting on the stewards to deliberate a result. He felt confident the decision would be a no-brainer, breathing new life into Ely village.

Danny stretched his arms and then clicked his stiff neck.

'I'd pay good money for this,' he said, pointing at the roaring fire. 'You're clearly better at making them than me.'

'I'm not falling for that one,' Meg said, on the settee reading her celeb mag called *Hiya!* 'You'll have me doing the fire every night.'

He'd abstained from the booze for months, but this was a day when willpower simply wasn't enough.

'Something else gets me about his stable,' Danny said.

'I'm guessing we're still on Toby.'

'All his horses were brown.'

'They are horses, Danny.'

'But no markings too, it's a bit strange,' Danny slurred. The wine had gone straight to his head. Recent months had seen him become a light weight in every sense.

Danny pulled his phone from his jeans and went online. 'According to this, nearly ninety per cent of thoroughbreds registered in the American Jockey Club's Stud Book were a variation of brown.'

'Which is why Toby's horses are brown,' Meg reasoned.

'But all twenty-eight of them?' Danny questioned. 'Not one of them is grey, roan, chestnut.'

Danny started typing on his phone.

'What are you searching for now?'

'I'm not.'

'Thank god.'

'I'm working out the accumulated odds of a twenty-strong string all being brown.'

'I thought you'd failed maths at school,' Meg said.

'Stuff like algebra was like a foreign language to me but give me odds, over-rounds or form figures and I turn into Rain Man. Wish the teachers knew that from the start.'

'It's just one of those coincidences you get in racing, let it go, Danny, please.'

'Ninety per cent, that's about the same as odds of nine-to-one-on or one-point-one-one-recurring as a return to a one unit stake. There are twenty-eight horses we know of at Arwen Vale, so it's like getting a twenty-eight fold accumulator up for every horse to be brown. One-point-one-one to the power of twenty-eight is eighteen-and-a-half to one. Add the fact all of them don't have any markings. Do you think it's a coincidence now?'

'Yeah,' Meg sighed, turning the page.

'In the eyes of the law, just ten jurors out of the twelve have to agree for someone to be sent down for life. I'm way beyond reasonable doubt on this Meg. The other thing I've noticed, the names of the horses.'

'What about them?'

'Well, they're all a bit cheap sounding.'

Meg laughed, lowering the mag as if to see whether Danny was being serious. 'Perhaps it's time we take that holiday we talked about.'

'I'm not cracking up,' Danny said. 'Look, Drinker's Elbow, Hasty Hedgehog, Smelly Socks, Fat Suit, I mean they're hardly going to draw in the top owners the same way as legends of the past like Galileo, Rock Of Gibraltar, Mozart, Dancing Brave.'

'They can call them what they like, Danny,' Meg replied, still smiling. 'As long as it's no longer than eighteen letters and nothing saucy.'

'But the names lack any class.'

'Never had you down as a snob.'

'I'm no snob, but a horse's name combined with a fancy pedigree and decent form does influence fees at stud. You wouldn't buy into a car brand called 'Rusty Banger'. And given their horses have unfashionable pedigrees, you'd think more than any of the top breeding operations, they'd sit down and call them something classier to add to their impeccable form on the track.'

'Maybe they didn't have a choice.'

'Why?'

'Perhaps they'd bought all of them already named, once they're registered in the Weatherbys Stud Book, they're stuck with the name,' Meg reasoned. 'I mean, they were after Red Ink at a horses-in-training sale. Either way, enough Carmichael for one night, no more mention of the C word.'

Danny sighed.

'You okay?' Meg asked. She came over and put a hand on Danny's tight shoulders.

'Can't stop thinking about Ryan Lawson. One minute he's got everything, the next nothing.'

'It sounded like he was lucky to escape with his life.'

'Don't think it was luck, all the other attacks were the same, the MO was to go for the hands and legs.'

Meg said, 'He'll have every bit of support available. Racing rallies round its fallen.'

'Yeah, but you didn't see his legs,' Danny said grimacing. 'Guess it shows just how fragile life can be.' He paused and felt the back of his neck. 'Have you put the kids down?'

Meg nodded.

'Think I'll look in on them later.'

'Jack wanted another one of your tales,' Meg said. 'Preferably not one about betting this time.'

'Did I mention we got an invite to a party?'

'Where?'

'It's a surprise,' Danny said, knowing she'd refuse if he'd mention Toby's name again. 'It's an Eighties theme party.'

Meg said. 'What? 1980s?'

'No, 1680s,' Danny replied sarcastically.

Meg frowned and said, 'Shame I got rid of my ruffs and cuffs last week.'

Danny looked over at her thoughtfully.

After a while, Meg said above the crackle and hiss of the fire, 'Stop watching me like a kettle waiting to boil.'

'I like the look of you,' Danny slurred. 'Can't a man look at his wife?'

Meg put her mag down. Its front page exclusive had two D-listers grinning at the camera and revealing to the world how incredible their lives are.

'Why do you read that drivel?' Danny asked. 'It's only an exclusive because no one else will have them.'

'Coming from someone who reads the formbook at night.'

'That's work,' Danny snapped.

'I was only teasing.' She leant from the arm of the chair and gave him a lingering kiss on the lips and then smiled warmly. 'I think I know what will make you relax, take your mind of things.'

Danny's phone rang. 'Hold that thought.'

'Who the hell is it at this hour?' she asked.

Danny looked at the screen. 'Stony.'

He left the room.

'Can we meet?' Stony asked.

'What's this about?'

'I can't say over the phone.'

'Where?'

'Say, the new bookies in town at one tomorrow.'

Reluctantly Danny agreed. He feared the anonymous donor had had a change of heart.

CHAPTER 9

On his way to new bookies, The Flutter House, Danny glanced at its sister shop Good4Cash next door. In the display, he caught sight of a saxophone, a trampoline and a bowls set. He decided not to window shop.

Instead, he disappeared into the bookies. The Flutter House had taken over the old Raymond Barton shop on Greyfriars Road not far from Queen Street in the heart of Cardiff city, a proven site for a turf accountant to thrive. Unlike its clients, bookies didn't like risk.

Behind the green counter, portly owner Trevor Hatton's lips were moving as he cashed up the till. As usual, his red braces were being severely tested and a biro was seemingly stuck behind his right ear.

On the shop floor, Stony sat at one of five green circular tables on a matching carpet. A blank betting slip rested on his open racing paper.

Danny called over to Trevor, 'Good business model you got going on this street.'

Trevor stopped from counting to nod smugly. 'Thanks, you can come back.'

'Might as well knock a hole in that wall so punters can pawn their grandpa's war medals with one hand, while betting it away with the other,' Danny said. 'Synergy, is that what they call it?'

Trevor stopped nodding and then disappeared behind the counter, presumably to put takings in the safe.

'Keep it light, Danny!' Stony said in a strangled whisper. 'Don't get us banned before I've even warmed my seat. They've got free nibbles at the counter here, can't go wrong.'

'What's this about?' Danny asked, dropping his bony arse on a stool.

Stony removed an A4 printout covered in spidery notes and comments.

'First, while you're here, will you indulge me in listening to my latest song I composed at evening class,' Stony said. 'It's about Emily Davison, you know the lass—'

'I know who she is,' Danny replied, sneaking a glance at his watch.

'It's not long, standard structure, two verses, three choruses and a bridge.'

'Let's hear it.'

Stony cleared his throat.

Danny sat silently.

Stony opened his mouth wide and out came, 'La, la, la, la, la, la, me, me, me—'

'Can I stop you there?' Danny asked, raising a palm. 'I think the lyrics need some work.'

'I'm warming up my larynx.'

'This isn't Cardiff Singer of the World.'

'Okay, okay. Here we go then... Oh, Emily, oh Emily, of all the king's horses and all the famous courses, you strode out with your message to the world—'

'For the love of God, isn't it enough that I'm blind!' came a gruff voice. Danny hadn't noticed Nye tucked away in one corner.

Stony stopped. 'I haven't got to the best bit.'

'I'd rather wait to hear the finished version on the wireless, thank you,' Nye said.

'It might never... oh, I see, smart arse.'

'Please tell me this isn't why you got me down here,' Danny said.

'Eh?'

'You had something to tell me.'

'Not me, it's Nye over there. He didn't reckon you'd come for a stranger.'

Stony and Danny stopped to look up at a spotty youth in a hooded grey tracksuit. He'd made a beeline for their table, holding a carrier bag in one hand and a packet of fags in the other.

'Nothing doing today, Crabs,' Stony said.

Danny didn't know, or want to know, how he'd got that nickname.

'You haven't seen what I'm selling,' the lad whined.

'What is it?' Stony asked.

'Rolls, ham rolls, finest ingredients mind.'

'Where's the ham sourced?' Danny quizzed, hoping the lad would get tired and move on to another table.

'Where's it from?' the lad questioned.

Danny nodded.

'A pig, I think.'

'How much?' Stony asked.

'Stony?!' Danny said indignantly.

'Want something to go with my nibbles,' Stony reasoned.

'Two for a quid,' the lad said.

'Ooh, I dunno,' Stony replied.

Danny sat back, glad his friend had finally seen sense.

Stony peered in the bag.

'Alright, three for a quid,' the lad said and gave Danny a toothy grin. 'Your old man drives a hard bargain.'

'I don't think it's the quantity we're worried about,' Danny replied.

'And he's not my son,' Stony said sternly.

'But these were made with by my own fair hands.'

Danny said, 'I thought you were trying to flog them.'

'What you saying?!' the lad replied, mood darkening. 'Hang on, I thought I recognised you. Danny... Danny...,' he clicked his fingers, 'That's it, you're a jockey, I backed one of yours, you owe me a fiver.'

'Oi, you,' Trevor snarled at the lad. 'I've warned you before, you're barred.'

Danny felt it a good time to slope off into a corner to find out what Blind Nye had to share. He sat down opposite Nye, who had put his white stick by his newspaper and a cup of coffee.

'Oh, it's you,' Nye said.

'How did you—'

'The smell.'

Danny sniffed his armpits.

'What do you want?' Nye asked.

'I was about to ask you the same thing,' Danny said. 'Stony over there reckoned you'd got something for me.'

'I couldn't help overhear you in the Castle Keep a while back, Cheltenham eve I believe. Thought you might be interested in something else I also heard there.'

'Why tell me now?'

'It's been playing on my mind,' Nye said and then removed his black shades to look him in the eye. Danny felt nervous. It felt like watching a PC taking off his helmet walking up the driveway.

Nye leant in close, nodding over at Stony, who was chomping down on a ham roll. 'You see, Stony was sat at the same table in that pub when *he* was handed the briefcase.'

'Who was it?'

'Don't rub it in, you know I can't see.'

'You're looking me right in the eye.'

Suddenly Nye stared slightly to the left

'You play darts, for Christ's sake, drunk!'

'I don't want you grassing me to the social, I depend on that handout.'

'Was it Toby with Stony that time?'

Nye said, 'I hadn't even planned on earwigging, it seemed they were old friends going to bore for Cardiff about the glory days.'

Old friends, Danny thought. It had to be Toby Carmichael, who'd shared the weighing room with Stony in their prime.

'But what struck me,' Nye continued, 'they were soon mumbling their words.'

'Mumbling?'

'Talking in whispers towards the end,' Nye said. 'That's not how old friends speak to each other. It suddenly got me intrigued, but I couldn't catch a bloody thing, except these words.' Nye leaned in even closer. Danny felt his warm breath. 'I'll finish Danny Rawlings.'

I'll finish Danny Rawlings.

'Thought you'd want to know,' Nye added.

'Are you certain?' Danny asked, swallowing.

'I know, some Secret Santa he's turned out to be.'

'Did he say anything else?' Danny asked, not really wanting to hear the answer.

'He said something else straight after and then slid the briefcase over to Stony, who took it and left. What was in the case?'

'Haven't looked inside,' Danny replied.

'Luckily I can smell a lie, too,' Nye said, grinning as he put his glasses back on.

'Cheers, Nye, it was worth coming down after all.'

Danny came back to Stony and sat, saying, 'Put the roll down.'

'But I haven't finished.'

'Nor have I,' Danny replied. 'Nye reckoned my "donor" said he'd finish me.'

Stony smiled.

'I'm glad someone thinks it's funny.'

'He was talking about,' Stony stopped to tap his nose, 'what's in the case. He said to me, if I don't pass on the... case, your career as a trainer would be finished.'

Danny breathed again. Stony's version seemed a lot less foreboding.

'Don't stress so much,' Stony added. 'I want you focused for Powder Keg in the Yorkshire Cup, stuck a tenner on at fourteen-to-one. Hope she's up to Group One level.'

'So do I,' Danny said. He noticed a purple crushed velvet smoking jacket neatly folded on the spare stool and an ebony walking stick with a carved silver horse head as a handle. 'Are they yours?'

Stony nodded.

'Where did you get them?'

'Good4cash.'

Danny stopped the questioning. He felt bad he'd eyed Stony with suspicion. He thought he'd make up for it by saying, 'Toby's got a party on Thursday. Fancy tagging along with me and Meg?'

'But I'm not invited.'

'Neither are we, not by Toby at least,' Danny replied. 'Get a taxi to ours and we'll go from there.'

Stony smiled. 'You're on.'

CHAPTER 10

YORK RACECOURSE. FRIDAY 12TH MAY.

1.05pm. Danny left Meg tending Powder Keg in the renovated racecourse stables beside the back straight. From there, runners would be walked across the track to the paddocks by the grandstands in time for their race.

As an apprentice on the Flat in his youth, Danny had never travelled this far north. He'd seen countless internet clips and footage of past renewals of prestigious Group Ones staged here, like the Nunthorpe, the Yorkshire Oaks and the International, though nothing beat actually walking the track to get a feel of the hallowed turf on ground known since pre-medieval times as the Knavesmire; 'knave' meaning man of low standing and 'mire' a swampy pasture for cattle. Now boasting four imposing grandstands, the third biggest prize money in Britain and some of the best quality racing in the world, the site had clearly come a long way since the Dark Ages.

Today's underfoot conditions had some spring in it, Danny reckoned, but very little moisture, despite having been watered earlier in the three-day fixture, better known as the Dante meeting after Wednesday's Derby trial. It wasn't enough to change the official going description of Good, Good to Firm in places, certainly not by the two-forty-five start time of the feature Yorkshire Cup. He'd be searching out for the good-to-firm patches.

Faster the better for Kegsy, Danny thought.

1.34pm. As the runners filed in from the pre-parade ring, Danny found a spot by the rail, partially hidden by a 'no alcohol' sign.

Unlike the surrounding paddock watchers, who were there primarily to view the condition and physique of the parading juvenile fillies, Danny was there to observe the connections huddled in groups on grass in the middle.

He could hardly miss Toby Carmichael, who was tucked into a grey three-piece suit and was animated as he ran through riding instructions for Drunken Mistress. His jockey was George Peters, who had emerged as an early leader in the Jockeys'

Championship and appeared to be intently taking notice of every word and gesture, possibly to avoid injury as Toby waved his cane around like a conductor's baton.

That didn't appear the case with Darren Cooper, who looked to be staring right through his trainer, Conor O'Brien. Clearly in the zone, Danny thought, possibly fearing it might be the last time he'd be wearing Malcolm Bernard's famous white and blue silks. He'd clearly dug out a spare after the last set of blood-spattered silks went up in smoke at Arwen Vale.

As Malcolm entered the ring in his trademark cream suit with blue handkerchief and tie, he reached back over the rail to shake the hand of a racegoer, presumably a fan. They chatted, Malcolm laughed and they parted with another handshake.

When Danny looked closer, the fan was the man in the waistcoat they'd seen at Ely bloodstock sales. Danny hadn't instantly recognised the stranger as he had since dyed his hair black from a bottle and grew some patchy stubble. Fearing he was a rival bidder, Malcolm had gone over to introduce himself. Judged by the warmth of their greeting just now, the leading owner had clearly made a friend and not an enemy at Ely Park.

Malcolm joined Darren and Conor connected to his seven-to-one chance Catchlight.

Danny looked back to the rail opposite but the waistcoat man was gone. He also felt it was time to leave.

During the private stable tour, he recalled Toby boldly proclaim that Drunken Mistress would win at York but it came over more as a statement than a prediction. He wanted a proper look at this 'good thing'. At the time, Danny wondered how he could possibly be that bullish without even knowing the opposition at the final declaration stage. Such bold words can make fools of even the best judges in the game. The racing cert was a myth.

He wanted a good vantage point to witness this. He felt some nerves, as if he badly wanted Toby to be wrong about this one. Perhaps Meg was right and he'd become bitterly jealous of his all-conquering neighbour. Keeping up with the Carmichaels was never a realistic prospect, he'd realised.

He pinned his trainer's badge on the lapel of his jacket and found a space from a balcony up in the Melrose Stand restricted to connections of the runners.

'And they're off for our opener,' blared from the speakers up in the overhanging roof which sheltered the private balconies above and the tiered viewing steps below.

'Drunken Mistress is up there vying for the lead early in this five-furlong sprint, with second favourite Celtic Charm also showing good early, in behind taking a tow are Milestone and Twinkle Toes. Catchlight brings up the rear after being caught napping in the stalls.'

'Go on, Twinkly,' shrieked the woman next to him.

'As they pass the three-pole there's five lengths from first to last and the market leaders show the way. Drunken Mistress by a half to Celtic Charm. Ron Chambers gets to work on Milestone, as they hurtle by the two-furlong marker and this is where the unbeaten Drunken Mistress asserts with George Peters yet to go for his whip, Celtic Charm showing distress signals in second, no answers to the acceleration of our leader, Drunken Mistress.'

The roar from the crowd below grew as the warm favourite had built a healthy advantage.

Danny was ready to look away and go to meet Meg, who by now would be preparing to walk Powder Keg across the racetrack to the pre-parade ring by the stands, but was stopped by a loud gasp from the twenty thousand racegoers below.

Drunken Mistress was hanging markedly left, but it was at the back of the field where the drama was unfolding.

'Darren has lost his irons and is slipping from the saddle,' said the commentator. Danny wanted to look away again as Darren hit the ground before summersaulting over and over.

'Oh, dear God, I hope he's alright,' cried an owner in front.

'That's got to hurt, poor soul,' said another, grimacing.

Danny hated Cooper for what he put Chris through at Bath but he wouldn't wish a fall like that on anyone, particularly in a five-furlong sprint where horses topped forty miles per hour, like suffering a car crash into an embankment without a seatbelt.

'Back to the leaders and it's Drunken Mistress's race to throw away as she lives up to her name, first veering left, then right, perhaps the Mistress is getting lonely!' That got a laugh.

Silently Danny urged the staying-on second Milestone to reel in the long-time leader, but once Drunken Mistress had straightened up again, she reasserted into a clear lead. Two lengths… three… four.

Why couldn't Red Ink have been a Drunken Mistress?

He knew he'd bought a dud. This was just rubbing it in.

'Have we seen the Queen Mary Stakes winner here folks?!' the commentator chirped. 'She seems to have the class for Royal Ascot.'

Now Danny really did want to leave for the paddocks.

'An eventful renewal, it's great to see Darren Cooper now sat up, being attended by medics,' the commentator added.

It was an eventful race, Danny agreed, but not for the same reasons. When a horse veered off a true line, it was either through greenness or something hurting. If the horse was edging away from the pain of an undetected injury or was looking for the far rail as a guide, why did she then veer right and then straighten up, without even a corrective slap of the whip? It was like she was remote controlled, with jockey George Peters a mere decoration on top.

He sought the big screen on the infield for the slo-mo replay but it was showing Toby on his lonesome, face dispassionate.

He really did expect this, Danny thought.

The TV cameras quickly cut to George Peters pointing to the cloudy sky. He apparently lost his mother only last week and the roving course reporter wouldn't let him grieve in peace. The tears came as he dedicated the win to her memory and the camera zoomed in closer. This made for better TV, Danny thought cynically.

2.23pm. Danny sat silently in the changing room, stomach turning. It was like being in a dentist's waiting room.

When Darren came storming in, jockeys without a ride in the Yorkshire Cup seemed keen to leave the room.

Darren stopped at the saddle tree beside Danny, who subtly slid along the wall bench until out of arm's reach.

The valet called over, 'Eh, that'll be a right shiner in the morning.'

'Yep,' Darren said. 'Do you want one?'

The valet returned to loading a saddle cloth – a larger leather pouch sat beneath the saddle – with lead weight.

'The racecourse doc was quick passing you fit,' Danny commentated.

'Do you want one 'n all?' Darren asked.

Danny said, 'Just saying.'

'I didn't go, alright?' Darren said. 'I landed softly. Bit stiff and sore, but the medics said nothing broken, only pride.'

He spoke slowly, deliberately. Danny was left thinking he'd landed on his head.

Darren kicked a metal leg of the wall bench. 'Fuck it!'

'Doing your best to break something,' Danny said.

'They reckon Dick Turpin was hanged on the Knavesmire nearly three hundred years ago,' Darren said and then slumped down beside Danny. 'I think I know how he felt.'

Danny wondered if Malcolm had had 'that chat' about his contract. After all, the bare minimum an owner asks of a jockey is to complete in a Flat race. 'Want to share?' Danny asked.

'What is this, daytime TV?' Darren asked and shot a scornful look across.

Danny took the hint and went to weigh out for the feature.

2.46pm. Danny was glad the fanfare of the nuisance prelims was over. The runners were now safely installed. Time for business.

Caged, he looked ahead at the half a mile expanse of turf stretching to the first turn. He dry swallowed.

Danny knew Powder Keg was good. It was time to find out just how good.

He kept telling himself, 'It doesn't matter. If she flops again, we can always take a summer break and return to hurdling in the autumn.'

Those words acted like a pressure valve when he felt anxiety rising up.

Danny reacted on the clatter of the gates flinging open. He needed to get a position near the rail to save ground on the bend. He rousted with all his strength.

Confidence bolstered by the Bath win just ten days before, Powder Keg responded generously, quickly shifting up the gears to race on the shoulders of early pacesetter, last year's Epsom Oaks fifth Magic Circle. His internal clock was telling him the early fractions were too hot. Just twenty-six seconds in and they'd reached the two-furlong mark where the rail on their inner disappeared as the offshoot joined the main oval circuit. They could never keep this up for fourteen furlongs.

Danny could see space on his inner. He quickly reined the exuberant Powder Keg back and slotted in behind seven-to-one shot Magic Circle, whose jockey seemed happy to tow them along despite the obvious stamina concerns.

The curving inner rail of the main track came up to guide the runners. Two furlongs to the first bend.

Hearing the growing thud of hooves, he glanced back and grimaced when he saw dual Group One winner Wold's Way Wanderer and Ascot Gold Cup runner-up Rebecca Riot within a length. Further back, he caught the black and orange of Darren's silks bringing up the rear. He'd clearly missed the break again, Danny thought; best to avoid him in the weighing room after.

Powder Keg saved ground hugging the rail as the field of nine banked left to embark on the five furlongs stretch along the farthest point from the stand which brings them back to join the long home straight.

Danny felt Kegsy was working that bit harder to hold a prominent pitch among some of the best Cup horses in the world.

The commentator's words were garbled this far away but Danny picked up on a change in tone and pace in the voice. He could hear the growls of a jockey on his outer. Danny looked across to see Darren was working hard on Marquee Moment, clearly intent on making a telling mid-race move on the fourteen-to-one chance.

Danny was content to let them by, demoting Powder Keg to third. They hadn't even reached halfway.

Now three-quarters of a length ahead of Powder Keg, Darren inexplicably forced his way into a gap clearly shorter than a horse length on the rail between leader Magic Circle and Powder Keg.

Danny shouted, 'Watch it!'

He was forced to check to avoid clipping heels, but still lost momentum and ground he simply couldn't afford at this level.

It was like he was trying to park in a space blatantly too small. What the hell was his game?

He could've bloody killed me and the horse, Danny thought. Perhaps that was his aim.

Only when he'd barged his way in, Darren looked back and grinned. While York racecourse's galloping nature and long home straight made it one of the fairest in the land, there was no accounting for the actions of other jockeys.

Danny suddenly found himself back in fifth, losing out to the heavyweights Wold's Way Wanderer and Rebecca Riot on his outer. Danny didn't react in anger. He gave Powder Keg time to right the ship and tag on to the leading quartet.

As they banked left on the second and final turn, Danny prepared to switch into the clear for an assault out wide.

But as they straightened up into the wide stretch of green, two more rivals came up on Powder Keg's flank. He didn't panic. Walking the track, he could tell the fastest ground was down the centre. As the leaders swept into the home straight, they headed for the middle and the rest followed. Horses are pack animals and generally performed best racing in company.

Danny now had space on his left.

Three furlongs to go.

Danny began to push the black glossy neck of his mount. She lengthened her stride and began to make up some of the lost ground. But he could see proven stayer Wold's Way Wanderer strike the front, closely followed by Rebecca Riot.

Danny administered a few sharp reminders. Powder Keg quickened again.

Unfortunately, the others were also accelerating. Danny could feel the gulf in class between the Group Two rivals here and the ordinary bunch they'd seen off at Bath. It was like being promoted from League 1 to Premier League. The mare was working that much harder just to keep up.

As Powder Keg's quick stride propelled her on Danny was still convinced the leaders were just within range.

Powder Keg overtook doubtful stayer Magic Circle, who was now paying the price for those early exertions.

Kegsy was now racing beyond her limit, giving everything for her rider's urgings, as if she were aware the future of her lodgings was on her muscular shoulders.

Come on girl!

Three lengths off Wold's Way Wanderer.

One furlong to go.

Powder Keg was breathing harder than Danny as they kept working hard.

Passing the half-furlong pole, a divot of turf kicked up by the second Rebecca Riot hit Danny in the face, showing how close they were.

Danny kept his head down and growled. He had the third Marquee Moment, ridden by Darren Cooper, in his sights. If he could get close enough, the stewards would surely reverse the placings having suffered bad interference from that errant rival.

As Powder Keg drew alongside Marquee Moment she found extra from somewhere. In the dying strides, Danny was a spent force, merely a passenger. Neck out, she stuck her head down where it matters to grab third on the line. In a way beating Darren felt like a hollow victory.

Danny felt Darren had robbed him of the chance to reel in the leading pair. Sixteen grand for filling third would cover training bills for the next few months.

Danny answered the stewards' chime and bit his lip as he made his case calmly.

On his way out to meet Meg in the van, Danny crossed paths with Malcolm Bernard, who had just appeared from the owners' and trainers' bar.

'Don't blame you for necking a few after Darren's ride in the first,' Danny said.

'It's Darren that was drunk not me,' Malcolm replied.

'Before going out to race?' Danny questioned. 'He was drunk riding?'

Malcolm nodded.

'Bloody hell, I just thought… I thought he was in the zone before getting on Catchlight,' Danny said, recalling Darren's glassy eyes in the parade ring. 'If I'd known…'

'None of us knew,' Malcolm fumed. 'Coming back in, Darren even blamed it on my horse. It's only when I saw the saddle was still on Milestone's back I knew it was human error.'

'She did overstep at one point,' Danny reasoned.

'But he didn't unseat for another furlong after,' Malcolm replied. 'This was entirely of his own making.'

Danny recalled Darren's mood and slow speech in the weighing room between races. 'It explains why he violently cut me up in the Yorkshire Cup. Cost me a place at the least,' Danny said. He felt spots of rain on his face. 'I hadn't made the link, he hadn't slurred.'

'But he was talking slowly,' Malcolm said. 'You can often spot a drunk when they're trying too hard to act sober.'

Danny thought the winning jockey George Peter's mount was the one showing signs of drunkenness. He hadn't imagined it was Darren. 'Many in the pressure cooker of sport turn to drink, look at George Best and Alex Higgins.'

'But they were geniuses. I assure you Darren is not a genius.'

They walked by the mighty Frankel's statue, sixteen point one hands of bronze overlooking the new gates in memory of his legendary trainer Sir Henry Cecil.

'He'll get a lengthy ban for this,' Danny said, trying to hide his glee.

'He'll get a lifetime ban with mine,' Malcolm said. 'I was looking for a get-out clause to rip up his contract and now I can avoid any release penalties.'

'Did he take it well?'

'What do you think?'

Malcolm zipped up his jacket and looked up at the darkening sky. 'Don't like helicopters at the best of times, least of all when the weather turns.'

'I can only dream of a chopper,' Danny replied. 'Results can't be that bad then. Clearly that bloke in the waistcoat at Ely Sales wasn't a serious rival bidder.'

'Quite the opposite, he's a bloodstock agent at another sales,' Malcolm said. 'Marcel Tailler is his name.'

'Don't be coaxed away, you can't beat Ely Park,' Danny reacted, finding it hard to put his ambassador's hat aside.

'Don't worry, it's a new bloodstock sale abroad,' Malcolm replied.

'Abroad?'

'Brittany, he's French. I quickly stopped him there,' Malcolm recalled. 'Don't waste any further breath, I said. I have enough trouble keeping track of all the sales at York, Newmarket,

Doncaster and Central London, not to mention Goffs in Ireland, which is just as well, as Marcel said he visits the UK to see family ties here, not for business.'

'I wouldn't rule out buying on the Continent,' Danny reasoned. 'I know only too well National Hunt prices in France are overinflated. I mean, bloody hell, a hurdle winner at Auteuil over there is suddenly worth six figures. But the Flat horses are still competitively priced. Mind, I'm not one to talk, barely have time to read the international racing news, let alone go over there.'

'Well the British sales have provided me with enough winners down the years,' Malcolm added, 'and results can only improve when I can finally get a decent rider onside.'

'I'm afraid I'll have to stop you there, Malc,' Danny said. 'I can see you're building up to make me an offer, but I'm just too busy.'

Malcolm smiled as he turned for the helicopter park.

Danny left with, 'Think of me on the nine-hour drive home in the van with all the roadworks.'

He felt it would seem to drag even longer as he kept thinking what might've been had the wayward Darren been stood down before the Yorkshire Cup. There would be other days, Danny consoled himself, and mercifully Darren would no longer be part of them.

CHAPTER 11

'It's party time!' Luke shouted, as he streamed another playlist of Eighties hits.

Danny looked at his watch again and took another long gulp of cheap bottled beer. He had an excuse ready to pull out of this but Meg had already set her mind on coming here. Themed parties were definitely not his idea of a good time. He felt the same about New Year's Eve and office parties, something about the idea of forced fun.

At least he had found a shady spot well away from the edge of a makeshift dancefloor between sofas pushed to the exposed stonework and timber of the walls, and lit by some cheap disco lights on the mantelpiece and a glitter ball hanging from a beam.

He looked again at Meg, who was channelling an early Madonna with a red ribbon in her frizzy blonde hair, a black corset dress, beads around her neck and rubber bracelets over lacy fingerless gloves. She pulled it off. Without trying, she looked simply irresistible. Earlier he'd caught some of the stable lads eyeing her up. When he started staring back at them, they soon sulked off to the punchbowl tended by Luke in the corner.

It didn't matter, as Meg's eyes were fixed on the dancefloor where Stony was showing the kids how it was done. Danny had to occasionally look away as his dance moves were almost hypnotic. His arms were synchronised as they swayed from side to side, like a carpenter planing wood while he stomped on the spot, occasionally hitting the beat. In his red and brown tank-top and green cords, he was in his element performing to the growing crowd as Tina Turner's 'Private Dancer' blared from the speaker system. Two of the younger stable lasses had even joined him under the swirling lights of green, red and blue.

Danny found himself smiling. At least someone there was enjoying themselves.

Host Toby Carmichael was doing the rounds, filling glasses and chatting to each group there, some twice. He'd yet to come over their way.

Increasingly, Danny felt the urge to move on to the stronger stuff. He hadn't got to travel to the track the next day and Jordi was in charge of the work rider's rota. But he was afraid his loose lips might tell Toby what he really thought of him.

Danny looked around the room. Barring Toby and Stony, he must be the oldest there. Most were in their early twenties, cheap watches and own-brand jeans and shirts giving off smelly aftershave and perfume. They all had the look of poorly paid stable staff, Danny thought. Where were the rich owners Luke had invited? This was supposed to be a chance for all connected with the yard to bond. Perhaps the owners deserting Silver Belle Stables to Arwen Vale had heard Danny was coming and declined the invitation, wanting the easy life. He began to think his former owners had left the game entirely, put off by their experiences at Silver Belle Stables.

Luke had switched from DJing to ladling punch into plastic cups from a giant bowl on the marble top of the open-plan kitchen.

Danny wanted to see the other side of Arwen Vale; the side that helped them sustain the unsustainable fifty-five per cent strike-rate with their runners over the last season and a bit; the side that they didn't even want the staff to see.

He looked back into the black of the hallway. Meg downed her vodka with cola mixer and went over to join Stony's groupies.

Toby and Luke were both busy. Standing alone and seemingly invisible in the corner, Danny knew there wouldn't be many better chances to quietly disappear unnoticed.

He slowly backed away from the lounge and headed straight for the stairs. At the top, the landing light was on.

The walls were panelled in dark wood and there was a red carpet strip running down the middle, exposing floorboards either side. It gave the landing a Hollywood feel, except this carpet led to the toilet at the end.

There were two other doors on the facing wall. He was drawn to the one ajar. He could feel the vibrations of the creaking boards with every footfall and was glad of Duran Duran's 'Hungry Like the Wolf' below to drown out the sound of his movements.

From the other side of the partly open door, he swore he heard a dull metallic thud.

He looked up to read the brass plaque engraved with: Office of Toby Carmichael Esq – Racehorse Trainer.

'Hello?' Danny pensively asked through the door, knowing he'd left the two Carmichaels downstairs. 'Hello?'

When he knocked firmly, the door swung open. Inside was a smaller than expected room. On his left was a mahogany and walnut desk against the wall with a lamp lying on its side and stationery scattered over its inlaid top. It seemed he'd already discovered what had made the dull thud. The far wall was dominated by wall units and shelves rammed with grey box-files.

Danny looked around the room to check he was alone. He didn't want to be one intruder disturbing another.

Before entering, he looked back down the landing and then ran to shut the toilet door at the other end. He wanted an excuse if anyone asked where he'd been, though he didn't think he'd be missed down there, not with Stony stealing the show.

Danny returned to the office. He could feel his heart thump as he searched the room. The desk drawers were locked and there was an empty wastepaper bin to the far side.

He pulled the handle of the closed wall unit door. Inside there was a large selection of boxed Star Wars plastic figures. In immaculate condition, they'd fetch a small fortune these days, Danny thought. Clearly Toby denied Luke a play with them, depriving his son of pleasure for the longer-term rewards. It also explained how Luke had got his name. They were being displayed on a weighty-looking combination-lock safe. If the collectors' toys were left on top, Danny wondered what the hell was being kept in the safe. He tried the handle but it was locked tight.

Suddenly there was a scratch of claws. Danny turned on his heels and saw a cat arching his back. He was standing by the kneehole of the desk. His coat was black and glossy like Powder Keg. His green eyes stared up with a mix of suspicion and distain. He licked his lips and then he was gone, scampering through the gap in the door.

Danny sniffed the air, picking up a salty smell in there.

Perhaps that's what attracted the cat in there, he thought, didn't they feed the poor thing.

As he moved closer to the desk, the smell grew stronger.

From the spilt stationery, he picked out a paperclip and fashioned it into a hook. He set about picking the lock. When it turned, he glanced at the door to the landing.

He pulled open the drawer. Inside, there were the May and June editions of the magazine *Desperate Farmers' Wives*.

This piqued Danny's interest, but not because of the cover's promise, 'Janet, 25, reveals more than her milking jugs, Page 7!' He was more intrigued to find out what could possibly be that secret or embarrassing to cover it with a stash of soft porn.

Danny slid the well-thumbed mags across. Underneath was a rainbow of plastic covers holding horse birth certificates and passports, each colour representing the specific year a horse was foaled. None of it seemed out of place in a racehorse trainer's office.

Danny dug deeper and fished out a clear plastic bag. Settled at the bottom was a rumpled sheet of paper.

From past experience, Danny recognised it as a police evidence bag.

The smell of salt was at its strongest now.

Danny smelt the bag. He then tried to decipher what was on the paper. Much of it was unreadable. It wasn't the handwriting but the water damage.

He made out: 'My loves Toby and Luke, I hope you can find it in your hearts to forgive me. It is for the very best. Soon you will see that. My passing will free us all from this misery. Please find the happiness I couldn't. Until we meet again in heaven…

Molly X.'

He dug even deeper in the drawer and pulled out a handwritten card. It was like a to-do list.

Much of the list had been blotted out with felt tip. There were two at the bottom uncensored. The first was, I'LL FINISH DANNY RAWLINGS. The man handing over the cash in the pub had said the same, according to Nye in the bookies.

But it was the second that made the card tremble. *KILL JACK AND CERYS.*

He looked up when he heard a creak outside the door, only then realising the distant thud of music had stopped.

He quickly took a photo of the card with his smartphone and tossed it back in the drawer as the door opened.

When he looked up, Luke was stood there in the light of the doorway. He was pointing the barrel of Toby's hunting rifle at Danny's chest.

Danny knew it was in working order from the air shots he'd heard up on Pen-y-Bryn.

'The door was already open,' Danny explained and waved the plastic bag. 'The cat knocked the lamp over, he must've smelt this and thought fish supper.' Danny waited for a reply that never came. 'I never touched the safe, it's locked anyway,' he added and then cringed. Shut up, Danny!

His brain was still processing the threat to his kids' lives on the card.

'And I left this door open to see if Dad was right,' Luke said.

'About what?'

'He reckoned you were spying on us,' Luke said. 'When I saw you go upstairs, I followed. Caught you red-handed I have, see?'

'What is this?' Danny asked, shaking the clear plastic bag containing the rumpled paper.

'It's Mam's goodbye,' Luke said. 'Put it down.'

'Where did they find it?'

'I rescued her from Lavernock Point near Penarth, she was walking right into the sea, up to her neck in it when I fished her out just in time. It will be two years ago tomorrow.'

'What's it doing here?' Danny asked.

'Dad wanted to keep it safe in the drawer. She said some lovely things in that letter, it was her goodbye to us,' Luke said. 'She was going downhill fast by then, this was written on one of her good days.'

'No, why is it in a police evidence bag?'

Luke shrugged.

'Did you report the attempted suicide?'

'What do you think?' Luke asked. 'They'd have only sectioned her. We just wanted her home that night. We were prepared to forget it and we knew she would, but it turned out I only spared her a few months extra.'

The rifle's barrel dipped.

Danny recalled reading in the local newspaper that a note had been found on her body hanging in the woods. He wondered if this note was planted there. 'And you definitely found it on her in the sea?'

'Smell it,' Luke said.

Danny suspected he was telling the truth, salt tears couldn't cause that much water damage.

As Luke turned his back, Danny took a photo with his smartphone of the letter before slipping it back under the May edition of *Desperate Farmers' Wives*.

'What now?' Danny asked, before Luke went grassing to Toby.

'I go tell Dad,' Luke said. 'Let him decide.'

'Like he does for every other part of your life.'

'I'm my own man.'

'Then why can't you get a ride, not even on the stable hack? I can see the gallops from up on the hilltop.'

'I'm working on it. I'm still young.'

'He's using you. And you're too dumb to see it.'

The safety catch clicked. 'Yeah?! Say that again!'

'I can help,' Danny said.

'How?'

'I can give you some work, gallops at first and then, if I like what I see, a ride somewhere.'

'Bunch of donkeys round your yard,' Luke said. 'Dad reckons—'

'Sod your dad,' Danny said. 'This is you and me now, man to man. I'll give you the chance to prove yourself, then, you never know what doors might open.'

Luke glanced at the door, smiling. 'I'm glad I opened this one now.'

'That's more like it,' Danny replied. 'Now put that thing away and both of us can forget this ever happened, yeah?'

'But you promise I can ride for you.'

'Yeah, sure,' Danny said. He'd have said anything to avoid Toby finding out he'd been in his office. He didn't want to be pulled aside for another one of Toby's private chats.

They staggered their return to the lounge.

Danny remained out of the spotlight of the dancefloor, as if to pretend he'd been in the shadows all along.

Meg looked across and came over, tugging his arm to get him up there.

Danny frowned and picked up the empty bottle he'd put down.

Stony also came over, sweating. 'God, haven't had this much fun since... I don't know when.'

'I was impressed by your moves out there,' Danny said. 'Put it online and it may go viral.'

Stony grinned. 'You should've seen me in my younger days, when I had real hips. My dancing is probably what destroyed them.'

Danny and Meg laughed.

'Only wished you'd said it was Eighties dress,' Stony said, wiping sweat from his brow. 'Would have saved wearing my best.'

Danny looked down at the tank-top and cords. 'I don't think anyone will notice.'

One of the stable lasses staggered over and put her arm on Stony's shoulder, slurring, 'I loved what you were doing out there. You'll have to teach me it.'

Danny looked to his right. Toby had finally found time to join them. He hoped Luke would stick to his side of the bargain.

Stony said, 'Fine lasses you've got here.'

'They're laughing at you, not with you,' Toby said.

Toby had killed the mood in seven short words. It felt like someone had farted there. Stony's shoulders dropped slightly.

'I thought you and Stony were old friends,' Danny said pointedly at Toby and then kicked his good leg.

'And old friends can be honest with each other, brutally honest if needed.'

'I know they're humouring me,' Stony said. 'I could be their dad.'

'And the rest,' Toby replied. 'Anyway it needed to be said.'

'No,' Danny replied. 'Some things don't *need* to be said. They were just having a laugh.'

'Sometimes, you've got to grab life by the balls, isn't that right, Stony,' Meg said, smiling. She wrapped a supportive arm round Stony's shoulders.

'I'd rather grab it by the arm,' Stony replied.

'You could be their sugar daddy,' Meg added.

'But he's skint, always has been, always will,' Toby said.

Luke came over and offered Danny a cup of punch. He was going to decline, when Meg pulled at his arm again, nagging him to go under the spotlights of the dancefloor.

'Just the one,' Danny said, taking the cup. 'Can't do any harm.'

CHAPTER 12

Danny felt too ill even to groan. It was like his eyelids had been glued down and a hammer had been taken to his skull repeatedly.

All he could say for certain, he was lying down and it was hot. *Too hot.*

When his stinging eyes did open, he needn't have bothered. It was pitch black. And there was barely any room to move. His left arm came up enough to touch hot metal. A radiator, he reckoned. His right hand could touch what felt like a leather wall with some give in it. What the hell happened last night? Was he being held captive?

He felt trapped. He then heard garbled voices. Silently Danny lay there, perfectly still.

When the voices stopped and there was a clatter of a door slamming, Danny pushed the leather wall. It began to shift, enough for him to sit up. He blew hard. His heart was thumping too fast for its own good. He got up and saw the makeshift dancefloor, sparking flashes of the night before. He groaned.

At the end of the evening, he must've crawled behind that sofa, the caveman in him seeking warmth and safety to hibernate the inevitable hangover off.

In the dark, he banged his knee on the coffee table that he swore wasn't there before.

He heard a distant engine fire up and rushed to the kitchen door. He saw the lights of the Carmichaels' Land Rover. It was parked on the drive with a horse trailer in tow. Danny checked his watch. 3.24am.

Where the hell were they going now? There wasn't a meeting far enough to warrant leaving at this hour and in any case the trailer was empty.

He saw ghostly swirls of the exhaust tinted pink by the brake lights of the Land Rover. Danny closed the kitchen door behind him and crept to the blind spot at the back of the horse trailer. He stepped on the bumper and hands hooked over the top of the stable door at the back, his trainers squeakily ran up the metal surface. As he swung his first leg over, the Land Rover pulled away. Momentum nearly threw him back out but he strained his arms as if recovering from a bad jumping error. He hauled his whole body in and fell to the trailer floor with a thud, pillowed by a thick bed of fresh hay.

Danny found it hard to keep still in the trailer as they snaked country roads. Without a horse in the back, they clearly weren't holding back. He was again glad to be cushioned by the hay.

Eventually, he felt them slow and then gravity pull him towards the front of the trailer as they descended a bumpy slope.

He bit his tongue and a metallic taste filled his mouth as the tyres rumbled over a rough stretch of ground. They then seemed to level off and stop. With the engine still ticking over, Danny didn't want to be trapped in here.

He quickly clambered to his feet and brushed the hay from his jeans. He climbed over the rear stable door. Back to the trailer, he could see they'd parked up at the base of a coastal path in a cove with a pebbled beach and jagged cliff face. He recognised the place. *Lavernock Point*. His school dragged him here fossil hunting once.

In the glow of the brake lights, Danny picked out a boulder bigger than him. He left the blind spot in the Land Rover's mirrors and sprinted for more cover. He slipped behind the rock and breathed out, hoping they hadn't glanced in the wing mirror for those few seconds.

Crouched into a ball, Danny listened intently as the engine died and the clap of doors shutting. There were distant voices. He could tell they were men but little else. He recalled teachers saying the first ever wireless radio signals were sent and received over open water from this beach way back in the day when the original Ely Park Racecourse was thriving. How the hell they could hear anything above those rolling waves crashing on the shore, Danny now wondered.

Suddenly a gust off the Bristol Channel carried the words, 'Patience, we wait here, let the sea come to us.'

'It's too rough,' came a reply. 'We should've picked another night.'

Danny knew these waters had the second-highest tidal range in the world. What the hell were they planning on putting in the sea?

He suddenly pinched his nose when he felt a sneeze brewing. He wiped bits of remaining straw from his legs. But it was too late to get rid of the pollen up his nose. In a hopeless attempt to stifle the sound, he let out a kind of sneeze-splutter, probably louder than if he'd just sneezed.

Shit!

He glanced round the boulder to see the two men growing larger.

Danny started to crawl and then run in the opposite direction. He measured his stride as he leapt cross the great slabs of rock at the foot of the crumbling cliff.

A loud crack of gunfire filled the night air.

Bullets pinged off the rock and splashed rock pools, spraying salt water up his jeans.

These were no longer air shots, Danny feared – they wanted him dead.

He didn't want to be placed there, as it would only confirm the Carmichaels' suspicions about him.

But surely they couldn't risk killing their nearest neighbour, he reasoned. Arwen Vale would be the first door police would knock after his body, bloated and bullet-riddled, washed ashore.

Danny saw his long shadow stretching out before him. Backlit by the torch, he took a gamble. He stopped, turned and squinted into the blinding white. He was no longer a moving target and held his breath waiting for a bullet to rip through his chest.

All he heard was the waves crashing against the pebbly beach and the screeching laugh of startled seagulls circling high above. The stark light died and the bullets stopped, leaving Danny to flee into the black of night. The gamble had paid off. He had been spared, for now. But he feared it would come at a cost. Toby would want payback for this some other way.

Loose rock and flint tumbled down as Danny started to scramble his way up the shallowest gradient to the clifftop. He heard a voice far below say, 'Yes, police please.'

Got to get the hell out of here, he thought. But it was impossible to quicken his progress up there. He started to shake as he struggled to find footholds in the dark, only thankful that he couldn't see the drop below.

He breathed out as he pulled himself up and over the lip of the cliff.

A beard of grass tickled his chin as he poked his head above the edge. In the silvery light of a full moon, he saw one of the black figures down below carefully remove a container from the driver's side of the Land Rover.

Danny recalled Luke saying his mother Molly had walked into the sea here two years ago to the day. Perhaps on this anniversary they were returning her ashes to the sea where she had first intended to end her life.

There was another rockfall. He saw the torch beam sweep up the cliff face. He was ready to duck but the spotlight stopped just short of the top. The men seemed to be checking Danny had escaped safely.

Danny recalled the anger in Toby's eyes after he'd been caught spying on his private land. He could only imagine the reaction to him intruding this very private ceremony.

Knowing these cliffs were unstable, Danny backed away. He walked by the lines of caravans in a holiday park as he joined up with the path that stretched the entire coastline of Wales. In the lightening sky, the path led him to Penarth. From there, he found a taxi rank.

When he checked his damp jeans pocket for a twenty, he also found a crumpled note in there. It was written in Meg's looping handwriting: *Don't you dare come home till you've sobered up! Megan.*

He spent the cab ride home rehearsing excuses: I know how it looks, it's not my fault, the bastards spiked my punch and with all the early mornings catching up with me, they offered me a couch.

As Danny crunched up the shale drive, he forgot the excuses and began to run. A police car was parked near the front door. Meg was talking to the two uniformed officers. *Kill Jack and Cerys.*

'Meg?' he croaked. 'Meg?!'

'Here's my husband,' Meg explained.

Between breaths, Danny blurted, 'Where are the kids?'

'Nothing to be too worried about sir, there's been a robbery in the area,' the taller officer said.

'And?' Danny asked. 'We don't have neighbourhood watch up here. There's no point, they're all a valley away.'

The officer pointed back at the shale driveway. 'Is that your car, sir?'

Danny looked over at his red Mazda CX-3. 'I'm guessing you've already run a check on it, so is there any point in answering?'

'You seem agitated, sir.'

'Look, what's this about?'

'Could you tell me what you were doing at two-twenty this morning?' the officer asked, looking down at Danny's wet jeans, stuck with bits of straw.

'I was in Arwen Vale.'

'A witness claims they saw that vehicle leaving there around the time of the robbery.'

'Arwen Vale was robbed?'

The shorter officer with red hair and freckles nodded.

Danny pictured the briefcase up in the loft. 'What was taken?'

'I was wondering whether you could help us with that... sir,' the taller officer replied.

'You don't have a search warrant,' Danny said, eyes flitting between officers.

When the officers looked at each other, Danny knew he might as well have told them it's in the loft.

'We never asked to search your property, sir.'

'Good.'

'But now that you mention it,' the officer said, looking over Danny's shoulder. 'Would you mind stepping aside for us to take a look around? We can get a warrant if needs be.'

Danny said, 'Why? You've got nothing on us.'

'A reliable eye witness saw a person fitting your exact description in that car leaving the crime scene,' the redhead said. 'And we've run a check on the prints found on the empty safe and we found a match.'

'Look, I was a kid back then.'

Meg looked at Danny. 'What was taken?'

For the first time she looked nervous, not sure whether the briefcase in the loft was what the officers were after.

'The no small matter of forty thousand pounds.'

Danny recalled hearing the figure at Lavernock Point phone the police. The bastards planted the cash on him via trusted friend Stony, he thought, and were now reaping the harvest. He was being framed. *Toby's payback.*

'For God sake, let them in, Danny,' Meg said. 'We've got nothing to hide. I'm sorry about my husband, he's got a thing about police, nothing personal you understand.'

She seemed unerringly confidently they wouldn't find the case in the loft. Had she moved it someplace even safer? More likely, she'd assumed Danny had got rid of it as she'd ordered.

Danny turned side on to give Meg a look when the officers snuck by his thin profile.

The officers smiled. 'Perfectly understandable, Mrs Rawlings.'

'It's just, we don't want to appear unwelcoming,' she said.

By 'unwelcoming', she meant 'guilty', Danny reckoned. He wished he'd pushed the briefcase away in the pub but then it would be Stony facing the same visitors now.

'Can I see your ID?' Danny asked. He'd been stung before by fake ID but these unfortunately looked like genuine PCs.

Danny quickly retreated and stood by the lounge doorway, as if to subliminally guide them in there, anywhere but the loft hatch on the landing.

'We won't make a mess,' the redhead reassured.

'The kids have already seen to that,' Meg said, smiling. 'Cup of tea either of you?'

Danny felt like pulling Meg aside. Perhaps she was in some kind of denial. He'd always admired her openness and willingness to help others, until now.

Without a word, the taller officer began to climb the stairs in the hallway.

CHAPTER 13

Danny looked down at the redhead officer sitting on the settee with a notepad open.

He heard the thud of the taller officer's boots on the landing above. 'Why start in the loft?'

'Why not?'

'More inside info from that witness I bet,' Danny fumed. 'Toby-bloody-Carmichael.'

'Danny!' Meg blurted.

'What?' Danny asked, still angry that she'd stood aside to let them in. 'You don't even want Carmichael's name being mentioned in this house.' Danny looked back at the officer. 'Calls it the other C word.'

The officer jotted something down. 'You and Mr Carmichael have a history then, sir?'

'Are you sure you don't want a cup of tea?' Meg asked. 'Coffee?'

'He said no,' Danny said, not wanting them here any longer than necessary.

The officer gave a look to Danny and then a smile to Meg. 'No, thank you, Mrs Rawlings. We'll soon be out of your way.'

'Don't worry about him, he hates the police too, you can tell when his nostrils start to flare,' Meg said and then laughed. 'Nothing personal, you understand.'

Danny started breathing through his mouth.

They all suddenly looked over at the hallway door. In plastic forensic gloves, the taller officer was displaying the aluminium briefcase, like an auctioneer's assistant.

Meg can't have moved it then, Danny thought. He felt like holding his wrists out to be cuffed.

'Is this yours, sir?' the redhead asked, standing.

'Don't recognise it,' Danny said, pretending to study it closely, not to appear too dismissive.

'Then it shouldn't have your prints on it when we get results back from the lab.'

Danny looked at Meg.

'Didn't know it was illegal to own a briefcase.'

'No, it's what is inside that interests us,' the redhead said. 'We have been informed that the stolen property was taken away in—' He glanced at his notepad, 'what looked like a silver case.'

Danny filled the silence with, 'Would you like that cup of tea?'

'Open it,' the redhead ordered his colleague.

Danny felt the tip-off was remarkably detailed. 'You were lucky to find such a good witness.'

The taller PC unlocked the case and peered wide-eyed inside.

Perhaps he'd never seen forty grand in cash, Danny thought.

'Well?' the redhead asked.

Silently, the taller officer turned the case upside down and shook. Nothing fell out.

Danny looked at Meg, who refused to react.

You little beauty, he thought.

He quickly looked back at the taller officer. 'You know what, I do recognise the case. Test it for prints if you like. I can autograph it if you really want.'

The officers looked at each other.

'Check for hidden pockets,' the redhead said.

The other office palmed the insides. 'Nothing.'

He then rested the case on the arm of the settee.

A metallic voice crackled over the redhead's breast radio. 'We won't trouble you any longer, sir. Apologies for the inconvenience.'

Danny shut the door firmly, making sure it was double-locked. Back in the lounge, he kissed the curls on Meg's head. 'Bloody hell, Meg, I was trying not to dry swallow or they'd hear my fear. I like the way you played it mean with me, just to show you weren't afraid to shop me if you knew something. Genius.'

'I wasn't playing.'

Danny frowned. 'I'm still feeling some tension in here.'

'Tension? You were out all night and then the police come knocking. I'll give you tension.'

'I'm sorry. I know not what I do,' Danny offered.

'Only cos you were bladdered.'

'Where did you hide it?'

'What?'

'The cash.'

She looked at the fireplace.

'Up the chimney,' Danny said. 'Bit obvious, but it did the trick I guess, should've known they'd try and frame me.'

'No,' Meg said and pointed at the black and grey ash on the fire among the logs.

'You burnt it?' Danny asked. 'You burnt the lot?!'

'You said they were fake!'

'Not to panic you, or tempt you into blowing it on a new kitchen,' he said.

'The other night you said you'd pay good money for a roaring fire like that.'

'Not forty grand!'

Danny knelt to examine the fragments of burnt paper. His heart sank when he saw a corner with a ten-pound symbol and half of Darwin's face on another.

'Why the hell did you-' Danny said and bit his lip. 'We needed that money. After Red Ink, we really needed it.'

'Don't shout.'

'I'm not, I'm speaking loudly,' Danny replied, holding his head.

'You were calling me a genius seconds ago.'

'Wait, I'd only told two people exactly where the cash was hidden: you and Stony.'

'Well it's not me that called them,' Meg said, ruling herself out. For the first time, he felt let down by his old pal Stony.

'That witness also gave them a tip-off,' Danny said. 'They make lying an art form. I'm on to Carmichael's secret and he wants me behind bars.'

'So that money was taken from their safe,' Meg said.

'Probably, but not last night, and by them, not me,' Danny said. 'Carmichael is my anonymous forty-grand donor.'

'Why would he do that?'

'It was a plant,' Danny explained. 'I'm being framed.'

'But forty thousand pounds!' Meg said. 'That's a high price just to get you in trouble.'

'They thought they'd be getting it back, that's why they asked Stony where I'd hidden it,' Danny said. 'If those officers had found the full case, the Carmichaels would have put me behind bars at no cost to them. It was their case, their money with my fingerprints on it and their safe. I'd be banged to rights.' Danny recalled Toby's threats at the Ely sales. 'Toby couldn't get away with gunning us down, but he knew the next best way to destroy me.' He groaned. 'Feels like I'm in quicksand. Every time I make a move, I'm sinking deeper.'

In the kitchen, Danny filled a tall glass with bitty orange juice and downed an aspirin.

She followed him in there, leaning against the kitchen island in the middle.

'You don't know what he's capable of, Meg.'

'Well, he was acting more human than you last night.'

'My punch was spiked.'

'We all had some.'

'Luke handed the cup to me, he didn't pour it out of the punchbowl like the rest,' Danny explained. 'I maybe down to a light weight, but I'm no lightweight when it comes to drinking.'

'You say that as if it's a badge of honour.'

'I say that to prove the Carmichaels have it in for me. I'd even seen it written down in Toby's office. *I'll finish Danny Rawlings.* And that's what he warned Stony when he handed over the money in the Castle Keep. I'm hoping that's why Stony agreed to pass it on.'

Danny recalled the final task on Carmichael's list was to kill Jack and Cerys, though stopped short of sharing that. She looked stressed enough as it was.

When she heard Jack crying upstairs, she stood from leaning. 'And that's your fault too.'

'How can you pin that on me?'

'He's seeking attention cos you're always busy working, either at home or away at the track… or partying.'

'Look, I'll go.'

'No,' she said. 'He doesn't want to see you in that state.'

She stormed out of the room, slamming the hallway door behind her.

Danny was never much good at reading the signals, but even he could make out she wasn't entirely happy.

Probably saw me as a dirty stop-out, he thought. He couldn't blame her. He'd think the same if it was her staggering back after a late night with the girls. What the hell had Luke put in that punch, paint stripper?

Danny was about to call Stony. There was no slack in the banded wads. He was interested to know where he'd got the money to buy the silver cane and smoking jacket. He suspected there'd been a transaction fee for him acting as a middleman between Toby and himself.

The tinny theme tune to Champions suddenly came from his mobile. There was no Caller ID. 'Toby, is that you?'

There was silence.

'Well, they've been and gone if you're wondering,' Danny said. 'And they didn't find a thing, let alone forty thousand things.'

'Danny,' a voice said down the line.

That didn't sound like Toby or Luke. 'Who is this?'

'It's Darren,' the voice said. 'I'm with Chris.'

'What?' Danny asked. 'Where are you?'

'I need to show you something,' Darren said. His voice sounded distant.

'I need to speak with Chris, make sure he's okay.'

'That's not possible.'

'Don't you dare do anything, even lay a finger on him,' Danny said. 'I'll meet you. Tell me where and I'll be there.'

'Ely... by the rail track.'

'By the racetrack,' Danny asked. There was a meeting there that afternoon.

'Rail track. Before it's too late.'

The line went dead. Danny checked the runners for the six-race Flat meeting at Ely. Darren had a ride in the first for Carmichael, an odds-on shot for the maiden called Foundling.

Danny didn't have a runner suitable for the entry conditions of any race that meeting, but he was booked to go there in his role as a racecourse ambassador.

'When Toby rings, you don't hang up,' Darren had said by the bonfire. Danny could now see why he wanted to meet conveniently near the racetrack.

Danny swiped the Mazda keys off the hallstand and headed for Ely.

CHAPTER 14

Danny parked up at Ely in the shadow of the red-bricked shell of the former brewery. He walked to the one point on the Swansea–Cardiff mainline he was familiar with – the ghost platform of the former Ely train station. He'd been here with town planners to discuss the viability of bringing it back to life as they had with the racecourse now stood on Trelai Park about half a mile south of there.

Danny hopped over the locked gates to the rear. Since the station shut not long after the old racecourse, it had been left to ruin. The coaching house and stabling behind the station were no more than crumbling walls overrun by vines and brambles. Weeds rose up from cracks in the paving slabs of the platform, and all that was left of the station master's building and ticket hall were faded black-and-white photos.

The large metal Ely mainline station sign on the platform was covered in rust and creepers. It was the only way to tell it was a former working station. He certainly knew trains wouldn't stop there now.

He glanced down the slowly turning track in both directions.

Darren had said to meet him 'by Ely rail track'.

With the first race at Ely only hours away, Danny knew Darren would be in the area. But there was no sign of him. Opposite he saw long, grey factory units, beyond conifers swishing in the morning breeze.

To his left, he could see the Old Ely Bridge, once at the heart of this village off the Llandaff suburb of Cardiff. Standing on the footbridge, made from the same bricks as the brewery, there looked to be a trainspotter in a leather jacket, staring down at the track holding what looked like a spotter's notepad.

Perhaps he'd also seen Darren and Chris. Danny thought about shouting over, but he knew he was trespassing, standing on the platform. He didn't want the town planners to have any excuse for rejecting the renewal project.

As a train cruised by, a wave of warm, gritty air brushed over him. The train appeared to be slowing down on the approach to Cardiff Central.

The trainspotter didn't note the number down.

Danny checked his watch again. He'd been told to come quickly. Darren was clearly playing games. He was probably crouched behind the trees opposite pissing himself laughing.

When he noticed the only other person there had climbed up on to the wall of the bridge and then dangled their legs over the edge, Danny began to question the reason why they were there.

Danny looked to his right and saw the cabin of a Swansea-bound train growing larger. The person on the bridge was now gripping the wall, as if ready to push off.

Danny looked back to the train and then to the bridge.

'No!' he shouted but it was drowned out by the oncoming roar of the three-carriage train as it flew by as a blur.

The train's horn blasted.

When he saw the kid push off and disappear behind the front carriage, Danny looked away sharply.

His head turned to see if anyone else was there to witness it. It happened so quick, he hoped he'd imagined the whole thing. But then came the pig's squeal of the train's automatic brakes grinding the carriages to a halt, some distance beyond the bridge.

Danny shouted, 'Help!'

It no longer seemed important that he could be caught there trespassing.

He ran to the edge of the ghost platform and jumped on to the grassy embankment to the side of the track.

He sprinted under the bridge to see if he could help but he knew the kid wouldn't have stood a chance.

He started to see trails of wet blood on the steel rails. He feared the body parts would soon follow and looked ahead rather than down.

As he ran by the middle carriage, he tripped. He thought it was a wooden sleeper. When he belatedly looked down, there was an arm in a leather sleeve sticking out from under the carriage and lying on the ballast of crushed stone.

The hand suddenly fell back and a rainbow band slipped down to the wrist. He had seen the same in the Bath changing room. *Chris!*

He was moving. He always knew the lad was a survivor.

Danny ducked down to see how he could set him free from the wheels. But he saw the arm had been severed clean from the body at the shoulder. There was a tapping at the window in the carriage above. Danny looked up at a girl only a bit younger than Jack with pink ribbons streaming from her hair and her nose pressed flat against the glass. Her dimpled face couldn't decide between a smile and a frown. She was probably wondering why the silly man was having a sleep under the train. Danny was thankful she couldn't see under the carriage. He motioned with his arms to shoo her away.

Her mother came to the window, saw the hand on the floor and yanked the girl away.

Danny then heard the crunch of stones. The driver had lowered himself from his cabin, muttering, 'I get a fucking jumper in my final month, happy fucking retirement!'

He wasn't moving fast, but then there was no rush. The damage had been done.

A little way back, Danny noticed a smashed phone in the grass, clearly thrown from the leather jacket. He also saw a piece of card fluttering down the track. Danny went over and stamped on the card to stop it getting away.

'Oi, you're my witness to this, I've called transport police,' the driver shouted after him. 'No way am I going to get a disciplinary for this.'

Danny studied the card. It was no bigger than a postcard. Beneath the dirty impression of the tread-print he'd left, there appeared to be a list. It was written by the same hand as the card he'd found in Toby's office on the night of the party.

Danny read: You poofs are all the same, limp wrists, prefer the back door, finish in rear to get an eyeful.

It was like reliving the ugly scenes in the Bath changing room. Was Chris seeing a shrink? This looked like some kind of exposure therapy to desensitise the abuse. Perhaps he'd been set homework to read these words over and over. *Poor lad.*

He recalled Darren's words that lured him here, 'I'm with Chris.'

Danny looked up at the bridge, shouting, 'Darren, I know you're there, hiding behind that wall. You might not have pushed Chris, but you pushed him into it. Come out you fucking coward!'

Danny looked back to see the driver throwing up on the embankment. He'd clearly seen the arm.

He slipped the card into his jeans pocket. It had his fingerprints and footprints all over it. He didn't want to be framed again.

'You've got to make a statement,' shouted the driver, wiping his mouth.

'He jumped,' Danny declared. 'And now he's dead.'

He needed to find Darren. He leapt back over the locked gates of Ely's ghost platform and sat in his Mazda. He was still breathing hard. When the screaming sirens and flashing blue lights of the police cars arrived, he slid lower in the driver's seat.

Time to go, he thought, and headed straight for the owners' and trainers' car park by Ely racetrack.

He was one of the first there, only beaten by those connections allowing plenty of time for a long journey.

With no runner to prepare, he sat there trying to blank the image of Chris jumping. It repeated over and over. Perhaps his brain was trying to expose himself to make some sense of it, like Chris had been with the Bath abuse.

He watched the horseboxes arriving one by one, slowly filling the car park. He looked at the trainers' names on the back. They were arriving from as far afield as Surrey, often a tip in itself. It wouldn't be long before the paying public started streaming in.

He slid lower again when he saw the luxurious four-berth van with *T. Carmichael, Arwen Vale, Glamorgan* painted on the back, more like a five-star hotel on wheels.

It made their van look like a grubby B&B in comparison, Danny thought.

Danny got out of the Mazda. The air was getting warmer by the second. He took off his fleece and went to the changing room not to put on his silks but a dark blue suit. Unfortunately he had to look the part as an ambassador, but he drew the line at wearing a tie. He was about to give the corporate VIPs an insight into the racing life of a trainer, an insider's view.

Right then, he felt like telling them where to go. Chris was dead and he kept thinking he could've prevented it. If only he'd chosen the old bridge as the point to look out over the track at Ely. Perhaps then he could've talked Chris down.

Meg was at home with the kids. Now more than ever, he just wanted to be with them. A morning like that reminded him how fragile and short life was.

CHAPTER 15

Danny headed straight for The Whistler Bar on the first floor of the grandstand when the chimes of a racecourse announcement crackled over the speakers.

'Would Mr Daniel Rawlings please come to the weighing room immediately, that's Daniel Rawlings to the weighing room, thank you.'

Probably the management checking he'd bothered to show his face, he thought, as he turned on the stairs and made for the weighing room overlooking the parade ring behind the grandstand.

In there, he was in fact met by Toby Carmichael, who wore an expensive looking black suit and a sombre, mournful expression. The clerk of the scales sat on Danny's left and the valet entering the changing rooms were similarly glum.

Danny assumed the death of Chris Ramsbottom had already reached the track. 'You've heard the bad news then.'

'Too young, far too young,' Toby said, stroking his second chin thoughtfully. 'Brings back the bad times with my wife Molly towards the end, grim, really grim.'

But Chris had lots to live for. He seemed upbeat having completed the JETS course, keen to start a new life not end one. Chris jumped to escape Darren Cooper not depression, Danny reasoned.

'What do you want from me?' he asked.

'To ride for me in the first.'

Did he really say that, Danny thought, one of us must be in shock.

After the police search that morning, Danny's first instinct was to stick two fingers up and go get some hair of the dog at the bar. He had wondered if this was another trap but the fact he couldn't even field a runner for his local meeting revealed the current state of his depleted string and with two kids at home, he wasn't in the position to turn down the offer. Principles took a backseat when mouths needed feeding and bills needed paying. He'd guessed Darren was right after all when he claimed, 'If Carmichael rings, you don't hang up.'

Danny had assumed Darren arranged to meet him half a mile from the track because he had a ride on Foundling in the first. Danny guessed he'd been called here because Darren had suddenly disappeared. Perhaps he'd been spotted urging Chris to push off from the bridge.

He knew Carmichael's runner in the opener was hovering around the even-money mark, so there was a decent chance he'd take home a winner's percentage of the prize money along with a riding fee. And it gave him an unexpected opportunity to find out what it felt like to actually sit on a racehorse from a yard that boasted a better than one-in-two strike-rate. He was keen to feel what ingredient was missing from the horses he usually worked every morning.

Danny nodded. He didn't dare ask questions, just glad to be picked for the spare ride.

He'd come here to give an insider's view of the sport but now set to ride one of Carmichael's, he might be the one about to learn some hidden secrets.

Danny collected the red and green quartered silks with white and red hooped sleeves on a hanger in a dust jacket from the valet. He felt nervous wearing the colours that had taken all before them over the past season and a half. From a confectionery van, he bought a bottle of water to keep hydrated and a Mars Bar for energy.

After he weighed out, he finished off the bottle and the chocolate.

Would he be the one to mess up? At least that would put him firmly out of the targets of the attacker, trying to ease the pressure.

In the parade ring, Luke nudged his father Toby, who then said, 'Luke here mentioned you promised to give him some work down your place and perhaps in time, a ride or two.'

Suddenly Danny had a better idea why he had been picked for this spare. He knew there had to be something. He had thought it was a trap but turns out it was a favour. The fact Luke's own father hadn't even given him a chance told Danny enough. But wearing the green, red and white colours of the Carmichael yard, he couldn't ignore the offer he'd made to Luke in Toby's office any longer. 'Call round in the morning, first thing. I'll test you on a tricky one.'

Danny was surprised by Luke's reaction to this offer. He seemed more worried than happy. Perhaps it was the fear he wouldn't measure up when finally put to the test.

'What are my riding orders?' Danny asked. He'd have liked them in writing so if he followed them word for word and got beat there'd be no one to blame but the trainer.

'Don't rely on the whip,' Toby said.

'At all,' Danny questioned. 'Even if it's tight and a slap might make the difference.'

'Even if it's tight.'

'What if my horse starts to meander? It's only his second start and he showed greenness at Sandown.'

'Hands and heels only. The whip only complicates things.'

'But the others will be allowed eight slaps,' Danny said.

'It won't do our chances any good.'

'It won't do them any harm,' Danny said.

'Do you want the ride?' Toby snarled.

'Don't blame me if I lose in a photo then.'

Danny was led out of the parade ring by Luke, who then let them go at the entrance to the course. He cantered Foundling to post quietly on a dirt strip outside the chase course. Near where the stalls were placed, there was another gap in the rails where the slowing runners fed through and then circled behind until the starting time at two o'clock.

Having played a big part in designing the jumps tracks there, Danny was keen to influence the racetrack bigwigs on the new Flat circuit. He had envisaged a sharp circular track inside both the hurdles and steeplechase courses.

While he realised horse racing was in the entertainment industry and knew funfair rides, picnic areas and best dress catwalks for ladies' days would all increase takings at the turnstiles, the trainer in him only wanted what was best for his horses. This was kicked into touch during the preliminary proposals, with the accountants and architects shaking their heads dismissively. Danny stormed out of there when he heard the reasons: it would limit space to maximise crowd capacity on the infield, it would cost too much and the viewing of Flat races from the grandstand would be distanced by the two outer jumps tracks. Next thing he knew they'd agreed to make a Flat track by taking the hurdles track and removing the hurdles between April and September. That way, they could fit the Big Wheels and candy floss vans in the centre for races like the Welsh Derby with a view to replicating the success of Epsom's Derby Day.

Danny wrote an email to the committee saying top horses wouldn't race on a track scuffed up and riddled with divots from a winter of frost, waterlogging and large field hurdle races. Keep the ground fresh with a thick covering of lush turf was the key to the track's success, he reckoned. For the committee, it was more about short-term costs and revenues.

With that in mind, Danny didn't hold out much hope for the revamp of Ely mainline station just down the road. Probably get a model steam railway chugging in, he thought.

Foundling had moved to post as well as he looked but, as with others from Arwen Vale, the youngster's breeding let the side down. The big, scopey bay colt was the son of a winning plater on the Flat out of a dam who'd failed to complete in three jump starts, hardly the ideal bloodlines to be making a big impact on the Flat. The strong vibes in the betting ring were based upon a hugely promising neck second in a Sandown maiden last month. That day, he finished strongly up the stiff home straight over an inadequate seven furlongs. With that positive experience to call upon, the tipsters in the paper and the punters on the track and in the shops widely expected him to go one better here, particularly given the yard's reputation and an extra furlong leeway to hit full stride.

Danny pinched the big ears of his mount and ran a calming hand down the proud, strong neck. Toby was bound to be studying and assessing Danny through binoculars from the stand. If he was to get beat, Danny wanted his boss to know he'd at least treated the horse right for a yard that didn't even want the horses touched with an air-cushioned persuader.

Given the lack of instructions he'd been given in the parade ring, Foundling was clearly expected to win whatever the tactics employed.

Even in the short canter to post, Danny could feel the difference in the quality between Foundling and Red Ink.

They were led forward without resistance by the strong arms of a stocky stall handler.

It made a pleasant change to sit on a juvenile with a touch of class. It reminded him of when he was put on some bright prospects as an apprentice jockey after leaving school. It felt rejuvenating, like listening to a song from his youth he hadn't heard for years.

Danny measured his breathing to slow his heart. He felt even more nervous than when he'd ridden Red Ink. He guessed it was the mix of greater expectation and responsibility of riding a hot favourite for others. It didn't help knowing what Toby was capable of if he didn't deliver.

For a brief moment as the flagman in a white coat and gripping a fluorescent yellow flag prepared to walk off the course a furlong ahead, he contemplated throwing the race. Payback for the police visit, he thought, though the instant gratification would be quickly spoilt by a lengthy ban from the stewards and a dent to his reputation as a rider.

Danny was stalled nine of nine on the outside. Even though there hadn't been enough races to collate a reliable draw bias, it was obvious he was going to be the most inconvenienced, positioned wide with only two furlongs to the first of two left turns.

As the stalls parted, Danny scrubbed hard to get to the front. Once they'd hit racing gallop, Foundling wanted to keep accelerating. He was doing too much, pulling at the reins to go even faster. This was a mile race, not a sprint. He needed him settled early if he was to conjure the same finish as his Sandown debut second.

Seeing a gap on the rails in behind the clear leader, Danny slotted the youngster against the rail to get some cover and go the shortest route.

The horse slotted in perfectly, like an experienced veteran, taking a tow from the twenty-to-one shot Job Well Done.

Even with nowhere to go, Foundling was still gassy, stubbornly refusing to relax. His big head was tossing left and right, tickled by the flashing tail of the leader. He clearly wanted an opportunity to show what he can do. Danny's biceps held him in check, just.

When they filed down another two-furlong stretch farthest away from the distant stands, Danny's flexed arms relaxed slightly. He was taking the handbrake off as they approached the final turn. With the help of momentum on the left turn, Foundling didn't need to be asked to switch out wide and quickly drew alongside the long-time leader.

Danny's hands started to nudge the neck of Foundling and the response was instant, like pressing a button. Foundling quickened two lengths clear.

Danny briefly looked over both shoulders. He saw a flash of colour as two runners began a forward move up the rail on his inner. Foundling kept accelerating, but Danny felt the first signs of greenness. The two-year-old began to lug left, as if getting lonely out in front and searching for a guide in the rail. Danny slipped his whip through and was about to give the youngster a firm slap to straighten him up and finish a job almost done. The instinct was as natural as putting his arms out before a fall. But he resisted the urge, having heard Toby's strict orders in the parade ring.

But the horse kept hanging to the rail forcing those on the inner to check badly. Danny heard loud protests from the jockeys he'd just cut up behind. Foundling brushed the white plastic of the rails but it didn't stop his forward momentum. He glanced up at the big screen stood on the infield and saw he was in a clear lead again. He needed to keep it that way as a winning margin less than a length might give the stewards ideas to throw him out. Danny kept pushing but the colt inexplicably started to drift off the rail back towards the centre of the course. There was no reason for it: he hadn't drawn the whip, the colt didn't feel tired, the going was sound, there was no side-on wind to buffer and no camber to the track.

Danny felt one of the runners he'd already hampered on the rail trying to challenge out wider but was then once again denied a clear run by the meandering leader. It reminded him of the wayward Drunken Mistress at York. Danny drew the whip through to his left hand. He knew if he used it Toby would be after him and if he didn't the stewards would be. He was forced to administer a few backhanders on the horse's rump passing the furlong marker. The colt straightened up almost immediately and then began to veer back to the rail.

Danny sat tight and put the whip down, aiming just to stay on board.

'And it's Foundling by a fast-reducing half-length but he's got enough in hand to hold on,' the race-caller said.

Danny blew out. He felt like punching the air. It had proved more a test of his riding skills and balance than the steering job he'd envisaged. Toby would surely be booking him for future rides on this evidence.

However, he felt a good deal flatter as he left the stewards room with a five-day ban for careless riding.

Returning to the parade ring, he heard the chimes again. 'Result of the stewards' enquiry… the placings remain unaltered, weighed in weighed in.'

Danny's stride quickened. He'd done his neighbour a favour. Perhaps they could call it quits. He beamed as he offered a hand to the winning trainer. It wasn't taken.

'Are you deaf,' Toby snarled. 'No whip!'

'I had to give a few taps just to straighten him up,' Danny reasoned, lowering his hand.

'We were bloody lucky to keep the race in the stewards.'

'I got a ban if it makes you feel any better.'

'Deserved more,' Toby said. 'It was dangerous not careless. I will personally make sure you will never ride for me again.'

'But—'

'Get out of my sight.'

No wonder he was running out of riders to call upon, Danny thought. He dreaded to think what the reception had been if the stewards had reversed the placings.

Danny walked back to his car. Being his local track, he'd shower and change back at the yard.

On his way, he signed a couple of racecards. When he started to hear a tinny ringing in his ears, his legs started to become leaden and wobbly. His vision began to blur and colours turned to smudges. The Whistler bronze ahead started to gallop across his vision as he spun. He caught enough to see the tarmac rushing up at him. He thought he was having some kind of anxiety seizure after the stress of the morning and the stewards' room. There was a cramping tightness round his chest. Was this a heart attack?

Close to face planting the ground, he was caught in time. It was if he'd been plucked from the air. He then felt like he was being dragged. Was he dying?

Danny blinked up at the towering bronze looking down. He was slumped against the brick plinth beneath the life-size statue of the legend The Whistler that graced the first incarnation of Ely Park on this site last century. He felt shittier than when he'd woken early that morning. He was glad of the shade and the cover from the milling racegoers the other side.

'Danny? Thank God you're not dead,' someone said. Danny didn't want anyone to see him like this. He managed to turn his heavy head enough and was glad to see it was Stony.

'Here, take a swig of this.' Stony put a silver hip flask to Danny's dry claggy lips. 'I'll get help.'

'Check my legs,' Danny said. He couldn't bring himself to do so. He couldn't feel any pain but wasn't sure whether that was a good or bad thing.

Stony looked down. 'They're still there.'

Danny found the courage to look also. His breeches were white and intact, no blood or bones visible.

'I know who did this,' Danny slurred, picturing Chris drop from the bridge. 'Darren, Darren Cooper.'

'You're in shock, you need checking over by the racecourse doc.'

'I'm fine.'

'Darren is dead.'

There was a silence, just the distant sound of chatter and laughter.

'He can't... you're wrong,' Danny said.

'He jumped under the eight-forty-five London Paddington to Swansea this morning,' Stony said. 'I heard the sirens on my walk to the track.'

'But Darren was taking out the top jockeys to give him more chances. Malcolm Bernard had ended his contract. I found him destroying evidence at Arwen Vale, Bernard's silk covered in Ryan's blood. I've got it back at the yard.'

'Just because it doesn't make sense to you now, it doesn't mean it isn't true,' Stony said.

Danny wasn't listening. 'And he's a bully, you should've seen him laying into Chris at Bath.'

'How do you think you got the ride in the opener?' Stony said. 'In the racecard, Darren was down to ride Foundling.'

'I thought he hadn't turned up, lying low after what happened to Chris. He'd be wanted for questioning. I can't believe he's dead, I didn't like the bloke but I wouldn't wish that on any one.'

'Go to The Whistler Bar if you don't believe me, they're all talking about it,' Stony said. 'They've even arranged a minute's silence before the parade for the feature race later.'

Danny recalled the rainbow wristband on the severed arm. 'Wait, Darren was married with three kids. You're wrong.'

'I've been called old fashioned, but even I know it goes on.'

'Darren was bi?'

'And living a lie it seems,' Stony said. 'Probably what pushed him over the edge in the end. I feel sorry for his little ones. They're the real victims in this.'

Danny recalled Toby say it reminded him of the bad times he'd suffered with Molly. Perhaps depression had made Darren take it out on others.

'He claimed to have kidnapped Chris just to lure me there. He knew I wouldn't have come otherwise. He said he'd got something to show me,' Danny slurred.

'What was it?'

'I got there too late,' Danny said. 'But there was a piece of card blowing down the rail track.'

Why was Darren carrying the card? Was that the *something* he wanted to show Danny?

It was like a transcript almost word for word of the abusive scenes in the Bath changing room.

Danny felt woozy when he tried to get up. Stony reached out.

'I'm fine, just need a minute to get my bearings.'

'You had a lucky escape given what the attacker did to the others,' Stony said. 'I must've disturbed him.'

'You didn't see anything, then,' Danny said.

'Nah, they'd have got away even if I had,' Stony said, hand on his hip. 'Seems I was wrong, you were a target. Guess the attacker saw you as a top jockey getting a ride for Toby Carmichael.'

Danny began to wonder if that is the reason why Carmichael chose him as the replacement jockey. Perhaps this was his payback. And this after Danny had ridden the bastard a winner. He felt a fool now for accepting.

'But I'm not a top jockey; I was flattered to be asked. Mind, there can't be many top jockeys available for Carmichael to choose now. He was scraping the barr—' Danny stopped.

'You feeling okay lad, want some more whisky.'

Suddenly Danny felt he'd made the link. The attacker wasn't targeting top jockeys. All the victims were set upon after riding for Carmichael. The fact they were all top jockeys was incidental.

'Yeah, feeling a lot better,' Danny said, shakily getting to his feet. He leant back on the plinth trying to stop the Tote offices from slowly turning. 'Did you take a cut of the forty grand?'

'No,' Stony protested. 'And I never would profit from tricking my best friend.'

'Where did you get the silver cane and smoking jacket?'

'Good4cash,' Stony said. 'I pawned a few of my jockey medals.'

'No wonder you told me to stop having a go at Trevor when I said punters might pawn their grandpa's war medals.'

'I was embarrassed for me not Trevor.'

At least he now knew Toby hadn't bribed Stony into it.

'I'm sorry,' Stony said.

'It's not you that should be apologising,' Danny said. 'It'll teach me not to doubt you again.'

'When's Powder Keg out next?' Stony said, as if steering the talk back to his comfort zone. 'Is she okay?'

'In better nick than me right now, going for the Goodwood Cup at the end of the month,' he said.

'That sounds like a tip to me,' Stony replied.

They shook hands, though it was more to keep his balance, as he stood upright.

Danny wanted to meet up with Toby. He needed to know why he was jumped upon straight after riding for the yard, just like Ryan at Bath.

When he switched on his phone, Danny saw he'd missed a call. He listened to the answerphone. 'Message received 10.42am on July 13th.' 'This is Darren, I can see you but I cannot reach you. I hope you hear this, tell my wife and kids I love them. I had something to show you – my behaviour at Bath, it wasn't me, it wasn't the real me, you must understand, my life is being ruled by another.' Darren's voice was being drowned out by a rumble getting louder and louder. 'Please forgive me. It's the coward's way out, I guess I'm the coward, it's all my fault, I shouldn't have got involved.'

Danny couldn't decipher the final words on the message, the last of Darren Cooper's life.

'Message ends,' the automated woman's voice said.

'It wasn't the real me,' Danny whispered, looking down at the phone. Had Darren been reading from the card he'd found?

'I'll finish Danny Rawlings,' Nye had reckoned the donor told Stony at the Castle Keep. The same phrase was also on Toby's cue card. Danny began to wonder if the card he'd found in Toby's office desk was also a script.

'If you weren't being paid, why did you take the cash from Toby Carmichael?'

'I had no choice,' Stony replied.

'Did he threaten you?' Danny asked.

'No.'

'Did he threaten me if you left without the cash?'

Stony nodded mournfully. 'And that's not all, he... he threatened—'

'To kill Jack and Cerys,' Danny interjected, recalling the other threat on Toby's card.

'I'm sorry, lad.'

Danny realised why Stony kept pushing the briefcase to him on the corner table in the Castle Keep.

'You've got nothing to be worried about,' Danny said. This time it was him putting a supportive hand on Stony's arm. 'You couldn't risk not taking it.'

'I'm a gambler but I couldn't cope with what was at stake.'

'You did right,' Danny said.

Danny began to doubt what was real and what was staged.

If the threats on those cards were scripted who was behind them?

He felt his skin crawl like it had when he saw the bridge jumper. It felt like he'd just heard Darren's words from the grave.

CHAPTER 16

That night, Meg had stolen most of the duvet, generously leaving a corner to cover his left foot. Right then, it was the least of his concerns. He'd worked up a sweat just lying there naked staring up at the grey ceiling. He'd wondered if it was stress or the body trying to sweat out any toxins left from the drugs that must've been spiking the bottled water he'd temporarily left to go weigh out. He could feel his heart kick.

It wasn't yet midnight but he'd already given up any hopes of getting the minimum five hours sleep before he had to rise for taking out the first Lot.

He was about to slowly lift himself from the sheet sticking to his back when he heard something downstairs. He stopped breathing and glanced nervously over at the closed curtains of the window looking out over the driveway.

Had the attacker come to finish the job? In the business to attract the public, Danny's address was on his website, along with online trainer databases and his business cards. He could easily be found, whether he wanted to or not.

He swore he heard something. It sounded like the slap of post landing on the mat he'd often hear when having a lie in, though he couldn't recall the last one of those.

But he wasn't expecting a delivery, certainly not at this hour. He slipped on his boxers and blue dressing gown.

Meg was a light sleeper. He knew even the soft yellow glow of the landing light seeping under their bedroom door would be enough to stir her. He wanted to face this alone. Passing Jack and Cerys' shared bedroom, he heard his son whimpering.

He tried feeling his way along the landing, but banged himself on the banister finial at the top of the staircase leading down to the hallway. He bit his lip and held his side. Since shedding fat and muscle, he felt every small knock, particularly to the ribs.

Bugger this, Danny thought, and flicked on the light. He'd escaped the attack with just a groggy head, he didn't want to push his luck and break both legs by missing a step in the dark.

He crept down the creaky stairs and in the dim light from the landing above, looked down at a small brown cardboard box sat on the Welcome-Croeso mat by the front door.

He bent to pick the box up and opened the lid. Inside was a scrap of paper. Danny squinted to read: *Remmember you're promis*.

He was more alarmed by the message than either the spelling or grammar.

Promise?

Danny pulled out the paper. With those mistakes, he reckoned it had to be a kid but he'd seen a lot worse from adults in online forums.

The back of the paper was blank, but the box was filled with a soft material. Danny wondered if it was another fragment of Darren's silk saved from the bonfire. He pulled it from the box. In his hand, he soon recognised it to be Jack's blanky. Danny sniffed it. The material smelt of his son. What the hell? How could this be posted through the letterbox?

Danny looked up the stairs. It explained why Jack was still awake and upset. He was about to return the pacifier to his son and then call the police. He was the victim here. He'd let this go too far. When he recalled the piece of card in Toby's office, he stopped himself. If he was being targeted after riding a winner for Toby, then what would be the payback for reporting it to the police? *Kill Jack and Cerys.*

He ran through any promises he'd made lately. It didn't take long as he made a point of not promising anything to anyone. He didn't want to let people down if he couldn't make good on that promise.

Luke Carmichael!

At Ely he'd realised the attacker was targeting jockeys riding for Arwen Vale. Toby had continually denied his son an opportunity in the family business.

That kind of rejection had got to hurt, Danny thought, particularly for a moody teen that had only recently lost his mother. It had clearly left serious trust issues. It seemed Luke still didn't fully believe Danny would give him a trial gallop at first light. At some point Luke must've removed the blanky from the spare bedroom. Even the thought made him feel sick. If he was trying to convince Danny to give him a job he was going the wrong way about it.

Danny opened the oak door and shivered at the rush of cold air sweeping in. The porch light came on automatically, fanning out yellow light over an empty shale drive. The deliverer of the gift was gone.

He was about to close the door when he looked down at the letter box. He put the cardboard box to the metal shutter in the door. The box was small but not small enough to push through. His fingers started to shake as he turned the box at different angles. The box was clearly too big to fit through the hole. He gently squeezed the box but there was no give in the cardboard. There were no creases either. The attacker had dropped the box on to the mat from inside the Lodge.

Danny stepped back in from the cold. He quietly double locked the door and then rushed to the kitchen. That door was already locked. He then checked the ground floor windows. All were shut and locked.

Danny quickly ran through the hours before they'd retired for an early night. He'd watched *Would I Lie To You?* on the telly and then told another bedtime story about knights and dragons to Jack, who again rooted for the dragon. He came back down at half-nine and locked up. They then checked everything was off and went to bed.

The attacker must've snuck in before that point. They had hidden somewhere inside and then delivered a gift Danny would never forget.

He shivered but it was no longer cold.

Remmember you're promis.

Danny quietly climbed the stairs and looked in on Jack and Cerys. They were both fast asleep. He'd put the blanky in the wash before reuniting it with his son. He didn't want the cardboard box in his house any longer. He went back downstairs, pulled on his boots and coat, and dropped it in the recycling bin by the barn and then returned to the kitchen. From the back of the kitchen cupboard, he pulled out a bottle and downed the last of the gin. He hated gin.

Standing there in the early hours wearing a coat, dressing gown, boxers and boots, and wincing as he downed the booze, he reckoned a shrink would say he'd got a problem.

They wouldn't know the half of it, Danny thought.

Danny pulled his mobile from his jacket and checked the wall clock. He'd normally cringe at the thought of ringing anyone at this hour, particularly his head lad, due in work just five hours from now. But this call couldn't wait.

Staying in the kitchen, Danny shut the door to the hallway and called Jordi on memory dial. He was staying in a one-bed flat above a Chinese takeaway in Rhymney. Jordi was looking to move. The sweet smells drifting up every evening were proving a test too far for a jockey constantly fighting the weight.

'Yes,' croaked down the line.

'Jordi, it's Danny Rawlings, nothing to worry about,' he said quietly.

'I'll be there in… five hours, Mr Rawlings,' Jordi said and then yawned loudly.

'You won't need to if you answer me this question.'

'What have I done?' Jordi asked suddenly sounding more alert.

'You've done nothing, you're not losing your job, I meant I'll give you the day off as a reward for telling me if you saw Luke lurking about the yard before you clocked off and I arrived back from Ely.'

'Toby's son?'

'That's the one.'

'Yes, but he said you already knew about it. He was looking about to get a feel for the place. He said you'd already given him the job.'

'Did he?' Danny replied. 'I can see why this call gave you a shock. Rest easy, your job is safe as houses.'

'Safe as…?'

'Houses,' Danny replied. 'I mean, there's no way Luke will be working with us. One more thing I need from you Jordi, and it's vitally important that you tell me the truth. Did you see Luke leave the estate?'

There was a pause. 'No, but he had gone, I checked around the yard before I left.'

He'd already be in Silver Belle Lodge by then, Danny thought.

'I'll still be in first thing,' Jordi said.

'If you like,' Danny said. 'I'll give you time and a half.'

'Time and a half?'

'Bit more pay,' Danny explained. 'I've got to go.'

Danny took off his jacket and boots. On his way back to bed, he looked in again on Jack in Cardiff City pyjamas and Cerys in her cot, both fast asleep. He felt like guarding the doorway for the rest of the night.

By four o'clock, sheer exhaustion won out over anxiety and he fell asleep. It seemed like he was only out for a few seconds when he sat bolt upright covered in sweat again.

In just a few hours, he would have to entertain the man who he believed had brutally attacked five of the best jockeys in the country.

He had a feeling he wouldn't be drifting back off to sleep before then.

CHAPTER 17

Danny had already been pacing the yard since dark, putting feed and water in the wrong trays, sending the lads and lasses out on the wrong horses and even getting their names wrong. His mind wasn't on the job.

He'd removed his phone several times, even typed Luke's mobile onto the screen with thumb hovering over the call button.

Everything told him to tell Luke the trial was off. He'd normally honour a promise, for fear of offending. But he suspected it wouldn't be Luke's feelings that would be most hurt if he called it off.

During the night, he'd gone over the moments before and after he'd ridden Foundling. Luke must've poured the drugs into his water bottle between hearing Danny had accepted the spare ride and briefly leaving the changing room to weigh out.

It was a ride Toby's son clearly felt had his name on. Danny had to pay for this just like all the others that had ridden for Arwen Vale. When Danny had then accepted a trial for Luke in the parade ring before the race, it was no longer in Luke's interest to attack Danny, who by then already had Rohypnol in his veins.

He could now see why Luke looked more worried than glad at hearing he'd been offered a trial.

After the race, Luke must've then followed Danny, ready to catch him when he dropped. He was the one Danny felt drag his limp body to cover and then leave him there to sleep the drugs off. That's when Stony found him.

If he backed out of this job interview now, Danny felt sure he'd become victim six. *Remmember You're Promis.*

Danny couldn't go to the police until he'd got something to back up his theory.

Let's get this over, he thought; just say to the boy I'll think about it. That would give him a few days to find some evidence that was more than circumstantial.

'You're early,' Danny said, disguising the tremor in his voice.

'Start as I mean to go on,' Luke replied, shouldering a rucksack as he crunched down the driveway. They walked round Silver Belle Lodge to the stabling at the back.

'Head lad Jordi has already tacked up Red Ink for you,' Danny explained. 'It's your riding technique I'm interested in.'

'You won't be disappointed,' Luke beamed.

'Confidence,' Danny replied. 'I like that.'

'I want this bad.'

'Tell me *why* you want this?' Danny asked. Luke shrugged. 'I mean, coming from a yard going places to one on the cold list. Some might see that as a comedown, a demotion.'

'Don't matter how big the yard is, if you don't get to ride for it,' Luke said. 'I just need to be given a chance to show what I can do.'

'Toby doesn't believe in nepotism, then.'

Luke shrugged again.

Danny explained, 'Giving you a head start just cos he's your father.'

'Have you invited me round to find out more about me or my dad?'

Danny paused by the entrance to the new stables. He clearly wasn't going to get any answers.

'Before we begin, the first house rule,' Danny said and pointed to Luke's ears. 'No jewellery allowed on all work riders. Put them in the dish in the kitchen window.'

Luke frowned and left with a sigh. Danny could see he would make the dawn gallops even harder work than normal.

As he watched Luke disappear in the kitchen, Danny glanced at the rucksack on the ground. He wanted to look inside for evidence but knew Luke would be seconds removing the studs.

They then teamed up with the black mare Powder Keg and the bay juvenile Red Ink, both ready and raring to go out on their regular morning workout. Despite being different ages and coming from different backgrounds, both these horses thrived on routine, which made it easy for Danny to plan the morning schedule.

Danny and Luke lined up facing the half-mile incline of gallop strip. Danny looked across, 'He's down to run in a maiden next week, so don't be shy, I want to get a good blow into that one.'

'After you,' Luke said.

'No room for manners,' Danny said. 'They don't get you far in race riding, you go first, I want to see your work.'

Secretly Danny just wanted to be in control of this. He needed Luke in his sights at all times.

Luke persuaded Red Ink forward. The gallop increased as they climbed towards the ridge at the top. Danny saw some promise there, albeit a little agricultural with the arms. But whatever the method, Red Ink appeared to be responding to the lad.

Danny asked Powder Keg to stay back, not to race. He wanted Luke and Red Ink kept in his sights.

'That'll do,' Danny shouted. They eased to a walk. Danny got off Powder Keg and went over to shake Luke's gloved hand. He wanted to at least appear like he was giving the lad an opportunity to shine. 'You're the first to get a proper tune out of that one.'

'That surprises me,' Luke said. 'He looks like he could be one of ours.'

'He nearly was,' Danny replied, recalling the Ely sales. 'Tell me, why does Toby go for attractive brown horses?'

'He fancies certain types.'

Farmers' wives among them, Danny thought.

'They must be lookers,' Luke added.

'But they're all so badly bred.'

'And therefore cheap, got to keep costs down, we're a business after all,' Luke said. 'The press call him the Midas Man. Like he tells them, the pedigree is only a recipe for success, not a guarantee.'

Luke looked down over either side of the Silver Belle Estate. 'Bloody good view up here.'

Danny was about to reply, 'Not as good as up on Pen-y-Bryn', but quickly thought better of it.

'Well, we both know I like your place and I like you,' Luke said. 'So will you welcome me into your family business?'

'I'll need to talk it over with Meg, it will impact on her and you'll be working under head lad Jordi,' Danny said.

'I'll soon take his place,' Luke said dismissively.

Danny was now even less convinced Luke would be a team player. He wouldn't get a job offer even if he wasn't a violent psychopath.

'Jordi is also the yard's declared conditional jockey who can take up to ten pounds off our runners in weight allowances,' Danny reasoned. 'His position is safe.'

Luke approached. Instinct made Danny want to back away.

Luke then embraced Danny. The hug felt really awkward and forced. It was either the inappropriate timing in what effectively was a job interview, or that Luke was just a gawky teen in need of some human contact stuck up here with a dad that rejects him and a mother that's dead.

'No one is safe,' Luke whispered, breath tickling Danny's ear lobe.

Danny broke from the embrace, fearing a blade might be thrust into his honed stomach. 'I think I've seen and heard enough.'

No one is safe.

In those four simple words, Danny's reckoned his theory had become fact. He was facing the attacker that had put the whole of the racing community into a state of fear. This long-overlooked, disenchanted son was draining his father's pool of jockeys, eliminating them one by one in the vain hope of *getting a chance* in the saddle. Until then, *no one is safe.*

'I know,' Danny said.

'What?' Luke asked.

'I think we both know.'

Luke looked away and started to grind his teeth. 'I'll stop,' he said. 'In my mam's honour, I swear—'

'Are you sure about that?' Danny asked. 'You'd already set your eyes on flooring Jordi. You said yourself, no one is safe around you.'

'But I'll have got my chance,' Luke pleaded. 'I'll have finally made it here, don't you see?'

'I see it alright,' Danny said. 'I'd be giving you the chance you needed to prove yourself to your father and your peers.'

'So when can I start?' Luke enthused.

'I'll get back to you,' Danny bluffed. He'd have said anything to get back to the yard in one piece when really there was more chance of Jack getting a contract. No wonder Toby had overlooked his son; he had a shrewd eye and could soon see his son was trouble.

'Too late for that, you promised.'

Promise, Danny thought, he clearly didn't know the meaning of the word, let alone the spelling.

'I promised nothing,' Danny said firmly. 'I did say I'd talk it over.'

The blast of a distant car horn made Danny flinch and scared birds from the trees down by the former ice house of Samuel House. He looked down to the broken hedgerow at the foot of the slope marking the boundary of Silver Belle Estate. There was a sporty black Citroen parked up on the Rhymney Road.

Luke was smiling.

'Do you know them?'

'Just an old friend,' Luke said.

Probably the boy racers Meg had warned him about.

'You go.'

'I won't be on a warning already if I do?' Luke said.

The car beeped again.

'No,' Danny replied, which technically wasn't a lie as he was never going to be working at Silver Belle Stables. 'You go, please, just to shut them up.'

'I'll make sure this one gets back safe,' Luke said. 'I like horses more than humans.'

Danny already knew that. Survival instincts urged him to gallop in the opposite direction but he stayed to see Luke trot Red Ink steadily down the slope towards the road.

Danny then turned and got back down to the yard in what felt like record time.

Luke had the look of a grandma's favourite, a boy band reject. Yet the curly blond hair and quiet, inoffensive demeanour hid a much darker side.

But it was Darren he'd caught burning the bloody silks of Malcolm Bernard on the bonfire. Darren had ridden in those colours to finish runner-up in the opener at Bath just minutes before the vicious attack on Ryan. There hadn't been a last-minute jockey change as Danny recalled vividly looking across at Darren wearing white with blue trim in the neighbouring stall down at the one-mile start.

Back in the kitchen, he grabbed his smartphone from the island and searched on the form database for the full result of that Bath maiden on Guineas Day. He scrolled down the finishing order. Ryan Lawson had won on hotpot Fat Suit and Darren Cooper was runner-up on Malcolm Bernard's Shoehorn, the three-to-one second favourite. Danny skimmed further down the page. He came to Red Ink, finishing ahead of just one home, Proud Nation – owned by Malcolm, ridden by Luke Carmichael, trained by Barry Dunn and sent off the thirty-three-to-one outsider. Leading owner Malcolm had two running in his white and blue colours. From the starting odds alone, Danny could see Darren was on Malcolm's first string wearing a blue cap, and Luke was on the second choice runner distinguished by a green cap. Danny had picked up a scrap of silk from the main body of the colours white with blue trim but the bonfire had clearly already consumed the green cap.

The form comment of Proud Nation read: Very slowly away, never travelling, well beaten.

Danny was never a factor in the race. He had no call to glance behind during the race as all the dangers were in front of him.

When he'd seen the silk colours and who was tending the fire, Danny couldn't see beyond the rider of the runner-up Darren Cooper as the attacker.

Danny went back outside and looked up at the ridge but there was still no sign of Luke returning Red Ink as he'd promised. Danny went over to the black rucksack dumped in the shade of the stable's wall. Concealed in a zipped inside pocket Danny found a small plastic container. Danny bunched the hem of his t-shirt and used it to cover his hand as he removed the container and then carefully unscrewed the lid. It was half-full of a clear, odourless liquid.

Danny recalled Ryan slur, 'I'm on Ruffie.'

This has to be the stuff that made my legs go at Ely Park yesterday, Danny reckoned. If it wasn't for Stony looking out for him, Danny might've choked on his own vomit or dehydrated in the heat.

Danny returned the container and carried the rucksack over to get a better view up to the ridge. With every minute passing, Danny suspected Luke would never return. He checked the copper dish on the kitchen windowsill for stable staff to leave jewellery and saw Luke had taken the diamond studs with him. There was nothing there to draw Luke back, he thought, just an old rucksack. Luke now knew Danny suspected him as the attacker. He must also have left the unsettling gift on the doormat on his way out of the Lodge last night.

Danny returned to Jordi, who was on lookout up to the ridge.

'He's not coming back,' Danny said.

'Why?' Jordi replied.

'He could tell I knew,' Danny said.

'Knew what, Mr Rawlings?'

'His dark secret.'

Suddenly a crack of gunfire filled the air.

Danny shouted over to a recent addition to the yard, stable-lass called Bev, a nineteen-year-old brunette from Somerset, who was in Powder Keg's stable. 'Leave the tack on.'

When he'd led the mare out, Jordi called over, 'He is coming back, see!'

Danny looked up at the ridge. There was a horse galloping towards them.

Jordi started making himself big by flapping his arms. As Red Ink got closer, Danny said, 'There's Red Ink, where's Luke.'

The colt had again bolted from the fright of hearing a loud bang.

Jordi expertly caught the reins as the scared youngster slowed approaching the white rails of the schooling ring.

'Where you going now?' Jordi asked. 'We got what we want, no?'

'I'm going to find that bastard,' Danny said. 'Jordi, if I'm not back in half an hour, or you hear more gunfire, call the police. Oh, and don't breath a word to Meg if she asks, she'll only worry and come after me.'

Danny slipped on his riding hat. He wouldn't normally bother, but he felt if it was strong enough to survive a forty mph fall perhaps it could deflect a bullet.

When he galloped back over the ridge and down to the Rhymney Road, there was no sign of the Citroen or Luke. After several minutes scouring the area with Kegsy tied to the gatepost, he found something in the grass. He studied the empty metal rifle cartridge. He looked back to see he'd found it at the part of the broken hedge where the Citroen sat beeping.

Danny pocketed the find and galloped back to the yard on the mare, still pulling for her head. She was clearly in fine fettle with her next target being the Goodwood Cup at the Glorious meeting.

Meg was stood arms folded in the gap between the schooling ring and the stables. 'Jordi said you went looking, did you find him?'

'No, but I found this,' Danny said, holding up the metal cartridge casing.

'Aren't you worried for him?' Meg asked.

'Not when he's the attacker in the news.'

'The one going after jockeys,' Meg said.

'It's obvious when you think about it.'

'I'm not Mystic Meg.'

'Luke saw these jockeys as a barrier to him getting on in the family business, something he felt was his divine right. He was at the crime scene at Bath and Ely, he'd even got wet hair at Bath after taking a shower to wash away Ryan Lawson's blood. When I looked in the rucksack he'd dumped here before doing a runner, I found a plastic tub. He used the date rape drug Rohypnol to make his life easier and ruin others.'

'Toby wouldn't reject his poor son like that, it hadn't been that long since his mam died.'

'The whole racing world apart from me seems to think Toby has a shrewd eye,' Danny said. 'But I'll give him this – he can see his own son for the loser he is.'

'So Luke went after you just for riding Foundling,' Meg replied.

'His father once again overlooked his needy son,' Danny said. 'I only wished I'd made the link before taking the spare ride.'

'Do you think he pushed Darren off the bridge?' Meg asked.

'Darren rode for Carmichael at Bath, and putting in a shift at their yard, even helped destroy evidence. Perhaps Luke feared he knew too much,' Danny recalled. 'Luke had come across as a sad, oily creep, not a murderer. But then, I had never imagined the kid had it in him to batter Ryan and the others.'

Danny pulled his mobile from his jeans.

'What are you doing?' Meg asked.

'Calling the police in,' Danny said.

'Don't call them, not yet,' Meg said.

'Christ, Meg, you know it must be serious if I want to call them.'

'But just look at what you'll be going to them with, an empty cartridge in an area known for its game hunting. When they came for the cash, you told them you had history with Toby and hated him nearly as much as you hated the police. I even saw the officer jot it down. This will look like you're getting some petty revenge by accusing Toby's son. You'll get done for wasting police time at the very least.'

'What do you mean, at the very least? I've done nothing.'

'You've been spying on them, even turned up there the other day.'

'Only cos we saw smoke,' Danny explained. 'And it's a good job I did, wouldn't have discovered the scrap of silk covered in Ryan's blood.'

'And your fingerprints,' Meg said.

'It's Luke's colours.'

'Michael Bernard employs dozens of jockeys alongside his retained rider Darren Cooper,' Meg reasoned. 'And what if it isn't Ryan's blood? What if Ryan put up a fight just like he did in his races? What if it's Luke's blood on that silk? You said his hair was wet in the Parade Ring before Powder Keg's race. Perhaps he got cut and had a shower to wash away any sign of the fight. How would that look if you walked into Rhymney station with the bloody clothes of a missing man from a family you hated?'

Danny wanted to reveal to her evidence suggesting Toby wanted to kill Jack and Cerys, but he knew she'd be the one on the rampage. 'We can't just leave it there, Meg.'

'We can and we will,' Meg replied. 'Luke will come back sulking when he runs out of money.'

'But he might attack again.'

'There's no motive anymore, he won't get a ride if he's gone into hiding. And if he's on the run, he'll be looking for hotel and hostel bookings, not jockey bookings. It seems to me he only thinks about one person: Luke Carmichael.'

'But he's already attacked again, you heard that loud bang over the ridge,' Danny said.

'Luke promised he'd return Red Ink,' Meg said. 'Perhaps he'd seen Red Ink react by bolting when Toby fired the air shot up at Pen-y-Bryn. He wanted to scare the youngster back to us.'

'Anything could've happened letting this one run loose. He could've at least ridden it back.'

'Not when you've effectively accused him of badly injuring several jockeys. Like you said, he's done a runner,' Meg said. 'Whatever happens, Danny, I don't want you to go near Arwen Vale. Not until all this is over.'

That evening, Danny slouched back on the sofa and ran his hands over his face like a flannel.

'If you're tired, go to bed,' Meg said.

'Everything but my brain is tired,' Danny replied. 'There's no way I'd get off.'

'What is it?'

'Today.'

'I know, that was so weird,' Meg said. 'He didn't even take Red Ink as a getaway.'

'He's not completely stupid, then,' Danny sighed.

'Eh, it's not the horse's fault he's no good, you chose him.'

'Toby chose him,' Danny said, 'I just got suckered into paying for him.'

'Has he rung us yet?'

'And the police,' Danny replied, nodding. 'Apparently, he'd heard the same gunfire from the next valley.'

'What did the police say?'

'Just that they found nothing to suggest a gun had been fired,' Danny said.

'That's because you picked up the cartridge.'

'Toby said they would make further investigations, but I don't hold out any hope. They reckoned it might be linked to the robbery at Arwen Vale.'

'But there was no robbery,' Meg said.

'That's why I don't hold out any hope.'

Danny ran over in his mind's eye the moments before Luke vanished. He was certain he'd heard distant gunfire. Moments later, he saw Red Ink sprinting over the ridge.

'Perhaps Luke thought I'd seen the liquid in his rucksack. He might have panicked and hitched a lift with his old friend in the black Citroen to get the hell out of there.'

'Do you think he thought you might think the liquid was steroids,' Meg said.

'One look at the lad would tell you he's not using steroids,' Danny said. 'There's nothing to him.'

'Perhaps it was for their horses, make them stronger and stay further.'

'The BHA test every winner, so it would only be a matter of time before a yard like Arwen Vale would get found out. No, this is Rohypnol. He wanted his chance to make it big as a jockey. If anything he wouldn't want the yard's horses winning, it would only remind him what he was missing.'

'And the success, fame and adulation that went with it,' Meg said.

'And acceptance.'

'Acceptance?'

'From his father, Toby,' Danny said.

He thought back to the times he'd met Luke. He was either acting as tea boy with a long face at the sales, or covered in muck at the yard. His father had never given him a chance to shine. It also seemed Luke had inherited his father's short fuse.

Meg continued, 'So you're certain it was Luke that attacked you at Ely?'

Danny nodded. 'And to think we were about to give him a job.'

'I'll fucking kill him,' Meg said.

'Doubt you'll see him again. Anyway, I got off lightly,' Danny said. 'Think of poor Ryan, might never walk let alone ride again. Not to mention the mental scars. He wasn't making much sense when I found him.'

'You've already had one lucky escape,' Meg said, 'I meant what I said earlier, I don't want you to ever spy on them again, I don't want you buzzing their gate, I don't even want you talking to them in the parade ring.'

'Alright, mother!'

'They don't exist, right?'

CHAPTER 18

Danny buzzed the gate of Arwen Vale. Meg didn't know he was there. Unfortunately, it seemed neither did the Carmichaels. He pressed the buzzer again and then waved up at the CCTV camera. He reckoned the recent addition of these taller iron gates was more about security than show.

He gripped the aluminium briefcase. He thought giving the impression he came bearing gifts would at least get an answer via the intercom. He'd weighted the case with old racing papers.

Taped to one of the gateposts, he saw a poster behind a crinkled plastic cover. It read: MISSING: Luke Carmichael. £10,000 REWARD for genuine information leading to his safe return.

Shouldn't that be a 'Wanted' poster, Danny thought. The reward seemed suspiciously generous for Toby. It only made Danny more certain Luke was hiding somewhere in the estate and the reward was set in the knowledge it would never be paid out, merely a false promise. It was a bit like the forty-grand gift in the pub. They knew they'd get it all back in time.

He switched the metal case between sweaty hands. He gave the intercom a knock. Can't be broken already, Danny thought.

He still heard nothing back except the chirping birds somewhere up in the canopies of trees that hid Arwen Vale's secrets from the world.

The refusal of the Carmichaels to even acknowledge his presence made him all the more determined to get in there.

Danny jogged all the way back to his yard. He picked up wellies, duct tape and rubber washing-up gloves from the kitchen. He then retraced the route they'd followed in the gallop that turned into a race.

He safely descended the craggy Pen-y-Bryn. When he reached the valley floor, he stood by the electric perimeter fence and then tugged on the gloves and wellies.

He looked through the fence at the cave in the hill the other side. Luke was in there, Danny was convinced of it. He needed to pay for ruining the lives of several top jockeys.

Up this close, he could hear the twenty thousand volts humming through the wire mesh. He taped the gloves to his shirt sleeve, as if to make it watertight. With one finger he touched the wire, it tickled his fingertips.

He then stepped back enough to give him the room to sling the briefcase over the fence, nestling softly in the lush grass the other side. It helped him commit to this.

He removed his fleece and tied it around his waist. He reckoned that would cushion him as he swung himself over the barbs.

Danny poked his fingers and tips of the wellies through holes made by the wire, all the time instilling in his mind that nothing else must touch the wire. His heart was working overtime as he inched up the fence. He knew the charge wasn't enough to kill him but he was less sure about the inevitable drop from up there.

Agonisingly close to the barbs, he saw through the fence that a figure had emerged from around the woodland and was limping towards him. Toby? Shit!

Instantly Danny knew this would be a tricky one to explain away.

Danny slowly lowered himself down and whipped off the Marigolds.

As the figure grew larger, Danny could confirm it was Toby, rifle under one tweed arm and walking stick in the other.

'Trying a different vantage point to enjoy the view are you?' Toby shouted.

Danny kicked off the wellies. 'I did buzz your gate.'

'And you clearly didn't take the hint,' Toby replied, now within speaking distance. 'Unlike your runners, you really don't know when to give up.'

'I was looking for your son, you know the one, Luke,' Danny replied facetiously, 'I saw the "missing" poster.'

'Why the hell would I put up a poster if he was already here? I thought dear Molly had lost it.'

Danny looked again at the cave.

'And he certainly isn't in there,' Toby responded.

'How would you know?' Danny asked. 'It's boarded up. It's the perfect place to hide away if you're running from the law.'

'Luke? On the run?' Toby asked. He seemed genuinely baffled.

Danny didn't share that he'd found what appeared to be Rohypnol in Luke's rucksack. He knew then that his chances of gaining entry would go from slim to zero.

Toby raised his stick and pointed back the way. 'Come round to the main gate and buzz again.'

He'd clearly seen Danny buzz the first time.

Danny didn't immediately accept the invite. He wasn't sure what Toby had planned that couldn't be done with a fence in the way.

'Come,' Toby added. 'I don't want you leaving here having the wrong impression of our yard.'

Danny left the fleece as a rough marker to where the briefcase had landed on the other side. Warily, he left with, 'I'll be twenty.'

He was let in through the main gates, which quietly glided apart, and was met by Toby, still with rifle and cane, standing by the trainer's house. He was led wordlessly to the clump of woodland in the middle of the estate. As they disappeared among the trees, it grew darker with every step of a well-worn dirt path.

Danny wondered whether he was being taken to some hidden stash of steroids kept in a clearing.

Suddenly Toby stopped.

Danny nearly walked into the back of him. He looked around. He was surrounded by trees. There was no obvious reason why Toby chose this spot. Was it to catch his breath? Give his gammy leg a rest? Or blow Danny's head off with that rifle?

Toby put a hand on the thick gnarly trunk of a tree.

'You okay?' Danny asked.

With sad eyes Toby looked up at the overhanging branch.

'Why have you brought me here?' Danny asked, eyeing the rifle.

'You see that branch?'

Danny nodded.

'It's where I found her.'

Danny immediately thought of the evidence bag containing the suicide note in Toby's desk.

'Molly hanged herself.'

Toby nodded and then sighed. 'I found her swinging from there. At first I thought she was still alive, but it was the gusts of wind playing tricks.'

But Luke had said he'd found the note when she first attempted to end it all at the beach.

The suicide note was crinkly. 'Was it raining that night?'

'Why do you ask?' Toby questioned, hazel eyes narrowing.

'Just picturing the scene.'

'You don't want to, trust me. I have tried to forget it. Lord, have I tried.'

Danny looked up. 'And it was summer?'

'Yes.'

There was no way rain could make it through that canopy, Danny thought. And even if some water did filter through, it didn't explain the salty paper. 'Did she leave a goodbye letter?'

'A note fell from her pocket as I cut her down.'

Lying bastard! He now knew for certain Toby had reused that letter found on Molly in her first failed attempt that went unreported to make her death here look like suicide.

'Why?' Toby asked.

Danny knew it wasn't a wise move to share his thoughts as it was Toby holding the weapon. He could imagine Toby faking another suicide note for this, Danny thought.

Danny filled the awkward silence with, 'Still, you've made a success of yourself since. I think I'd dive into work if anything happened to Meg, touch wood.' He also reached for the trunk.

'I loved Molly with all my heart, she was my life, but she was also hard work towards the end. I'd still trade all our successes on the track for another day with her. We were never a tactile family,' Toby said. 'But even Luke and I hugged once the coroner and police had all finally left.'

'Did they leave with the suicide note?' Danny asked.

'Yes,' Toby said cagily and blew his nose. 'It was for the best, I keep telling myself.'

For who, Danny thought. You or her?

Toby managed the ghost of a smile as if satisfied he'd finally won Danny round.

Exiting the woods the way they came, Danny asked, 'Okay if I nip to your loo?'

'You live minutes away,' Toby said.

'By car maybe,' Danny said. One look at Toby's face told Danny to hold it in.

Back in his own racing office, Danny was reclined in his leather swivel chair when Meg entered.

'Early night for both us,' he said.

'I like the sound of that,' she said and sat on Danny's lap, spinning the chair and laughing.

'I mean, it's a sod of a journey to Goodwood, we both need to have clear heads.'

Meg got up. 'You're no fun before these big races.'

Danny didn't think Toby was reading off that cue card when he fought back the tears retelling the moments he'd found his wife in the woods. For once, this felt like the truth but he must be holding something back. He said he'd cut her down when it was too late. Perhaps he'd got there in time.

Why hold on to the suicide note? This was planned, Danny reckoned. At Ely, Toby confessed that sharing a life with her was grim towards the end.

'I know you went round there,' Meg said.

'I went to return that briefcase,' Danny explained.

'But it's empty.'

'That's why I went,' Danny said. 'He'd get the payback he deserved.'

'Brilliant. That won't get Toby worked up at all,' Meg said sarcastically. 'Seriously Danny, what good will that do?'

'Well, I now know he planted the suicide note found on Molly's body in the woods.'

She sat on his desk. 'Really?'

'Luke reckoned they hadn't told anyone about her first suicide attempt walking into the sea at Lavernock Point. Toby saw his chance to make use of the note, planting it on her as she hung from a branch in the woods.'

'Why would he do that when she committed suicide?'

'Because she didn't commit suicide,' Danny said, 'Toby killed Molly, using the suicide note to make it look like suicide. This was premeditated murder.'

CHAPTER 19

GOODWOOD RACECOURSE. THURSDAY JULY 29TH.
2.33pm. Danny stared out at the grey mound of the Isle of Wight rising up from the glittering blue of the Solent dotted with yachts. He was marking time by the white-canopied grandstands of Goodwood perched on the sloping green and brown patchwork of the Sussex Downs.

He felt the warmth on the back of his neck as he breathed in the fresh coastal air. Suddenly life didn't seem so bad. With Luke in hiding, the attacks had stopped and with Darren gone, so had tensions among those in the weighing room.

For the sake of marital harmony, Danny had even come to just about accept Carmichael's inexorable climb up the training ranks, though wins for a second-season trainer in the Queen Mary and the Chesham at Royal Ascot only served to stoke up past resentment. Even the biggest yards in the land were thankful to leave Royal Ascot with a single winner pitted against the top-class international fields coming over from the US, France, Germany, Australia, South Africa and Japan, attracted by the splendour and history of the occasion.

Next stop on the summer festival circuit was this five-day Glorious Goodwood meeting and true to form Carmichael had already got on the scoresheet by taking the Group Three Molecomb the day before. Thankfully, Danny hadn't been there to witness either the win or the smug look on the trainer's fat face afterwards.

While Carmichael was busy establishing Arwen Vale on the world stage, Danny was stuck supplementing income with tipster talks to pissed-up middle management in corporate boxes at Ely Park. Whenever he was heckled, he just kept thinking of the cheque to help cover some of the owners deserting the yard.

Meg was happy with a runner-up prize in the regional ballroom finals for her foxtrot and the fact she'd dropped two dress sizes, though she'd claimed it wasn't her size that mattered to her most, it was the goal of reaching a racing weight for the Flat that spurred her on. The thought she could team up with Powder Keg apparently made giving up the chocolate bars and glasses of wine less of a chore. The mare had spent a fortnight bucking and kicking in the lower field with Salamanca – Danny's top-class chestnut steeplechaser now fully retired and loving it as a family pet, though he was still a champion in the Rawlings' eyes. If there were any designs of Powder Keg returning to hurdles in the autumn, Danny needed to get a refreshing holiday into her or risk a burnout later. The tiny mare left everything out on the track and if over-raced, she might take a year just to get herself back to where she was.

Jack was still making progress in his riding, despite catching the measles a few weeks back. He could actually stay on Zola and had even sat on Powder Keg walking round the yard.

Danny broke from his reverie and headed to meet Meg in the stabling behind the grandstand. On his way, he threaded through the growing crowds of men in white linen suits and Panama hats and women in bright summery dresses around the parade ring, inspecting the condition of juveniles about to be sent out for the Group Two Richmond Stakes. Passing the quieter pre-parade enclosure set further back, he saw two men talking intently in the cover of a thick tree trunk in the middle of the oval ring and the shade of the green canopy above. He stopped when he saw who it was. Toby Carmichael and Marcel Tailler.

Danny recalled the pair had stood at opposite sides of the Ely sales ring. They'd also blanked each other at York. He'd never seen them together before and neither had a reason for being down there. For a few steps, Danny hadn't even recognised Marcel, who had ditched the colourful waistcoats for a white three-piece suit and Panama hat. It seemed he wanted to blend in.

Danny wouldn't have looked twice if they had been together sipping Pimm's at one of the trendy bars near the Tote terminals in the paddock. But they had no reason to be in this restricted area. Toby didn't have a runner to saddle in the Goodwood Cup, and Marcel, a bloodstock agent with no connection with a runner, wouldn't be allowed access. They'd clearly met for a quiet chat with no danger of being overheard there.

Marcel only came to the UK to visit family, according to Malcolm at York, so Toby was either related, or the business was so private it was worth breaking rules by entering the restricted area.

Since the Midas Man had become a face around the UK sale rings, he'd attract rival bidders on reputation alone, greedily hoping for some of that golden touch to rub off. And Danny couldn't judge, he had been suckered into buying Red Ink at Ely.

Danny recalled all the colourful horse passports in Toby's office desk were purchased in the UK. Perhaps Toby had become a victim of his own success and was being forced to hire a foreign bloodstock agent to seek out the bargain buys on mainland Europe where he wasn't yet a name.

Danny flashed his jockey's pass at the racecourse official guarding the break in the plastic railing.

As he approached, Toby and Marcel were too lost in conversation to even notice. Danny swore he heard Marcel say, 'Have you planted the rice in hip twenty-seven?'

Toby replied, 'The triangle is complete.'

'You've done your part,' Marcel said. 'It's over to me now.'

He didn't sound French, Danny thought.

'But this is the last one,' Toby said. 'Greed is good to a point. I noticed changes at Ely Sales. We have enough solid foundations to build a lucrative breeding operation.'

What changes?

Danny recalled the armed police officer guarding the entrance.

Planted the rice? Hip twenty-seven? The triangle is complete? It felt like he was listening into a game of Chinese whispers. It would have made no less sense if Marcel had been talking French. He knew it had to be some code. That, or they'd hit the hospitality early.

Toby added, 'Be patient, hopefully he'll be out late spring next year.'

Danny was about to duck in behind the trunk in the centre. He hadn't understood a word just then but he wanted to hear more. As if sensing a presence, Toby turned and said, 'Well, well, Daniel Rawlings, how the devil did they let you in here?'

'I was about to say the same thing.'

'A two-time Royal Ascot,' Toby smirked. 'I'd have expected appearance money.'

'Any news on Luke?'

Toby shook his head. 'A few possible sightings but nothing concrete.'

'You didn't tell me you had another son,' Danny said.

'He's not my son.'

'Nephew? It can't be brother, he's not old enough,' Danny said.

Toby shook his head.

If he wasn't a relative, Marcel and Toby must be discussing business.

'*This* is the neighbour I was telling you about,' Toby told Marcel. 'Where I go he seems to be there.'

Danny was quick to notice a racecard sticking out from the pocket in Marcel's jacket.

'He just won't stop until he finds out what he wants,' Toby added. 'And if he can't find what he wants, he just makes it up.'

'What have you found out about my friend Tobias?' Marcel asked Danny. They both listened intently.

It suddenly occurred to him perhaps Toby and Marcel had stayed away from each other on purpose in the Ely sales arena. They'd both been chatting on their mobiles prior to the first lot being put through the ring. They also hung up at exactly the same moment. At the time, it didn't occur to Danny that they might be talking to each other. But if they were just a few dozen steps away from talking face to face, why discuss it over the phone?

Obviously they didn't want to be seen together in public, Danny reckoned, but that only added more questions in his mind.

'You two know each other but you don't want others to know that... for obvious reasons.'

Marcel gave Toby a look of surprise.

'We've never met,' Marcel replied assuredly. He was clearly an experienced liar.

'You don't have to meet someone to know them, Marcel,' Danny said.

'I'm afraid this might well be a case of mistaken identity,' Marcel replied.

'Daniel, I'd like you to meet Charlie Foster,' Toby said, grinning.

Danny looked down at the metal member's badge strung from the man's lapel. *C. Foster Esq.*

'But you spoke with Malcolm Bernard... twice... at least.'

Charlie shook his head. 'No, I'm afraid I don't know a Malcolm...'

'Bernard,' Danny helped out. 'Is this some kind of joke?'

'Are we laughing?' Toby asked.

'Charlie, he introduced himself to you at Ely sales ring and you even shook hands and laughed with him around York parade ring. He's a black man, wears a cream suit like yours, blue tie and handkerchief.'

Charlie shook his head again.

'You need your eyes checking,' Toby said. 'No wonder you're picking duds at the sales.'

Danny raised his arms in exasperation. 'He was there!'

'I seem to have got about a bit,' Charlie said. 'Did I enjoy myself?'

Danny huffed, 'Christ, Toby, you were there too.'

'Oh, the owner, Malcolm Bernard,' Toby said.

'Yes, finally, hallelujah,' Danny said, thankful he hadn't gone completely mad.

'I'm glad someone knows him,' Charlie said.

'But you do work in France?'

'I'm a bloodstock agent,' Charlie said. 'Which means some of my work is in France but I really do think this Malcolm has been having you on.'

'Why would he do that?' Danny asked. 'We were never likely to meet, you and me.'

'And we never did,' Charlie said. 'For the last time, I'm not Marcel Tailler.'

Danny had never mentioned the surname. Malcolm wasn't the one lying.

'I've heard enough,' Danny said. Without giving Toby's guest the chance to back off, Danny leant forward and kissed both his cheeks.

Danny was quickly pushed away but not quick enough to prevent him deftly dipping his jacket pocket for the racecard.

'This is what they do on the Continent,' he explained but really the kisses had been a means to distract.

'But we're not on the Continent,' Charlie said.

'Not right now,' Danny said, hoping for a reaction. 'I'll let you get on to planting rice. The rain we get up in the Valleys, I reckon paddy fields ought to thrive.'

Again, Charlie looked to Toby.

'Don't worry, he's all bluff,' Toby said quietly.

Danny left the pre-parade ring before Charlie had time to realise his racecard was gone.

Back in the changing room, Danny opened the pamphlet. It was thicker and heavier than he'd expected. He looked down lists of horses. But they weren't runners with trainers, jockeys and form figures. Each entry had the sire and dam and grandsire, along with the vendor name. It wasn't a racecard but a sales catalogue. He then saw above the first column the header LOT/HIP.

Hip! Danny thought. Have you planted the rice in hip twenty-seven?

Danny was angry he hadn't already made the link. He'd always known the lots were sometimes called hips as that's where the lot number was placed on the horse before it went out into the sales ring.

He then noticed Hip Seven had been circled, just like Red Ink had been in the Ely catalogue.

Danny checked the international racing news. He saw reams of articles on a recent spate of horses that had gone missing from sales rings around mainland Europe. He reminded himself to check the world news now and again. Horse racing was a microcosm of society, almost in a world of its own. It was all too easy to get wrapped up in the bubble of that small world.

But what was the rice?

Inside the cover, Danny saw the sales director was an Adrien Thibault. But there was no sign of Marcel Tailler.

Either Malcolm Bernard or Charlie Foster had lied to Danny.

He felt an impression in the pamphlet as if something was hidden in between the pages. Danny shook the catalogue and out fell a small black car fob. It was embossed with silver wings either side of the letter B.

A Bentley, Danny thought. He must be one hell of a bloodstock agent. Perhaps he was the real success behind Arwen Vale.

Striding out the gates of the racecourse, Danny tilted his pass at the official in a blazer who looked baffled when he saw the silks and breeches.

'Going to get an extra pair of socks,' Danny offered as an explanation.

'Have you got cold feet then?' the official replied, making himself laugh. The fifty-something then opened his racecard to see who Danny was booked to ride.

Danny shook his head. He wasn't in the mood. 'I'll be back in five.'

He headed straight for the members' car park nearby; like most things in life, money buys convenience in racing.

Unsurprisingly, it wasn't going to be easy to find a Bentley in there. If you could afford a member's ticket for such a high-profile meeting, chances are you could afford a flash motor. He kept pressing the car fob when nearing a Bentley. Four rows in a gleaming grey Bentley Mulsanne answered the call with a flash of the indicators and click of the doors.

Bloody hell, Danny thought, considering branching out as a bloodstock agent. His eyes devoured the sharp lines, the Flying B of the radiator mascot, above the familiar silver grille and round headlamps. It was a car that deserved to be displayed in nothing less than a glitzy showroom, not in a car park. Danny looked around and saw that he was alone. Everyone else was on track excitedly anticipating the feature. Having a ride in the race, Danny knew he had more reason than most to be on track.

Danny opened the door and slid inside on the cream leather of the driver's seat. He glanced at the round chrome clock on the instrument panel. Twenty-one minutes until post time. Danny looked through the windscreen over at the grandstand. He shouldn't be doing this. Missing the weigh-out time was punishable. It wasn't a fine or a ban that bothered him, but the fact he risked disqualifying the horse Powder Keg, who had been brought to the boil for this very day and her owner Meg, who, he could vouch only too well, had barely slept a minute all week in anticipation.

But he couldn't leave there without something to pin on Charlie Foster or Marcel Tailler, or whatever the hell his name was. Danny searched the driver's side. In a white leather and polished wood compartment beneath the arm rest, Danny found racing badges and parking ticket stubs. On the passenger seat, there was a *Racing Post* and a tailor's brochure for waistcoats.

Danny slid further inside and stretched to release the glove compartment in the dark wood panel.

From there he pulled out an ID badge in a plastic pouch. There was a passport photo of a person bearing a striking resemblance to the man talking in tongues to Carmichael in the pre-parade ring. On the ID it claimed he was indeed Marcel Tailler. It seemed Malcolm Bernard was telling the truth after all. The badge was on thick laminated card in orange with job title down as bloodstock agent.

Danny looked at the clock again. 2.51pm. Nineteen minutes until the Goodwood Cup was due to start. And being a championship race, he'd forgotten there would be a parade of the runners in front of the grandstands to a fanfare.

Yet he hadn't even seen the clerk of the scales. *Shit!*

He was about to return the pouch where he'd found it when he saw through the clear plastic that the back of the card was blue.

Danny looked over at the grandstand and then slid his fingers into the pouch to pull out the ID. Out fell a rainbow of coloured cards, falling on to the white leather seat, six in all.

They all had the same job title and the photos were clearly of the same person he'd just seen in the paddock, albeit going for a very different look in each, either with or without a beard and glasses, and hair dyed black, blonde and brown. He could've filled a row in *Guess Who?*

The names on each were also different. Adding to Marcel Tailler in France, there was Dirk Hofwegen in Holland, Lucas Peeters in Belgium, Dietmar Bechert in Germany. Charlie Foster was right about one thing, he did get about a bit. Danny bet each pseudonym was to deal with separate rich clients. These fake IDs were used to cover their tracks. He was looking down on proof they were up to no good on an industrial scale.

Danny heard the commentator say, 'We move on to our feature race, the Group Two Goodwood Cup.' He then heard a recorded fanfare of trumpets.

Danny felt sick. He was nowhere near ready to pair up with Powder Keg and he could hear the clock ticking. It was like being in an anxiety dream. He quickly took a photo of the IDs spread out on the passenger seat. He slipped the ID cards back into the one holder, making sure the Marcel Tailler card was showing through the plastic at the front of the pouch. As he returned it to the glove compartment, Danny saw a sheet of paper in what looked like the maroon of a UK passport. He took a closer look. It was a printed boarding pass for a flight departing Birmingham and arriving at Brest airport that evening. There was another security pass. It was for entry to the inaugural Morlaix Bloodstock Sales. Danny took photos of all the documents. He predicted this was where the next case of the vanishing horse would be.

He glanced again at the clock in the dashboard. 2.54pm. He had to weigh out at least ten minutes before the start time at 3.10pm.

Danny pushed himself from the driver's side and slapped the key fob on the gleaming roof of the Bentley. As he walked by the gate, he said to the official, 'The owner of a Bentley four rows in has only left his key on the roof.'

'Thanks, sir, I'll go find it and the owner,' he replied. 'And you look like you've got a horse to find.'

Danny smiled politely. A jog to the weighing room soon turned into a sprint. He gathered up the saddle and grabbed his goggles and whip.

Strangely, he felt trying to make the weighing out deadline was helping as he didn't have any time to stew over the race. This was the only race on his mind right now.

He looked up at the circular wall clock. 3.00pm. He needed to be sat on the electronic scales outside the changing room right now.

'Jockey coming though,' Danny called, as he shouldered the door into the foyer and then jumped on the scales, saddle draped over his forearm.

'You're late,' the clerk said, checking his Rolex.

'It's 3.00pm.'

'Six seconds ago.'

'Your watch is seven seconds fast,' Danny said.

The clerk checked the electronic screen glowing nine-stone eight pounds in red. Dead on.

The clerk noted something down, probably a caution.

'Go on, your steed awaits,' the clerk muttered. 'Don't leave it so late next time. This isn't some National Hunt meeting out in the sticks.'

'Right you are, sir,' Danny said, leaping from the scales. Desperate to see Meg, he made a beeline for the parade ring, explaining away autograph hunters with, 'After the race, cheers, thanks, not now, cheers, I'll sign after, cheers.'

He made an exception for a suited boy clutching a racecard open at the Goodwood Cup centre pages. He can't have been older than Jack and was stood by the security guard at the entry to the ring. Danny didn't want to put off any youngsters from getting into the sport with a snub; there weren't enough as it was.

When he saw Meg, his pulse began to thump against his body protector as if it was the first time he'd set eyes on her. He didn't want to let her down, any more than he did the horse.

CHAPTER 20

'The runners are parading for the Goodwood Cup run over the two miles, and ladies and gentlemen we have a renewal as hot as the weather,' could be heard over the speakers. The tannoys were a lot clearer here than at other courses, possibly the lack of background noise from traffic and industry in this idyllic rural setting, with only the ancient cathedral city of Chichester within a five-mile radius.

Danny knew everything would have to go right for Powder Keg to have any chance in the prestigious Group Two that had attracted Langland Bay, who had to shoulder nine stone twelve pounds with a four-pound Group One penalty added for winning the Ascot Gold Cup in a photo, Rebecca Riot, who beat Powder Keg into third when winning the Yorkshire Cup and then franked the form by plundering the Prix Maurice de Nieuil at Longchamp, and Swift Cider Black, who made it four wins from five starts in the Group Three Lonsdale Stakes at York.

Powder Keg couldn't match these credentials but she hadn't gone unfancied in the market at a steady ten-to-one, mostly on the strength of her rallying third after suffering interference in the Knavesmire, and he hoped she could improve again for only her second start on the level with an extra two furlongs covered. Her neat, compact action was made for galloping over the rollercoaster undulations and sharp turns facing them on these historic downs.

The stalls for the two-mile start were positioned facing in the opposite direction to the packed stands, with the runners initially travelling away from the finish line before sharply doubling back on a loop. It was a test of endurance, poise, timing and tenacity.

He was pleased with the way she'd handled her first parade. She had coped with the wall of noise up the Cheltenham hill, so the polite ripples of applause here barely registered. Cantering to post, the mare was relaxed enough not to take a tug and alert enough not to feel sluggish. In these stamina tests, it was all about preserving energy both before and during the race.

Circling down at the start, Powder Keg was on her toes, head turning, as if inspecting her rivals, while Danny adjusted his tinted goggles on this sunny July afternoon. He could hear the racecourse commentator run down the final betting show. 'And Langland Bay is our seven-to-four favourite, Rebecca Riot is into nine-to-four from five-to-two, then it's eight-to-one Swift Cider Black and ten-to-one Powder Keg, twelve-to-one bar these.'

They were safely installed at the first attempt, slotting into box nine. Another in a long list of potential problems out the way, he thought.

The commentator continued with, 'Last to load we have Swift Cider Black moving forward into stall eight.'

Danny felt a slight jolt as the giant Swift Cider Black filled the stall on his inner and the gates shut behind.

'All in,' the race-caller shouted.

Danny bunched up the reins and blew out. Sitting perfectly still, he waited for the starter to do his job.

The clunk of the gates springing apart released a surge of energy as the eleven half-ton equine athletes quickly found their stride. The silence away from the stands was soon filled by the growls of jockeys and the thud of hooves on the springy turf.

Danny pushed Powder Keg's neck forward as they began the long climb to the loop at the far end of the track. From her regular homework, he knew she wasn't fazed by attacking a hill climb and felt it was a good opportunity to gain some places to negate a wide draw.

Having studied tactics in past renewals, Danny suspected the runners would head for the outside rail just a furlong into the race, helping to cut an early left turn as they headed away from the forty thousand sell-out crowd.

Danny thought he'd made the rail first, but Langland Bay was soon pressing on his outer. Danny wasn't surprised by this. Having last been seen taking the Ascot Gold Cup over two miles four furlongs, the warm favourite for this race clearly had stamina in abundance and his jockey Conor Fahey planned to make full use of it by dictating out in front.

Danny felt the early pace was fast enough for a two-mile marathon and the clock in his brain told him to rein Powder Keg back into third as they began a stiff five-furlong climb to the first bend of the loop. The field made a steady diagonal over to the inside rail in preparation to take the shortest route round the loop. Now away from the rail overlooking an infield of yellow crop, Danny found the room to sit on the flank of the new leader Langland Bay.

As hoped, Powder Keg handled the climb with ease. Both her stride pattern and breathing were metronomic. They'd found a rhythm and synchronicity as if Meg had been on the feisty mare.

The strong initial gallop showed no sign of relenting as Danny eyed the sharp right-handed turn marking the first section of the loop. He wanted to hug the rail to save ground but he had to think again when beaten to it by Yorkshire Cup heroine Rebecca Riot. Danny held his place one horse-width from the rail when the gallop eased a touch as the field of eleven banked right. With every stride, Danny felt stiffness flow out from his tense limbs. He was buzzing from the adrenalin as he held a prominent third, market leaders firmly in his sights. He was actually starting to enjoy this. But he knew overconfidence can also result in defeat, either from striking the front too far out or leaving the challenge far too late.

He saw Conor Fahey's gloved hands start to move. Clearly he had been instructed to keep cranking up the gallop from the front and then repel the challenges one by one when it became an endurance test late on.

Danny wasn't going to let the favourite steal this and moved ahead of George Taylor on Rebecca Riot. Powder Keg kept her balance as she quickened up on the turn.

He looked left and saw the colt Swift Cider Black make his considerable presence known. Less nimble and agile than Powder Keg, the massive four-year-old was steering a more gentle turn three horse-widths wide. He guessed any ground lost was worth it just to prevent his giant stride becoming unbalanced.

When they'd straightened, Danny could see the grandstand quivering in the heat. The field wasted no time drifting left to the outer rail sheltered by mature trees and bushes.

Up front, Langland Bay was travelling slightly off the rail. Danny was eyeing the gap. He was convinced Powder Keg's small conformation could fit through there. But he knew it would be race over if Conor Fahey shut the door on them. There were no indicators or hand signals out there and he wasn't a mind reader.

Patience, Danny thought, it's a marathon not a sprint.

Swift Cider Black appeared now on his right. He'd clearly been switched and had recovered well from swinging wide off the loop. The progressive colt was aiming for another personal best and began to apply pressure to the long-time leader Langland Bay.

Like slalom skiers, always seeking the shortest way round this twisting track, they began to say goodbye to the outer rail and cross the track to meet the one on the inner as they prepared for the final sweeping turn into the downhill straight.

Many riders were guilty of fanning too wide as they straightened up for the final stretch, losing momentum and vital ground with just four furlongs to go. Danny had found a space behind joint leaders Langland Bay and Swift Cider Black. The rail temporarily gave way to yellow cones to help keep runners on the right course. There was no way Danny would take a wrong turn. Studying online footage, he felt like he was a regular here, despite having never previously set foot on the track.

He was perfectly positioned in third on the rail, but knew it would quickly turn bad if anything drew alongside on his outer to box him in, as the classy front pair just ahead would form an impenetrable wall.

They banked right. Danny kept the shortest route, riding boot inches from the curving plastic rail.

Nearing the two-furlong marker, Danny glanced left. It was time to make his move. He was about to pull on the left rein when he saw the fifty-to-one outsider Marquee Moment, who had caused interference and mayhem in the drunken hands of Darren Cooper before finishing behind at York, move up under a strong drive from Jimmy Atkins. That gelding was clearly responding better to sober handling. He was pleased for owner Malcolm Bernard but not *that* pleased. With the rail and Marquee Moment either side of him, Danny had nowhere to go. Checkmate.

He was left fuming with himself, having not been quick enough to react. Unlike the National Hunt game, there were rarely second chances on the Flat.

Marquee Moment didn't possess the quality to sustain the finishing burst and was merely plugging on at the same pace which meant Danny couldn't pull back or push on to find some space.

Despite a wide expanse of straight, he was pinned to the rail. He'd get slated in the forums for this.

Ahead, he could see the two jockeys had resorted to their whips and weren't getting away from the rest. There was still some hope. He sat lower, arms and legs urging Powder Keg to keep with them until a gap appeared. The mare still had more to offer.

Approaching the furlong pole, Danny had no option. He had to edge out. He'd risk a ban for dangerous riding, but a lengthy holiday wasn't a deterrent when he had no runners to ride and Meg was planning a trip away. But she'd much rather be picking up the golden trophy and the one hundred and seventy grand winner's cheque.

He calculated there was zero chance he'd get thrown out for the interference providing Marquee Moment didn't finish second, which meant he'd be directly affecting the result. The placings would then be reversed. But seeing how hard Jimmy Atkins was working just to hold his place, there was no chance of that.

Danny pulled down on the left rein. Powder Keg could see she was going to make contact, but obeyed her master and the horses barrels touched.

Jimmy looked over and snarled.

Danny kept nudging the rival. Marquee Moment was starting to flounder.

He'd soon leveraged enough room to kick on. Seeing daylight, Powder Keg lengthened her stride willingly. Danny administered a sharp reminder. The roar of the crowd grew louder as the finish line came closer. Urged on by the cheers, Powder Keg began to eat into the lead held by Langland Bay and Swift Cider Black, who both were now in desperate need for the line.

On his left Danny heard another coming up to challenge. Head down he pushed and pushed. His arms and legs felt the burn. Under his flapping left arm, he caught a flash of the yellow and black hoops of Rebecca Riot's jockey finishing to similar effect further out wide.

Danny growled and yelled. 'Come on, girl!'

He pictured Meg up in the stands somewhere.

Flashing past the half-furlong marker, Powder Keg's bold head struck the front, edging out the pacesetters on the far side.

The four pounds she was receiving from the penalised Langland Bay was beginning to tell. But Rebecca Riot was off level weights with Powder Keg and her jockey had clearly saved a bit by also sitting off the pace early.

Danny was determined not to be beaten again by the rival and pushed with all his might when his body was screaming to stop. When he started to see red dots, he filled his lungs, feeding the blood with much needed oxygen.

'And it's Powder Keg hanging on, but Rebecca Riot isn't done with yet, Langland Bay only third. Powder Keg by a neck, by a head, by a short head. Oh that's close, one for the judge. A real thriller between two ultra-tough mares, number seven on the far side Powder Keg and number eight Rebecca Riot on the near side.'

The crowd was crackling with tension and excitement as everyone there waited on the judge to study the photo on the line. It was all done digitally now and the anguish of not knowing wouldn't last long.

He saw Meg in a Silver Belle Stables t-shirt. She ducked the rail and ran out on to the course to meet them. She led them back to the offshoot heading to the parade ring and winners' circle.

'She deserves a break,' Danny panted. 'Whatever the result.'

Meg slapped the shiny black neck of Powder Keg, whose ears swivelled like satellite dishes. 'You little star, Kegsy.'

Meg didn't seem bothered about the result. The fact she'd once again run to her very peak was enough. Like a proud parent, it was the effort and the taking part that meant most. But Danny was after the prize. A six-figure sum would mean the yard wouldn't only survive but thrive for at least the next year.

'Here is the result of the photograph,' the speakers blared. The crackle of the crowd hushed to an eerie silence. 'First, number seven Powder Keg, second—' the rest of the announcement was drowned out by the cheers from the crowd.

Meg jumped up, clenched fist punching the air.

Danny smiled. He'd leave the proper celebrating until he was out of camera shot.

George Taylor steered the tired third Langland Bay over and offered a hand in congratulations. 'Make sure you turn up for a rematch at Ascot next June.'

Danny suspected Taylor was confident he would reverse placings when he tried to retain his title in the Royal Ascot Gold Cup. While there was nothing to the tiny Powder Keg, Taylor didn't yet seem to realise she possessed the heart of a lion. 'You're on.'

Danny kept touching the peak of his riding hat to acknowledge his name being called out as he was led by Meg on Powder Keg behind the stands.

While the National Hunt would always be in his blood, he could get used to this Flat game. Perhaps taking out a dual licence would be the making of Silver Belle Stables. He'd always heard diversifying was good for business.

In the winner's circle, the press cameras clicked like a Geiger counter as Meg kissed the white blaze down Powder Keg's face.

'And can we have one with Danny in it?' asked one of the photographers. 'For the family album.'

Danny hated having his photo taken almost as much as dancing but knew he'd regret not doing so later. This was the kind of publicity that advertising couldn't buy. In just three minutes and twenty-four point seven seconds, he'd proved he could both train and ride a Pattern race winner on the Flat.

Now that's what you call a result, he thought, as another flurry of camera clicks captured Danny and Meg's image, holding the rein either side of the real star. Surely owners like Malcolm would at least now make enquiries to putting a few horses his way.

'You deserve a good rub down later,' Meg said.

Danny turned hoping she was talking to him, but she had whispered into Powder Keg's ears. The unassuming mare was probably left wondering what all the fuss was about.

In the hotel room that evening, Danny lay back on the cool fresh linen with a miniature bottle of Jack Daniels held by his side. He'd booked a hotel room in Chichester. He'd done well to get a room due to a late cancelation. If he'd lost, he couldn't face the tiresome journey all the way back to mid-Glamorgan while if he'd won he'd want a drink to celebrate. He'd left the heroine Powder Keg at a livery nearby.

Danny lifted himself from the bed and looked out from the sash window at the cathedral spire towering above tourists laden with rucksacks and cameras below.

He finished off the little bottle and savoured the warm tingle as it went down.

He returned to the corner of the bed and turned on his tablet. In the reflection of the screen, he could see Meg in just her bra and knickers, towelling her hair.

She came up behind him, and locked her arms round his neck. He looked up at her face and felt a warm glow, unsure whether it was feeling her soft skin against his neck or the alcohol. Either way, he liked it.

'I'm surprised you're not rewatching the Goodwood highlights,' she said.

'I stopped it three furlongs out, when I got boxed in.'

'Don't worry, I can reveal you got out of that hole and won the day.'

Danny smiled. 'Thank you.'

'I didn't do anything,' Meg said. 'I should be the one doing the thanking; I owe you big time for turning Powder Keg's career around. I feel so shitty sometimes. I totally let her down at Cheltenham.'

'You'll soon be partnering her again,' Danny said. He didn't want her to feel like he had taken over and stolen the limelight. 'I'm just like a supply jockey.'

Meg sighed.

'You sound a bit...' Danny paused trying to find the right word. He was nearly as bad as Stony at talking about feelings. Sometimes he'd say things meaning well only to make it worse. Moody? No. Sulky? No. Grumpy? No. 'Disgruntled.'

'I'm not disgruntled,' she replied. 'If anything I'm... gruntled.'

Danny laughed.

He smelt her sweet scent as she pressed her soft lips against the crown of his cropped hair. It sounded like she was more in need of the drink, certainly after the news he had yet to share with her.

'What's that?' she asked inquisitively.

No point in lying and prolonging this, he thought. 'A boarding pass I printed off down at reception and a passport.'

'I know I said we ought to go on a break, but this is for the morning. I've promised Jack and Cerys I'd be back before then.'

'I haven't promised,' Danny explained. 'It's for one adult. Southampton was by far the nearest airport doing direct routes to Brest in France.'

'Why do you—'

Danny showed her the sales catalogue he'd lifted from Charley's jacket. 'There's a Bloodstock Sale near Morlaix in Brittany tomorrow afternoon. We can't stand still, remember?'

'But we don't want to rush in, blow the prize money just cos we've got it.'

'I won't,' Danny said though he stopped short of revealing the real reason he was making the short flight over to the north-western province – the circled Hip Seven in the catalogue. 'I know the National Hunt stock there is overpriced right now. I want to see if the Flat-breds are the same.'

'Just keep in mind the winner's cheque hasn't even cleared.'

'I've already expressed an interest and emailed my trainer's licence as proof of ID and status. Just drop me off at the airport and I'll be back tomorrow evening.'

CHAPTER 21

Danny caught the one-hour flight from Southampton to Brest Brittany airport, northwest France. He then rode the half-hour train journey east to Morlaix, a Breton port between the Léon and Trégor regions, nestled in the sloping foothills of the Monts d'Arrée. He was here for the bloodstock sales held for the first time on the outskirts of the town.

Rucksack slung over his shoulder, Danny left the unassuming white flat-topped Gare de Morlaix and caught a taxi through the medieval town bustling with families now that schools had broken up for summer holidays.

Danny stared out the taxi window, but was too lost in thought to enjoy the pretty three-storey half-timbered houses, with their high, pitched, slate roofs, overhanging tiers and shuttered windows, lining the narrow cobbled streets of the Old Town. He glanced up at a Paris-bound train as it crossed the towering viaduct of pink granite a couple of hundred feet up. He reckoned he could set aside some of the newly acquired prize money for a short family break here.

He was dropped off at the quayside looking out at the estuary of Morlaix Bay, peppered with tiny islands and islets. He would walk the rest, in need of some time and fresh air to clear his head.

Studying the town map, he heard the clink of tall masts on moored yachts and distant chatter from those enjoying an al fresco lunch at a quayside restaurant nearby. According to a potted history on the map, the bay had a notorious history of piracy. That got Danny thinking.

He sat on a bench and removed the map of mainland Europe he'd picked up at the airport shop. He'd already marked the bloodstock sales Charlie had previously visited with an X. Each sale was in a different country, suggesting they were trying to stay a step ahead of police. Perhaps more significantly, all of the sales were either on or near the coast.

Danny turned and stared at the boats. The plane ticket he'd found in Charlie Foster's Bentley was one-way. Whatever was being planned, Danny reckoned he was looking out on their getaway vehicle back home.

Danny left the hubbub of the town centre and made the walk to the sales site, a purpose built new-build sandwiched between stabling and a pavilion.

He registered in the sales office and went straight to the ring, already half-full with buyers, consignors, agents, trainers and press.

Danny put in an ear piece for a translation of a brief opening ceremony. The town mayor declared the inaugural yearling and two-year-old horses-in-training sale open, followed by a fanfare from the Breton bagpipers.

He scanned the room. There was a small rock garden in the middle of the sales ring and red, white and blue flowers livened up the dark wood of the telephonist stall. There was a smell of newness to the place. A digital screen hung by the auctioneer podium. Above, there were circular clocks telling time for Paris, London, New York and Hong Kong. Large wall murals of the Prix de l'Arc de Triomphe and Prix du Jockey Club coloured the whitewashed walls. If he couldn't pin anything on Marcel, at least he could take some style tips back to Ely.

From a safe distance, he soon spotted the waistcoat man with raven-black hair who'd talked with Toby in the secluded Goodwood paddocks. Danny was no wiser as to what to call him. He shied from getting any closer and risking being spotted. In his favour, the man wasn't expecting to see him there.

Even from a distance, Danny could see an orange ID displayed in the plastic pouch round the man's neck. Danny viewed the gallery of photos on his phone, most were of Jack and baby Cerys in Meg's arms. He touched the image showing the IDs spread out on the cream leather of the Bentley passenger seat. He zoomed in to see the name on the orange ID card. It appeared the bloodstock agent with more faces than the Big Ben clock-tower was, for today at least, Marcel Tailler.

A suited auctioneer, slim, with slicked-back greying hair, climbed his podium, cleared his throat and called upon the gavel twice to get some order and silence for the sale to begin.

Stood two tiers behind, Danny looked down and off to his right at Marcel, who had just put a phone to his ear as lot six began to circle the black rubber of the ring below.

Just one lot away, Danny recalled.

To Danny's untrained ear, he could only pick out the 'I've got' and 'I want this' prices in the bids. The auctioneer chant made less sense than Toby and Marcel's words he'd overheard in the Goodwood paddock. *I've planted the rice in Hip Twenty-Seven.*

'We move on to a lovely lot now, Hip Seven in the catalogue.'

Danny looked down at the circled seven in the catalogue he'd stolen at Goodwood.

'I noticed changes at Ely,' Toby had said to Marcel there. Danny now knew he'd meant the armed officer guarding the sales entrance. The police clearly had a tip off there'd be another kidnapping. Toby and Marcel had both been present at the Welsh track, so the leads were at least partly right. Perhaps they'd been scared off at the last minute.

Had Toby planned to take Red Ink that afternoon? It still didn't marry well with the types being taken on the Continent, all six- and seven-figure purchases and royally bred. Hip Seven was an unraced son of Derby runner-up Heraldry out of Epsom Oaks winner Burning Shore, half-brother to six winners, including a Group Two Lennox Stakes. Even without seeing the specimen, Danny knew he was one of the star lots on paper and it was no coincidence the sales ring was at its fullest right then.

Easier to get lost in the crowd, Danny thought, but harder to keep track of Marcel.

With the bidding well underway, Marcel remained on the phone but had still to raise the paddle or his arm.

'Six hundred thousand euros, six hundred, six, six-fifty at the back, seven hundred thousand back with you on the telephones, seven-fifty at the back, eight hundred new bidder online, eight-fifty on the phones, nine hundred at the back.' There was a pause as if everyone was taking stock. Danny was mesmerised by the nine hundred thousand euros on the digital screen. He wanted it to reach a million, like Jack watching the milometer turning to a round number in the Mazda. Danny didn't mind that, it made a nice break from the usual cries of 'Are we there yet?'

'Nine-fifty back on the telephones,' the auctioneer beamed. 'Nine hundred and fifty thousand, with the telephone bidder to my left. Final warning.' His hawkish eyes then scanned the room and the bid spotters in the ring below. Suddenly, the gavel came down firmly to a warm round of applause. 'Another record price for our debut sale at Morlaix.'

And it will take some beating, Danny thought.

It would've barely got a mention at some of the bigger sales like Goffs in Ireland and Tattersalls in Newmarket, but the impact would be felt in future sales here, influential owners taking interest in a new player on the sales circuit.

Danny was equally confident the sales would hit the headlines but for all the wrong reasons.

He glanced back to see that Marcel had gone or had moved.

Lot seven was led away by the stud hand. The shimmering dark bay was blissfully unaware he'd broken records just by showing himself.

'Strange,' Danny thought aloud.

The spectator stood nearby. 'I know, who would have thought they'd be fetching telephone numbers at a provincial sale in its first year. No hope for us little guys.'

Danny wasn't baffled by the price but the fact Marcel had played no part in the bidding for the only lot he'd circled in that sales catalogue.

He politely nudged and squeezed his way out of there. Stood outside the sales office in the chilly evening air, Danny wondered what the hell just happened in there. He looked back to see Marcel sign the purchase ticket, confirm payment details and pick up the stable release, a permission slip to take the yearling through security at the stables behind the pavilion.

He felt like storming in there, revealing the man was a fake. He hadn't bid at any stage of the auction yet he was walking away with the star lot worth almost one million euros. He hadn't raised an arm or a bidder's paddle and neither the auctioneer nor the bid spotter had pointed or even looked his way. Danny could sort of understand Marcel coming all this way if he'd put in a few early bids and then given up when the auction flew by the upper limit he was willing to spend.

Marcel hadn't remotely looked like getting involved at any stage, even at the opening offer. Toby had advised Danny to bid aggressively. Marcel clearly wasn't of the same opinion.

He saw the sales team shake Marcel's hand. No wonder, Danny thought, the auctioneer's fee would be five per cent. Forty-seven thousand five hundred euros, he calculated, not bad for a few minutes work.

As Marcel turned to leave, Danny quickly sidestepped left of the sales office's glass doors. He would be safe there as he knew the stables were off to the right.

In the dark, he watched Marcel disappear round the back of the red-bricked main building.

He saw a white horse-van creep from the parking area. Danny thought it might be a courtesy van put on by the sales company to take sold lots to their new homes, though he knew some sellers agree to look after the horse for a day until travel arrangements can be made.

Danny entered the sales office.

At the desk, a man with hair as suspiciously black as Marcel's looked up with a smile. 'Ah, hello again, monsieur…'

Danny showed his pass he'd been handed after registering there earlier. 'Danny Rawlings.'

'What is the Hip number of your purchase please?'

Danny looked down at the form Marcel had signed, still in front of the sales team member.

The M. Tailler signature was barely legible and as fake as the orange bloodstock agent ID that had hung from the winning bidder's neck. Lower down on the form, he could clearly make out: *Purchased by Marcel Tailler on behalf of Malcolm Bernard.*

By the Frankel statue at York, Malcolm had told him he'd knocked the agent back, saying he hadn't the time to buy abroad.

But the form seemed legit. It had been stamped red with Verified and Authorised Payment Confirmed.

Danny wondered who had authorised the payment. Malcolm was a big owner, but even he wouldn't splash out nearly a million euros for a yearling on spec.

'No sale this time,' Danny replied. 'But I've certainly learnt a lot.'

'Maybe see you again, non?' the man said. Danny nodded politely. 'Bon voyage, Monsieur Rawlings.'

Danny left and selected Malcolm from the contacts list on his phone.

'Yes?' Malcolm began with.

'It's Danny Rawlings.'

'I've already promised to return to the Ely sales ring, Danny.'

'It's more important than that,' Danny replied. 'Did you change your mind about that bloodstock agent Marcel Tailler?'

'After you suggested I looked further afield for shrewd buys, I decided to call upon Marcel's services.'

'I didn't say go with him,' Danny replied, already cringing from the guilt he might've steered Malcolm into buying a one-million euros scam.

'Don't worry yourself, Toby Carmichael was the deciding factor,' Malcolm explained. 'He gave me the heads up about Marcel, said he was a good man who had sourced some of his best horses. The Midas Man called upon Marcel; that was enough of a rubber stamp for me.'

'Can I ask the bid limit you'd agreed with Marcel?'

'You can ask, doesn't mean I'll tell you,' Malcolm replied. 'Look, if this is about me keeping my powder dry at Ely Sales, I've already said I'll return there.'

'Is it under a million euros?' Danny asked.

'Yes, of course.'

'Half a million?'

'Yes, I wanted to trial the man before trusting him to buy big.'

'So you wouldn't trust him with a million euros then.'

'Now you're worrying me.'

'Would the amount bounce from the account details you gave him?'

'I would very much hope not,' Malcolm said sharply. 'Darren did more harm to my reputation than my bank balance.'

Danny recalled Malcolm's anger right after witnessing Darren Cooper's drunken show on Yorkshire Cup day.

Perhaps Malcolm was more involved in this than Danny had imagined. Could Malcolm have pushed Darren off the Old Ely

Bridge? Suddenly Danny wasn't sure whether to hang up before he gave anything else away.

'Let's hope you're wrong and the payment is returned.'

'Now you're really worrying me,' Malcolm said. 'Danny?'

'Do you want the good or bad news?'

'Both.'

'The good news is Marcel's unlikely to charge his agent's fee. The bad news is, he's shelled out nearly a million euros of your hard-earned on an unknown yearling.'

'What? Where are you?'

'Just call your bank and stop the payment being processed, if it already hasn't.'

'Where is he now?'

'You'll probably never see him or your horse again but there's still a chance to get the money back.'

'Thanks,' Malcolm said. 'I'll be in touch.'

Danny put his mobile away. The white van reappeared. He saw a glimpse of Marcel in the passenger seat. Was he using a courtesy van?

He'd learnt from Toby and Marcel talking on their phones at opposite sides of the Ely sales ring, all was not as it seemed. Most in the room would assume the bloodstock agent was called Marcel Tailler and was on the phone to a rich owner giving instructions and bidding limits from somewhere like the Cayman Islands, waiting to be given the okay to raise the bidder's paddle.

Marcel was somehow placing bids without even raising a paddle or an arm. Danny realised Marcel Tailler was in fact talking to one of the telephone bidders by the auctioneer's podium over the other side and not his client Malcolm Bernard.

A telephone bidder had won the lot. Marcel was on his mobile throughout. He was placing bids indirectly. After all, he'd been talking to Toby from the other side when both were on the phone at Ely.

But that didn't explain why he'd flown here in person. Danny feared he knew the answer. Marcel was primarily here to pick up the goods.

Danny avoided the cars with a courtesy driver put on by the sales. He didn't want to be implicated in the disappearance of the horse.

Instead, Danny jumped in a taxi from a rank waiting for the owners to emerge and said, 'Allez la van, s'il vous plait.'

The driver turned and said, 'I suspect I speak English better than you speak French.'

'Allez, allez,' Danny said, seeing the van turn left and rev away.

'The English,' the driver muttered under his rattling breath.

Danny looked out at the fingers of flickering light cast over the black waters of the quay. They sped under the towering viaduct now up-lit yellow.

Danny wondered where the hell they were heading. He recalled the one-way flight ticket in the Bentley. Perhaps they had no intention of leaving the country. Perhaps it was a coincidence all the sales were on the coast. But why would Toby be so involved if this was a mainland Europe job?

He felt his pocket, suddenly concerned he wouldn't have enough to cover the eventual fare. The more rural and dark it became, the more suspicious it would look to have two headlamps trailing them, Danny thought.

Suddenly the van took a sharp left after cresting a steep bend.

'Woah, there,' Danny said, thinking it was near enough international code for stop.

The driver stopped and shrugged. 'I am not a horse.'

Danny more than covered the fare and then jogged after the van down a dirt track. He could see Morlaix Bay ahead. It seemed they'd only moved the short distance to a quieter part of the bay.

The cove was as secluded as Lavernock Point, but with a sandier, shallower beach. There was a medium-sized fishing trawler moored by a granite jetty. The van had already parked up by the boat.

Danny held back to assess the situation. He didn't take a photo as the darkening sky would set off the phone's flash. He could see two men slowly positioning and then lowering a large wooden crate into the hold of the boat with an on-board crane, normally reserved for removing the catch of the day.

Danny crept up to the back of the van.

When he saw the silhouettes return to the van, Danny knew this was his chance. He ran and leapt over the steel handrail that skirted the deck of the boat.

He saw the black shape of a third man standing in the trawler's cabin.

Danny ducked below window level and then crouched into a ball by a red metal box housing life jackets and a fire hose on the outside cabin wall. He felt sheltered there on the opposite side to where the van was parked on the jetty.

Crouched still, he felt the boat rock twice. The other two must've boarded.

Danny slowed his breath. He heard the mooring rope slap on to the granite and the boat's engine cough and splutter into life.

Once they began to chug away from the mooring and join Morlaix Bay, Danny knew there was no turning back.

CHAPTER 22

Danny remained huddled beneath the gallery of windows wrapping around the cabin as they carved up the still waters of the bay.

Going at a fair old clip, Danny reckoned, must be eight knots at least.

Despite giving a wide berth to the rocky islet of Île Louët, he could still make out the white lighthouse and cottage perched there.

With the lights of Morlaix fading fast, the boat sent waves up the rocky slopes of the Château du Taureau, a forbidding granite structure rising up from the sea. It was built as a fortress to repel English invaders, according to the town map he'd read, before being turned into a prison dubbed the French Alcatraz, and finally a tourist attraction.

When he smelt smoke carried on the wind, he was quick to cover his mouth, fearing a cough would be heard above the engine.

He peered over the red metal box shielding him towards the bow of the trawler. In the celestial light, he made out the black shape of a man who'd lit up the orange glow of a cigarette. It's only then he noticed that his own breath was turning into ghostly swirls of steam, showing in the window behind Danny's head. He tucked his knees up even further and breathed into his thighs.

He felt he had to move before either he was discovered or his body fully seized up. Exposed to the northerly gusts, he already felt like he was encased in a block of ice.

Carefully, like Jack taking his first steps, he crept towards the stern of the trawler. Every few feet, he anxiously glanced back at the smaller windows to the rear of the cabin. He could see the two remaining crew staring out toward the sea ahead and the third member having a smoke.

They'd soon be crossing one of the busiest shipping lanes in the world and had clearly booked a captain as experienced as he was willing to turn a blind eye to the cargo below; one that could readily bounce off any awkward questions posed by a coastguard or water police on the sea or over the radio.

Aware they might catch a reflection in the cabin glass Danny was slow in lifting the grey lid to the hold below containing half a ton of horseflesh worth the best part of a million euros.

Inside, he could see a metal stepladder soon swallowed up by the blackness down there.

Danny slipped through the gap he'd made and descended the steps until his boots planted on the floor with a hollow thud, thankfully drowned out by the engine rumbling loudly through the wall in front.

Danny stamped again. They'd levelled off the hold with a sprung floor to take the weight of the horse and keep the crate level. Clearly this was no amateur operation.

He fished for his phone and used the torch function as a searchlight to scan the hold.

He was faced by the wooden crate he'd seen lowered in there. Peering in the gaps between the struts of the box, Danny made out the shape of the young son of Heraldry, standing quietly. He'd clearly got a temperament to match the pedigree. He wondered if they'd sedated the colt for the journey, but the darkness probably helped, acting like the blinds put over a reluctant horse's face going into the stalls.

Behind the crate, there were two brown glass bottles sat in a metal container on a desk fastened to the wall in case the weather turned.

Danny pictured the Carmichael string, all a variation of brown. He was left wondering whether it was some kind of paint or skin dye to colour the horses.

Wouldn't need to waste any on this one, he thought.

Off to the left, there were the double doors of a grey metal locker, again bolted to the floor.

Danny went over to the desk and saw a gun just lying there like it was perfectly normal. There was also another metal tray containing what looked like two tiny computer chips encased in glass.

In the drawer, he saw a half-empty bottle of whisky. There was a square of card. On it was a handwritten list, much like the one in Toby's desk and the one fluttering down the rail track from Darren's dismembered body.

It appeared to be answers to awkward questions if stopped by police out there. It looked like all the crew were prepared for the worst.

He flinched when he heard a whinnying from the crate. 'Are you okay in there, boy? We'll be there soon enough.'

Though he wasn't certain 'where' was.

Thankfully there was plenty of room and slats for him to breathe and stay cool.

He wondered what would become of the colt. The fact he was worth a small fortune was very much in his favour. Danny then began to worry about his own fate if found down here. He was certainly not worth a small fortune to Carmichael, who'd probably take pleasure in throwing him overboard. Never to be seen again. They were too far out from either coast to swim.

He went over to the locker. There were also thin slats in those doors. The right one was unlocked. Inside he saw a mop and bucket on the left and what looked like a tool bag to the right.

Danny unzipped the bag. Inside were syringes in vacuum-sealed sterile bags, a blue plastic plunger and a small scalpel.

Suddenly he heard the creak of the fibreglass ceiling. Danny pictured the room in his mind's eye and switched off the phone. He didn't have time to go back for the gun. Instead, he stepped into the locker, careful not to tip over the mop and bucket.

He soon heard the squeak of boots on the metal steps of the ladder.

Danny stood behind the locked left door and kept the tool bag and mop in view on the right side, just in case the man now lowering himself into the room might have come down for them.

Danny pressed his face to the thin slats. He watched as the man flicked on a naked bulb above the desk, and then snapped on a surgical mask and gloves from one of the drawers.

Danny was ready to jump out as the man opened up the crate. But the colt showed no sign of any distress as he was led towards the desk and then fastened to a makeshift harness hooked to one of the metal beams on the red ceiling.

Even in the dim light from the single bulb, Danny could see the colt's eyes were bright and alert. Perhaps he hadn't been sedated. Danny was dying to give him a comforting pat on the neck.

He saw the masked man head for the locker. Danny quickly backed away from the slats. The right metal door shuddered open noisily.

Back pressed firmly to the inner wall of the locker, he stared intently at the arm reaching in there and picking up the bag with the syringes.

Danny held his breath and kept still, countering the sway of the boat. The bag was gone and the locker turned black again.

He returned to the slats of light and saw the man in the surgical mask pull what looked like a ruler from the desk drawer and then measure some way down the horse's mane. Stopping in the middle third of the neck, not far above the withers, the man measured a couple of inches down. Danny swallowed. Perhaps the horse's fate wasn't as assured as he first hoped.

From his pocket the man removed two small handheld devices, and a marker pen. He scanned that part of neck with one device and read its small LCD screen. He then passed the other device over. It bleeped, like a metal detector. He scanned again. He pulled the lid off the marker pen and scanned yet again, stopping this time when the solid bleep sounded. The man made a black mark with the pen on the brown neck.

Danny knew every horse in Europe had to be microchipped about there, on the left side of the horse's neck, a few inches under the skin in the large nuchal ligament.

Each horse was injected with a computer chip programmed with a unique fifteen-digit identification number held in a database with the relevant equine authority of the country of birth, as well as backup details about the horse, like colour, sex, birthdate and any markings, along with a hair sample for DNA.

As with phone numbers, the chip ID started with a code to link the horse with the country it was foaled. For the French-bred in the room, it would start with 250.

The man ripped some cotton wool from the tool bag and went to the desk. He used the wool as a stopper as he tipped the bottle, turning it a yellowy-brown.

He then returned to the horse, and gently wiped and dabbed the neck where he'd left the mark.

Some kind of antiseptic or anaesthetic swab, Danny reckoned.

He saw the masked man remove the blue plastic plunger from the bag and a tiny tube from the sterile wrap. Having seen this done before, Danny knew it would just feel like the prick of an injection, as the chip was no bigger than a grain of rice.

Have you planted the rice in Hip Twenty-Seven?

Danny was convinced he was witnessing more rice being planted, but this time in Hip Seven.

The man attached the sterile nodule to the blue plastic plunger and slowly inserted it where he'd marked X.

There was just a flash of his black tail as the needle went in and was then carefully removed.

Danny heard the rattle of metal on metal when the man dropped something in the tray on the desk.

'That wasn't so bad was it boy,' the man said, voice muffled by the mask.

It seemed he'd actually removed the chip, Danny realised. But this was a yearling, he'd already been chipped. The bleeping device had appeared to show this.

The air began to smell chemically like a hospital.

The man wet some more cotton wool from the brown glass bottle. This time he wiped an area on the rump of the harnessed horse. Back at the desk, the man removed one of the tiny glass-encased chips he had seen in the metal dish.

Was he about to move the microchip ID to a hind leg? What would be the point in that?

He watched the man change the needle attached to the blue plunger. It was inserted into the off-hind leg without the horse even turning a hair. A morbid curiosity made it hard for Danny to look away as the man followed the same procedure on the near-hind leg.

The man then returned from the desk with another device, small enough to fit comfortably in his gloved palm. He pressed a button on the device and the horse's off-hind leg kicked out.

'Good,' the man said.

No, Danny thought. Not good!

The man looked down at the buzzer and pressed again. This time the near-hind leg twitched.

'You'll feel it more when the local anaesthetic wears off,' the man said into the horse's pricked ear.

Countless times he'd been stopped by security at racecourse stables to scan the chip reader over his runner's neck after arriving on race days. The encased chip must emit some kind of radio frequency to tell the reader the ID number of the horse, Danny reckoned. Security can then check it matched with the horse's name in the racecard. He knew microchips had been introduced in the UK and Ireland partly to prevent 'ringers' – a horse masquerading as another – getting into a race they shouldn't, after some embarrassingly high-profile mix ups and scandals. Serious money could be made backing a physically and mentally stronger three-year-old that was snuck into a race restricted to juvenile two-year-olds. A man against boys.

But where were they going to find a replacement ID for these smuggled imports?

Danny recalled the press dub Carmichael 'The Midas Man' as he'd consistently and successfully bought cheaply. He then pictured the bullet hole in the horse's skull hidden among other bones in the cave. He wasn't buying the horse. He was buying the chip inside. A new identity.

He had later regretted beating Toby to Red Ink at the Ely auction. It now looked like he'd saved the colt's life that day.

That didn't explain why they were they all brown lookers with poor bloodlines.

Toby was clearly buying based solely on appearance in the search for a doppelganger for the import. Its pedigree wasn't relevant, as Toby could turn a bad family tree into a fashionable one within a generation of putting a blue-blooded ringer into the mix. Soon, he'd build the reputation and breeding empire to attract the best broodmares on offer to pair with the Group-class winners of Arwen Vale.

Beneath the porno mags in Toby's desk, he'd seen passports of the rejects now just scattered bones in the cave. The horse drawings in them had no shading for distinctive markings or X's for whorls. After the stable tour, he'd discovered that nearly ninety per cent of horses in the American Stud Book were a variation of brown. They must be choosing brown horses with no markings to increase the odds of a physical likeness, Danny reckoned. Once the passport and ID number matched, the horse would likely go undetected through its entire career. Blood samples sent to the integrity unit of the BHA after the horse won would only be tested for banned substances as the identity was already assumed.

No wonder many of Carmichael's horses hadn't made the track, Danny thought, they were on death row waiting for a match, and then cast aside like some waste by-product in the process of manufacturing a classy thoroughbred racehorse.

But Danny knew an attractive pedigree on paper was no guarantee to the success of the progeny on track. There had been many examples where seven-figure purchases at the sales struggled to win a lowly maiden worth a couple of grand at the races.

How could Toby possibly maintain a fifty-five per cent strike rate over a season and a half?

Danny didn't believe in miracles. He reckoned the answer was more likely to be found in the colt facing him.

The microchips he'd just seen taken from the metal tray on the desk and implanted into the hind legs must also respond to radio signals, Danny reckoned.

He recalled Toby's instructions in Ely's parade ring before he got on the spare ride. *Do not use the whip.*

They'd got their own whip, Danny thought. They must be sending a small electric impulse, like a static shock, to the muscles. It would replicate a firm reminder with the air cushioned persuader. Whips tended to be drawn in the final few furlongs when horses started to tire and well within range of that device held discreetly in the palm of a racegoer up in the stands. The shock wouldn't leave a mark – at least physically – and they could administer it as many times as they liked, unlike the rivals whose jockeys were limited to the number of hits depending on the race distance and the places to strike the horse by the whip rules introduced in 2012, or they'd risk being handed a suspension.

He could now see why Foundling had inexplicably drifted in his hands, left towards the rail and then right to the middle of the track as if remotely controlled. Using the whip would risk spooking the animal, unseating a jockey unaware of the scam.

No wonder Toby had been so angry when Danny had disobeyed orders with a few cracks of the whip at Ely to correct the horse's path. It only made the meandering worse as the horse was receiving mixed messages with the whip and the electric impulses.

Despite the waywardness, Foundling had kept finding extra to win once he'd put the whip down. He could now see it was more to do with those tiny responders rather than his strong arms.

Danny needed this to stop. While the owners and punters of rivals were being ripped off, it was the horses he was worried about. The colt here hadn't shown any distress but if he could talk he might say different.

He watched as the masked man led the horse back into the crate and then removed the whisky bottle from the drawer. He wondered if the alcohol would be used as an added antibacterial agent. But the man snapped the elastic mask away from his face and gulped back a generous measure. He sat down, facing the wall, seemingly glad to be out of the cold for as long as he could get away with.

You can fuck off now, Danny thought. He'd been stuck in that cramped locker for what seemed like hours. He wondered if the man at the desk had drifted off. But he couldn't open the stiff locker door quietly. He had to play the waiting game.

Then, he heard the creak of the rusty hinges above. He looked up and saw a slither of blue light from the night sky.

The others were probably wondering what the hell was keeping the surgeon, Danny thought. He looked over at the gun on the desk to the left, well within reach of the man.

Even with the element of surprise, Danny would still struggle to get there first.

He then heard the second man climb down and walk the hollow floor into the light by the wannabe veterinary surgeon.

Marcel! Who the hell was behind the mask then?

'Here,' Marcel said, handing over a small pamphlet.

'I'm busy, can't you see? I'll be up in a minute,' the seated man replied, resting the bottle down.

'You'll want to see this,' Marcel replied.

The man swiped the booklet from Marcel's hand.

Danny's face creased as he hurriedly patted down his jacket pockets again, as if he'd locked himself out of the house. They were empty. The sales catalogue he'd stolen was back with Marcel.

'And?' the man asked, gloved hands thumbing the pages. 'They were dishing these out free at the sales office. But you'd still better throw it overboard. We've kidnapped one of the most expensive horses since Shergar. We don't want anything linking the Morlaix sale with this boat.'

The sales catalogue was handed back to Marcel, who said, 'It more than links the boat with the sale. Look at the opening page. I'd circled the lot we were taking. Hip Seven.'

'Why the hell would you do that?' the seated man fumed. 'We might as well have walked the horse out of the ring shouting we're stealing this.'

'I only had this on me at Glorious Goodwood,' Marcel said. 'I'd circled it to show Toby in the paddocks but was thrown by that Danny Rawlings turning up. I must've dropped it sometime after.'

'You careless fuck, you do know he's done time for theft,' the man replied. 'And if they found this here, it wouldn't only link the boat to the sales, it would link the stolen horse to the sales and, with your prints all over it, link us with it all. Throw the bloody thing, now! It's toxic.'

'I will,' Marcel said, 'but that doesn't explain how the hell—'

'It ended up on this boat?' the masked man finished the question off like a twin.

The pause was broken by the seated man saying, 'He's on board.'

Danny felt his heart work harder.

Through the slats, he saw them turn to look at the locker.

Danny pulled his face from the light. He looked down at the mop handle. He'd do more damage with his fists and boots.

His stomach turned when he could make out the pair of them slowly creeping towards the locker. Danny braced himself to burst out the unlocked right door. He pushed down on the handle and flung the door open like a spring-loaded stall.

Head down he brushed by the surgeon and then shouldered Marcel to the hollow floor with a loud thud.

Danny's new-look lighter frame nimbly climbed to the top of the stepladder. He pushed his way over the lip of the hold's mouth and out into the cold night air. He turned back and winced as he discovered the ladder was neither detachable nor telescopic like the one from his attic.

Danny looked over at the third crewmember steering the boat with his back to him in the cabin. It was no good sitting on the fibreglass lid as he couldn't then move from there when the driver inevitably came out to see what was keeping the other two below deck.

Beyond the cabin, Danny could make out an undulating black strip against the dark blue of the lightening sky. Land was approaching fast. Further downcoast to the right, he could see the warm glow of city lights. Danny flicked on his mobile. They were now close enough to get an internet signal.

He heard the thud of boots on the stepladder.

According to the GPS app on his phone, they were off the coastline of South Wales. The city was Cardiff.

He saw Marcel's face appear from under the raised lid of the hold.

Danny looked back at the coastline. Directly ahead, he could make out a dot of light, far too small for it to be a lighthouse. It was circling and flashing. He remembered the torch sweep up as he looked down from the cliff top. They were heading right for Lavernock Point.

It explained why Molly had been stopped from walking in the sea there. She'd probably wandered off when the husband and son were busy loading up a previous smuggled import.

He bet the Carmichaels hadn't even gone to the cove to spread her ashes. They had been on the pebbly beach to meet the latest shipment. Perhaps it was the Hip Twenty-Seven Marcel and Toby had discussed at Goodwood.

It felt like someone else's fingers as he tried to type 'skull in cave' on a text with hands shaking from a mix of fear and cold but it was 'sky in cave' that appeared on the screen. Fucking autocorrect, he thought, as he clicked send and threw the phone in the sea. He didn't want the crew seeing what he'd seen from the photos of fake bloodstock IDs and horse passports, and the warning text he'd sent Meg.

Danny hoped Meg and her phone were both switched on to decipher the message at these small hours.

He knew the sea foreshortened the distance, but he still reckoned he could swim it, particularly with an incoming tide to carry him home once into the sheltered cove.

The man in the cabin turned.

Danny grabbed the handrail and pulled himself over, toes balancing on the deck's edge like it was a pair of stirrups.

He looked over to see Marcel had picked up the gun from the desk.

Danny flung off his jacket. It floated on the swell of the water but was soon left behind in the frothing waves carved up by the boat.

He quickly lowered himself down. He knew every second he could stay with the boat was precious as it meant a lot less work in the water. But he knew a second too long and he'd end up like the horse in the cave.

His hands clung to the bottom of two slippery steel handrails. His boots kept skidding as they tried to grip the wet fibreglass of the hull.

When he saw Marcel looking down from the deck, Danny pushed off the hull with his feet.

Sinking in the water, the muffled rumble of the engine soon faded to nothing and time seemed to slow.

Danny opened his stinging eyes to see white patterns of moonlight in the rippling and sloshing water at the surface.

Hands cupped, Danny scooped water and kicked to reach the light. Suddenly he heard bullets fizz either side, leaving a trail of tiny bubbles.

Danny stopped kicking and turned his hands to push water in an upward motion to keep him submerged for as long as his lungs could take or for the bullets to stop.

The light also faded to nothing. It wasn't the moon but a spotlight on the boat. The bullets had stopped.

They clearly weren't going to waste any time saving him. Danny wasn't surprised. His death would be seen as a problem solved by all involved.

He blew out loudly as he resurfaced and trod water while he got his bearings. Catching his breath, he suddenly felt his arms and leg muscles starting to seize up. He couldn't afford cramp in water this cold.

He began to swim in the crawl stroke towards the black of the coastline, now tantalisingly close.

When he felt light-headed some minutes later, he stopped to slow his heart and was encouraged to make out details on the coastline. He then started to feel the push of the waves carrying him into the cove where he'd seen the dot of the light. He heard the crash of waves on the pebbly shore and saw the craggy face of Lavernock cliff he'd clambered up the last time he was there. Moments later, he caught sight of the luxurious Carmichael van; special treatment for a potentially special horse.

He started to swim breaststroke, not to splash so much, as he closed in on the smugglers.

Danny felt like he'd already made it as his feet could reach the shallow seabed but when he started to walk, he went under as his leg muscles were moving on memory alone. He still kept going. He never thought he'd be that glad to see a pebbly beach.

His wet clothes felt like chainmail as he staggered the final few yards, waves pushing him forward and then cruelly pulling him back. It felt like he was walking up an escalator the wrong way.

As he crumpled on to the pebbles, frothy water trickling around his body. He squinted into the dazzling white light shining down.

'Good of you to wait,' Danny choked between rapid breaths.

'Shoot him,' came from the dark.

'Not here,' said another.

'But the tide is coming in, it'll wash his blood away.'

'But we don't want to risk his body being found here,' the other voice said. 'Our tracks are in the dirt over there. No, throw him in the van. We'll kill him and the other reject in the cave, let the rats do the rest. Remember, we always keep this behind closed doors.'

And an electric fence, Danny thought. He recalled the skull in the cave. He heard a tinny noise and couldn't stop his eyes from shutting.

And then, nothing.

CHAPTER 23

Danny felt something warm and wet slide up his face, tickling his cheeks as it went.

Am I dead? Was this then the afterlife?

Someone there needed a shave and a mint, he thought, delirious.

He quickly opened his eyes to see the bristly and toothy mouth of a young horse. The waves of warm breath acted like smelling salts.

Danny dragged himself away and sat up, wiping the white streaky deposits of sea salt from his face. He could see enough from the lightening sky outside to know he was back in Carmichael's cave: the bones, the cave art, the dripping water.

However, the wooden boards once guarding the mouth were now leaning against a boulder by the lip of the cave, presumably to allow them to shift the horse and his unconscious body in there.

He was alive, but for how long? He recalled the voice he'd heard shining dazzling light in his face at Lavernock Point. 'We'll kill him and the other reject in the cave. Let the rats do the rest.'

In the half-light, the colt certainly looked like the million-euro blueblood he'd seen in the trawler hold: a flawless bay coat, a bold strong physique for a yearling and large intelligent eyes and ears. He seemed to possess a similarly laidback temperament.

But this had to be the reject for the more expensive ringer, Danny reckoned, probably already moved into his box in the stable nearby.

He saw a red nick on the left side of the horse's neck, a couple of inches from the glossy black mane. The microchip had already been removed. They were probably planting the rice in the blueblood assuming this one's identity right now. He glanced down at the skull with the bullet hole. The colt here was no longer a name or a number. In the eyes of the racing authorities, the horse didn't exist. His fate was already sealed. Soon, both Danny and the horse would be a memory. *Bastards!*

Danny's hands felt tingly and as heavy as his damp shirt and combats. They were held in an unnatural position out in front.

He saw the leather hand ties holding them there. Panicked, he tried to pull them apart but there was no give at all. He rubbed his wrists trying to find some leverage.

He looked across at the colt.

Bound to be hungry, he thought, perhaps he could gnaw on the ties, but conceded he'd have to be one hell of a horse whisperer to convince the colt that was a good idea.

It felt like the pair of them was waiting on death row. Danny tried again at the ties. He then noticed his ankles had also been bound.

He looked down at the mix of charred and broken bones in search of something with a serrated edge. There appeared to be slightly more this time. Had they killed another horse since he was last there?

There was plenty of ash in the mix. Seemed it wasn't just bloody silks put on the bonfire behind the stables, Danny thought.

He suddenly stopped searching as something had caught his eye. He could see a glint among the bones. He leant forward and scooped up the shiny thing from the black bed of ash. His restricted fingers clumsily brushed it clean. He instantly recognised it. He'd ordered Luke to remove his diamond ear studs before the trial gallop. Danny recalled the empty copper dish on the kitchen windowsill after Luke went missing. The lad had clearly put them in his fleece pocket. It wasn't Luke who'd fired the rifle shot he'd heard back at the yard. It must've been the driver of the black Citroen. Luke had said it was an old friend. Couldn't have been that close, Danny thought. He now viewed the black ash, both on the floor and his fingertips, in an even darker light. He tried to brush clean his black fingers.

They must've put Luke's body on his own bonfire where he'd burnt the bloody silks, still wearing the fleece containing the ear studs, and then bagged up the remains and dumped it with the rest here.

He wasn't on the run. He wasn't running anywhere. No wonder the attacks suddenly stopped.

It seemed Toby was even more evil than Danny had previously feared. In the parade rings, Toby had always looked at his son with a mix of distain and shame, never even trusting him with a ride. But would he really kill his own son?

Danny looked over at the cave mouth. He knew it wouldn't take long to implant the chip into the blueblood. He scoured the ground and picked out a small fragment of bone with an edge that was pleasingly sharp. He set about cutting the ties that bound him. They soon began to fray.

He heard a noise above the constant drip of water. He looked up at the blue circle of light that was the cave mouth.

Two black figures had appeared. They entered the cave. *Toby and Marcel.*

Danny wedged the diamond between the looped ties.

'Can we kill him now?' Marcel asked, holding a torch.

'We wait for the boss,' Toby said.

The boss?

Toby was the boss of Arwen Vale, Danny had thought.

'The Midas Man is as fake as the horses then,' Danny said.

Toby shot Danny a look.

Marcel smiled.

'Don't know why you're grinning, you've got five fake identities, saw them in your Bentley,' Danny said. 'Charlie Foster.'

'Six,' the man replied. 'I assumed the role of Charlie Foster for a bloodstock sale west of Pau on the Atlantic side beneath the Pyrenees.'

Danny heard footsteps outside the cave. Another man entered. Danny knew the odds of getting out of there alive were lengthening.

'But Malcolm reckoned you only came back to the UK to visit family,' Danny said.

'He does,' Danny heard a familiar voice from the dark.

Closer, Danny could see it was the surgeon on the boat. The man snapped the mask away from his mouth as he stepped into the pool of light from the torch.

Chris?!

'I see you've already met my brother, Sean Ramsbottom,' Chris said, lowering the mask to hang round his neck.

'You're brothers?' Danny questioned. 'But you don't look anything alike.'

'For a reason,' Chris said. 'He's touring mainland Europe casing sales rings undetected under fake names and guises. But underneath the chemicals, he's a strawberry blonde like me.' He glanced at Toby and Sean. 'The final triangle is complete.'

On the boat, Danny had seen the two hind chips had already been implanted. Chris had clearly inserted the ID chip taken from the horse here into the neck of the import. The three points on the horse implanted made a triangle.

He recalled Chris say he'd taken a retraining course with JETS to stay in racing. 'You retrained as a vet.'

'Our imports are bred to be the best,' Chris said, grinning. 'Combining horsepower and electric power, we had created the very first hybrid. Seven Group race winners in our first season, we are well on the way to transforming modest pedigrees and building a breeding powerhouse to compete with the likes of Coolmore and Darley. And it can all be done without leaving a trace on the horse, as painless and harmless as keyhole surgery. No marks on the beast. Everyone outside this electric fencing believes we're buying extremely well and they have no reason to believe otherwise, all horses have valid documentations and an authentic ID number programmed into the microchip in the neck.'

'It's just that the IDs weren't theirs originally,' Danny said. And then he saw that Chris was holding the gun he'd seen on the trawler desk.

Trying to buy some time as he continued to work the bone fragment against the ties, Danny asked, 'Why risk being found out by racing the kidnapped horses? Why couldn't you lay low and breed from them? The stud fees will always be greater than the prize money.'

Chris said, 'It's not like the black market in stolen art where masterpieces can be sold on to private collectors, never to be seen again. Racehorses need to race, otherwise they're just horses. While they can earn far more at stud, they're judged on their achievements on the racetrack. An unfashionable bloodline can turn on its head if a modestly bred horse can deliver at the highest level.'

'How the hell did someone like you get others on board with all this?' Danny asked.

Chris sucked in air as if displeased by the thinly veiled insult. 'I had something on all of them. Who needs brawn when you can blackmail.'

Danny recalled Darren on lookout near the attack scene by the Roman pillars at Bath racetrack. He'd clearly witnessed Luke attack Ryan there but did nothing about it until Danny arrived.

Had Darren Cooper been part of this?

'Do you know what Darren's last words were over the phone before he jumped under a train?' Danny asked. 'I'm with Chris.'

'He was,' Chris replied. 'We were lovers.'

Danny paused to take it in. He recalled the matching rainbow bracelet they wore. 'It didn't seem that way in the Bath changing rooms.'

'I know, he did a good job, there should've been an Oscar buzz about that performance. You see another jockey caught us holding more than hands at Warwick the day before. The rumours needed extinguishing before they spread like wildfire, which would have forced Darren to come out.'

'So you were thinking of him first,' Danny said.

'I was thinking of myself first,' Chris replied. 'Once he was outed, I had no power over him, no control.'

Danny recalled the card fluttering down the rail track. Darren had called him to the bridge to show him that he was speaking the words of another, a script. 'So that's why you staged the argument.'

'And what better way to quash any rumours than have him ridiculing me in front of a crowd in the Bath weighing room. He convinced you to stand up for me. The boy did good.'

'It didn't do him good in the end,' Danny said. 'Couldn't he just call it off with you? Walk away from all this.'

'That wouldn't change the fact he'd been unfaithful to his wife,' Chris said. 'That secret meant he was mine and always would be, whether we were together or apart.'

'Did you push him off the Old Ely Bridge?'

'No,' Chris said. 'At least, not directly.'

'You pushed him into it then,' Danny said. 'You threatened to go to the press. He'd then have a marriage to save and custody battle for the kids.'

'Why would I do that?' Chris asked. 'For this whole operation to work, I needed someone onside in the weighing room, an alibi, a pair of eyes on the erratic Luke, a pair of ears to hear if anyone became suspicious of our horses. He had a growing drink problem and losing his retainer with Malcolm Bernard couldn't have helped. Above all, I believe it was the fear of revealing to the world a long-held secret and the misery it would cause those he loved that pushed him, his choice alone. Often the fear of the outcome is worse than the actual outcome.'

'So the shy guy routine was also just an act.'

'My riding career was going nowhere fast – I had that in common with Darren. That's what first broke the ice; that and the fact we saw each other most days at work. Over time we grew closer. I did some work riding down Toby's on Darren's recommendation. It soon became clear Toby's yard was on the verge of going bust. When I was training as a vet, I saw there was now an overreliance on the chip number by authorities in identifying horses. I saw that as a weakness in the system. I needed help from others to make this work but years of abuse from my father left me unable to trust anyone. I needed to find weaknesses in others, find dirt that stuck to each of those involved, enough to stop them turning whistle-blower.'

'How did you control this one?' Danny asked, glancing over at Toby. He recalled the script in his desk. Kill Jack and Cerys.

Toby said, 'I confessed to him at a previous yard's party that I had got to Molly in time to save her, like Luke had saved her from walking into the sea. I saw her enter the woods. She was walking purposefully, as if there was an important job to be done. She was carrying a kitchen stool and a rope was trailing behind her. I followed her into the woods, I can only hope she didn't sense me there, as she'd know I was still watching her stood perched on the stool as she pulled the noose tight and remained behind a tree trunk as she kicked the stool away. I only stopped looking as she gagged and gargled. It seemed to last forever. I looked back when it fell silent. I should have stopped her,' he cried. 'Then I went to my office to fetch the suicide note I'd kept since the first attempt, which we hadn't reported to the police. Luke wanted to keep it because he could hear his mother's voice in his head saying the words. I planted the suicide note on her as I felt paranoid the police would tell I was lying to them that I hadn't seen her do it. I later told all this to Chris when I was drunk at the party. He said it wasn't a problem. He seemed quite happy. Luke had become erratic since his mother's death. I couldn't risk leaving him alone if I was sent down for assisted suicide and falsifying evidence.'

'And Chris here didn't want a loose cannon about the place,' Danny said, now able to move his hands some more. 'A bit like me spying on your yard. I was on to you. You planted cash on me via a trusted friend with a view to framing me with stolen goods. When that didn't work, you saw a chance for me to become victim six by offering a spare ride.'

'It wasn't for your riding ability,' Chris smirked.

'But Luke didn't finish the job, I'm still here in one piece. He got cold feet.'

'He's a fool, but he's not a complete idiot,' Chris said. 'It seemed he saw a permanent job at yours was better than trying to pick up the odd ride at ours. It wouldn't be long before he'd attract the police to Arwen Vale. I had Darren help destroy all evidence of the attacks with a bonfire. I wasn't going to be implicated in covering up those crimes.'

'And my boy hasn't attacked since,' Toby said.

Danny held the diamond earring tight. He felt he'd need it. 'You're a control freak. You controlled those around you like chess pieces.'

'And it was working well.' Chris said, raising the gun.

Danny's eyes didn't waver from Chris' hands despite seeing another small figure appear in the mouth of the cave.

As the figure crept closer, he recognised those womanly curves. *Meg!*

Danny still didn't react to give her away.

He couldn't believe she'd already read the text by this hour and was even more surprised that she'd deciphered it. *Sky in cave.*

But part of him wished she hadn't. He couldn't bear to even imagine Jack and Cerys becoming orphans while they slept.

Sean suddenly turned and saw Meg. 'Brother!'

But before Chris had the chance to look behind, Meg ran screaming and leapt on his back.

Meg needed backup. Danny furiously worked the bone's edge against the wrist ties until they snapped.

'Get the bitch off me,' Chris cried as he stumbled forward under her weight. As he fell, he tossed the gun to Toby.

Meg stayed on board, fingernails clawing at his face like a feral cat, drawing blood.

Sean hooked his arms round her and separated them.

'Finish him!' Chris snarled.

Toby turned the gun back on Danny, who had now also freed his ankles.

'Don't let him control you any longer, Toby!' Danny cried, palms up. 'You're nothing to do with them. They want you implicated in this by killing me.'

'I'm already in this too deep,' Toby said. 'They couldn't implicate me any more than I am.'

'You can still walk away from this,' Danny said, staring down the barrel of the gun. 'Molly committed suicide. It wasn't her first attempt.'

'I had a chance to stop her, but I didn't. I just hid like a coward and heard her die, slowly, gagging for breath from the rope.'

'She wanted to die, and you always wanted what was best for her.'

'Assisted suicide is still a crime,' Chris said. 'Particularly when you plant a note on the body to cover it up.'

'You feared Luke wouldn't cope with his mam dead and his dad inside,' Danny told Toby. 'It's understandable.'

'Toby, can't you see, Danny's trying to save himself,' Chris said. 'He's the one using you.'

'You did nothing wrong,' Danny cried.

'I killed her.'

'You didn't stop her killing herself, there is a big difference.'

'Good luck in telling the judge that,' Chris said.

'It won't need as much luck as you,' Danny said, as he displayed the diamond he'd been pinching between finger and thumb.

'Where did you find that?' Toby asked.

'It was among the bones,' Danny said. 'There's a good reason why the attacks stopped. Your son is dead.'

'What?'

'They murdered him. I saw their Citroen, we all heard the gunfire. They feared he was going to share your trade secrets with a rival. Luke didn't go into hiding, he was killed by Chris and Sean. His body was cremated behind your stables and the ashes carried here.' Danny showed his black fingers.

Toby turned the gun back on Chris.

'I had to,' Chris explained. 'Police would soon link the attacker back to Arwen Vale. They'd already questioned Darren.'

'You... killed... my... son,' Toby growled, jowly face trembling in the dim light.

'Luke was one of only two risks to the success of building our breeding empire. You know I don't like risks'

'What was the second risk?' Danny asked.

'You,' Chris replied. 'Toby had told me you had been spotted up on Pen-y-Bryn several times. You'd accused him of wrongdoing. There was a risk someone at some point might listen to you.'

Danny saw similar sadness in Toby's eyes when he'd been taken into the woods to show where Molly had died. Toby wasn't acting here. He was grieving.

'Don't do anything stupid,' Chris said.

There was a click of the safety catch.

'I don't think what I'm about to do is stupid.'

'The lad's mother had died,' Chris said. 'And his father rejected him. No wonder he went off the rails.'

'Because *you* weren't prepared to risk my boy on our horses.'

'Not until we got a successful foundation crop to build upon,' Chris said. 'We were all in this together to the end. And here is our chance to eliminate the second risk.'

'You said my role was to train horses,' Toby said, confused. 'I'm no killer.'

'You're right,' Chris said. 'Now, give the gun to me.'

'No!'

Chris said, 'Had I not killed Luke, he would've no doubt gone on to cripple jockeys riding for our yard in the future.'

'No!' Toby howled. 'You can't have!'

'Well I can, and I did. It was all over very quick, he didn't suffer, unlike his victims. And it will be worth it in the long run. Just think of the future champions not yet born,' Chris explained. 'And you will be credited as star of the show, the face on the newspaper covers everybody congratulates and wants to be associated with.'

Toby pulled the trigger and Sean fell to the ground like he'd fainted, blood leaking from his chest. Meg screamed again.

'No!' Chris cried. 'Brother!'

'Now you can feel some of my pain,' Toby cried.

'Give me the gun,' Chris growled. 'Give me the fucking gun!'

'You're not speaking to Luke now,' Toby said, teary.

Chris charged Toby. The gun went off again with a loud bang. Chris dropped to the ground, face burying in a bed of bones and ashes.

Danny and Meg looked at each other anxiously. They had just witnessed two murders. And while the murderer still held the gun, Danny knew they weren't safe in there.

Hands and ankles freed, Danny bunched up the ties in his hand, pushed himself up and then ran for Toby, who was bent checking the pulses of the bleeding brothers. Danny rugby-tackled Toby, sending him crashing into the wall of the cave. The gun went flying. Toby took a swipe with his cane but Danny whipped it from the stricken man's grasp. 'This is for the dead horses over there!'

'Don't!' Toby cried. 'Enough! I'll confess everything. Just no more pain.'

Danny kept the cane raised behind his head.

Meg cried, 'Danny listen to him, we need him conscious to explain us out of this. The two in charge got their justice. Toby was just a pawn in their game, the fall guy if it all went wrong.'

Danny breathed out as he let the long pent-up rage simmer down. He set about tying Toby's hands and ankles. 'Call the police Meg.'

They left the Arwen Vale trainer inside the cave.

Meg pulled the sleeve of her Silver Belle Stables fleece down over her hand and carried the gun outside the cave.

Danny freed the colt tied to a rock and he joined Meg by the mouth of the cave. They sat on a boulder next to the wooden boards stacked up and waited for the sirens.

He asked, 'How the hell did you guess to come here from my 'sky in cave' text?'

'It didn't make sense, so I typed in s and then k and it tried to autocorrect as skull, and there haven't been that many caves you'd been obsessing over, so I came.'

'But I wasn't here for hours after sending it.'

'I had to drop the kids round your mam's. You'd better call her, stop her worrying.'

Danny patted his empty pockets.

'The gates were locked, so I waited near the bushes until I saw the van enter and then snuck in before the gates shut.'

'I've taught you well, young one.'

She laughed. 'When I saw those men go into the cave, I knew it wasn't to say hello.'

He kissed her. 'Without you I would have added to the bones in there,' he said. 'And I'd never be found in a cave boarded up as unsafe. The Lord Lucan of the racing world.'

'I couldn't cope with that.'

'I dunno, you're stronger than you think,' he replied. 'If you owed me at all for helping turn around Powder Keg's career, I think we're quits after that. Ever thought about being a rodeo?'

Meg smiled. 'Still amazed I didn't unseat. You know me and my dyspraxia.' She rested her head on his shoulder and then straightened. 'You're soaking.'

'Leaks in the cave roof,' Danny lied.

'Guess I was wrong to doubt you about the Carmichaels.'

'You're just too trusting of people.'

'What the hell were they up to?'

'You don't want to know the details, let's just say there are more ringers in Toby's yard than a campanologists' convention.'

'He's a handsome fella,' she said, offering a pick of grass to the rescued reject. 'Has he got a name?'

'He hasn't even got a number.'

'The way he looked at me just then, I simply can't let him go.'

'Is that what you thought when you met me?'

She shook her head smiling. 'Give us a job, more like.'

'Seriously, Meg, we're not a charity.'

'You took me on.'

Danny paused and then sighed. 'Alright, just this one mind, but we then reinvest the Goodwood money, agreed?'

'Agreed.' She kissed him as if to seal the deal. 'What the hell do I tell the police when they arrive?'

'Just stick to the truth,' Danny said. '*We've* done nothing wrong. I'll show them the photos I took of the fake horse passports in Toby's office and the IDs I found in Marcel's, sorry Sean's, Bentley. They're on my—' He recalled his mobile was at the bottom of the Bristol Channel. 'I've still got the bloody silk, and when they take DNA samples from the Carmichael string, they'll soon see that none of the ringers match the microchip number in the database. And they'll have a field day with all the evidence in the cave back there, which is on Toby's land.' Danny glanced up at the electric fence skirting round the cave's mouth. 'Never thought I'd say this, but I hope they go lenient on Toby. He forced into following orders of the Brothers Grimm in there, and he's not got the support of his wife or son when he's inside. He's won plenty on the track, but lost more off it.'

'At least finally you now see that we'll always be winners,' Meg said, 'we've got Cerys and Jack, what happens on the racecourse comes second, just a bonus.'

Danny couldn't stop himself saying. 'A bloody big bonus mind, if we can just find say a dozen more Flat winners before the season is out and then—'

'Danny!'

Printed in Poland
by Amazon Fulfillment
Poland Sp. z o.o., Wrocław

51921943R00114